"An ambitious and curious venture . . . straddles historical drama and dystopian fiction, and yet manages to cross the divide."
Thuy On, *Sydney Morning Herald*

"A brilliant, deeply unsettling work with the unapologetically feminist rage, passion and awareness of books such as *The Natural Way of Things* or Margaret Atwood's seminal *The Handmaid's Tale*."
Books + Publishing

"This is one of those rare books that penetrates deep into the reader's most secret self. Read it and hold it close."
The Saturday Paper

"By turns horrible, sweet, erotic, tense, challenging, beautiful, disgusting, solemn, abhorrent and moving, *A Superior Spectre* is a novel no serious reader will forget in a hurry."
John Purcell, *Booktopia*

"*A Superior Spectre* doesn't just transcend the genres of its protagonists, it transcends the act of reading. You can't help but emerge from the novel . . . and be struck by both the temporal magic of reading and the responsibility it bequeaths you."
Craig Hildebrand

"The amazing, wonderful, talented Angela Meyer."
Heather Morris

"Pared-back brittle language . . . a sophisticated piece of writing . . . a beautifully rendered work of literature."
Eloise Millar, Mslexia Novella Award judge,
on *Joan Smokes*

ANGELA MEYER

A Superior Spectre

CONTRABAND

Contraband is an imprint of Saraband

Published by Saraband,
Digital World Centre, 1 Lowry Plaza, The Quays, Salford, M50 3UB
and
Suite 202, 98 Woodlands Road, Glasgow, G3 6HB, Scotland

www.saraband.net

ISBN: 9781912235483
ebook: 9781912235490

1 3 5 7 9 10 8 6 4 2

Designed and typeset by EM&EN
Printed and bound in Great Britain by Clays Ltd, Elcograf S.p.A.

MIX
Paper from
responsible sources
FSC
www.fsc.org FSC® C018072

Supported by
The National Lottery®
through Creative Scotland

One need not be a chamber to be haunted,
One need not be a house;
The brain has corridors surpassing
Material place.
Far safer, of a midnight meeting
External ghost,
Than an interior confronting
That whiter host.
Far safer through an Abbey gallop,
The stones achase,
Than, moonless, one's own self encounter
In lonesome place.
Ourself, behind ourself concealed,
Should startle most;
Assassin, hid in our apartment,
Be horror's least.
The prudent carries a revolver,
He bolts the door,
O'erlooking a superior spectre
More near.

Emily Dickinson, *The Complete Poems*

'Those whom their nature keeps away from the community . . . need no defence because incomprehension cannot affect them because they are dark, and they find love everywhere. Nor do they need any sustenance, for, if they want to remain truthful, they can draw only on their own substance, so that one cannot help them without first doing them harm.'

Franz Kafka in *Kafka: A Life in Prague*, Klaus Wagenbach

I am not afraid of the dark. I have missed the complete darkness of the Highlands, and the quiet. But there is a drip somewhere. And the more I look into the darkness the more I notice that it is not absolute. There are blotches of light, of colour. Even when I close my eyes.

I yell, and then feel impolite, and then yell again. I brought myself here; should I not play by the rules? But then this is unnatural, to lock a person up.

Time moves slowly. Has it been minutes or an hour? Will I be here all night?

The blotches become shapes.

Round, draped, thatched.

A full image, painted. A basket of ripe, verdant fruit, and browning leaves. White folds of robe. A muscled shoulder and deep collarbone crease. Trace the neck to a tilted chin and parted peach lips, to bite to the seed. Heavy-lidded eyes. Dark curls in just-woke tufts. Shadows at his shoulders like wings. The image is delicate but strong.

I gasp. I fear this vision but it is breathtaking. I have stared at this painting for a long time. Somewhere.

I feel warmer. My mouth is open; I pant almost like a dog. Ecstatic light in my chest, to the tips of my nipples. Time, in my chest. I am not sitting in the dark.

When the woman opens the door the image shatters. I realise I cannot feel my legs; I have been sitting on them. There is drool on my chin, my eyes are dry. I can't see beyond her candle flame though I think she is studying me. She holds out her hand and helps me up.

I knock the pins and needles out of my feet as we walk through to the room with people in it. The cold descends upon me and I shiver. She hands me a cloak, silently, and I sit on a wooden chair, joining a circle of shadowy figures.

'Everyone welcome Miss Duncan,' she says firmly.

'Welcome, Miss Duncan,' is a chant.

'Good evening, thank you,' I say. The warmth of the image is departing, and this chamber holds an aged, mossy cold that seeps into my bones.

PART ONE

At the back of the cottage she sat, skirts tucked up between her knees, swapping the limp animal from hand to hand to push her sleeves back. Smell of peat smoke and sweat. She pulled off her bonnet, one-handed, and placed it on a squared-off stone. She slicked back a stray hair, getting a little blood on it.

The young woman worked quickly and calmly, jutting her jaw in concentration, taking short breaths to not draw in too much of the sweet, permusted smell. Once she had removed the hide from both legs it hung down like a pair of dirty socks.

She reached her juice-slicked hand beneath the rabbit's genitals and in under the warm skin of the belly, loosening it gently to pull it off. She then worked her hand in above the tail – the moment that always caused a brief sad stirring in her breast, that small puff of fur – and drew across the back, lifting, separating, and then moving up to the arms.

She busted the thin skin between the arms and neck with a pinch, and as she pulled the fluffy suit up, catching the sleeves, a hollow cramp moved across her lower abdomen. She stopped for a beat, two, and sighed. And then cracked the rabbit's spine beneath its head.

Her old cairn terrier, Duff, came out the back door behind her, followed by her father, in his work clothes. He'd had a job up at Knockallan, Mrs Grant's place, fixing the wooden frames of the windows.

'Did you no hear me talkin tae Moggach just noo, Leonora?' he asked.

'No, Father, I was at ma task, I'm sorry.'

'It's all right, Lae, just thought ye might huv said hullo.'

'I'm feeling a wee bit ill.'

'Ye did hear him then.'

Leonora stood, and Duff yipped and leapt at the rabbit carcass.

'Go catch yersel one,' she said to the hairy mutt, and Duff turned her eyes on Leonora for a moment before padding off down toward the woods.

'I'll make supper,' she said, and smiled warmly at her father.

He returned the smile, his red beard fanning out. 'Oh, Lass, I forgot tae tell ye, Miss Cruikshank will be coming by at e'en. I bought some o the tea she likes frae Tomnavoulin yesterday.'

Leonora nodded at her father. Miss Cruikshank had been visiting more regularly this past month. And her father always washed with the good soap, humming 'Ae Fond Kiss' before she arrived. He always offered her a dram of the better malt, which sat on a higher shelf as though Duff might think it were a piece of meat. He'd not yet offered Leonora a taste.

As Leonora cooked the rabbit in the pot hooked above the fire, heating some bannocks alongside it, she thought of her mother. She often did when she was cooking, or cleaning – wondering if she was doing it right, wondering how her mother would have done it. And had Isabella felt this way at this time every month, too? The moon high but her heart sunk, fluttering, like a bird fallen from its perch. And her lower belly swollen, with something inside it pinching and then pulling and then clawing. Soon the bleeding would come. So much of it, and by the end her head would feel full of heather, her temper would be quick and she would want to sleep well past dawn for almost a week, with not many good days before it began all over again.

Had it been the same for her mother? And was it the reason Leonora was feeling unreasonably angry all of a sudden towards her father?

Luckily, her friend Abby had gone through it first, and had passed on her own mother's advice about coverage and washing, and lady-of-the-meadow tea to relieve pain and ease stomach upsets.

Miss Penuel Cruikshank arrived in a pretty, soft yellow dress. Leonora was not good at guessing ages but she figured Miss Cruikshank to be five and thirty or perhaps forty at the oldest, but a young forty. It was the lines at the neck when she turned her head that gave her to be older. The 'Miss' indicated that she'd never married, and Leonora didn't know the exact circumstances. Leonora had spent the first years of her childhood, to almost the age of four, away from Chapeltown. And she knew her grasp of social mores was rudimentary: she'd read some of the novels of Jane Austen and George Eliot, Elizabeth Gaskell and Charles Dickens. And there were the poets, such as Lord Byron: 'Vice cannot fix, and virtue cannot change / The once fall'n woman must forever fall.' But the lives described in these books seemed grander, more complex and, quite thankfully, far removed from her own.

'Leonora, this is a fancy spread, is it no?' said Miss Cruikshank, as Leonora added the butter and salt to the table.

'It's no much,' she said.

'But it's always enough,' said her father.

'How are the berries doin, John?' Miss Cruikshank asked. Leonora noted the switch from 'Mr Duncan' that had recently occurred.

'Too delicious tae last afore the other critters get at them.' He grinned. But Leonora knew he'd picked and put some aside for tonight. His garden was a source of pride to both of them, as old as their residence here when he'd carried a wee lass and three small sacks of seeds back from Edinburgh after Leonora's mother's death. He didn't often speak of it but Leonora knew of the threads to his regret: that he'd left the Highlands in the first place; that he'd lost his wife in Edinburgh; that despite learning a trade that may have saved his own father's life, he hadn't come back sooner. His mother – Leonora's gram – was left alone at Aignish but still he did not return until Leonora's mother had passed away. He'd once told Leonora that her mother couldn't get the kind of treatment she needed in Chapeltown.

Her father had been able to put his trade to use and soon became a known joiner and carpenter in the village, and further afield, as well as contributing to the food production. He worked well in the harvest, as did Leonora, once she was old enough and allowed. And they had a fine garden from which they could swap: perfect cream tatties, big juicy strawberries in summer, and a selection of herbs for taste and medicinal purposes.

It was strawberries they ate after supper. Outside it was moony and dark. Inside, candles burned sedately. Miss Cruikshank's face pinkened in the soft light when she bit into one of the berries. She smiled at Leonora's father, and it made Leonora feel strange, as though she'd lost her appetite.

Her father cleared his throat. 'Now, Leonora, ye've finished at the schoolhouse two years ago. Penuel has discussed with an opportunity with me.'

Oh dear, Leonora thought. Miss Cruikshank will have a long-lost cousin come to Tomintoul, someone about my age.

'Aye, Leonora, ma brother, he's keeper o an inn up in Tomintoul,' said Miss Cruikshank, lips wet with strawberry juice. 'Yer father agreed with me that ye might think aboot workin there a few days in the week. It's good experience if . . .' She looked at Leonora's father.

'It would be good for yer prospects, Lae.'

This was not exactly what Leonora had expected. She felt hot. She tugged at the ruched fabric at her wrist, wanting to draw up her sleeves. 'Would I stay there, in the hotel?'

'For half the week, aye,' said Miss Cruikshank. 'A coach be doublin weekly from here tae there, and in good weather it's really no sae far tae walk.'

'I ken' said Leonora, too quickly, 'I've done it afore. But Father, I've work tae dae for you. And the harvest is soon.'

'There are hands enough for the harvest. We need tae think aboot your life ahead o ye.'

'Ma future.' The words shook up an image of her hands slick after having reached inside Dona, the cow, to shift and deliver a calf; the brown and white calf taking breaths, wobbling on thin legs. If Leonora had thought about herself in the future she pictured her hands dirty and pressed against life. The fast-beating hearts of animals. Or roots deep in the soil.

She wanted to express this, but she was polite, and Miss Cruikshank was a guest. Leonora had to control this burning. So she told her she would certainly consider it, while not looking the woman in the eye, and her father nodded his assent. The topic was done with for the night. Miss Cruikshank rose from the table first, insisting on cleaning up, which made Leonora feel embarrassed – had she stalled too long? The guest shouldn't have to clean. Another part of her, which she tried to damp down, understood the gesture as Miss Cruikshank taking a step toward making herself at home.

The woman perturbed her thoughts on this too-bright night, as Leonora gathered a sheet in her fist and fought the burning in her throat. From the inside of a dirty inn in Tomintoul to what? Was her father aware of Miss Cruikshank's motives? Did he really want the best for Leonora? How could he not know what that was? At least, at least, it was only half the week. She would try to let that thought sustain her.

I came up slowly out of the trip, into a dark, unfamiliar room. I gasped, as from a sob, or as though someone had been holding my head underwater. I tried to take a proper breath, as I reached over and flicked on the lamp. Leonora's dread, and melancholy, were lodged inside of me. I, too, loved her father, and dreaded the thought of life moving in a direction away from the place she called home. And what was incredible, I thought, as I sat up and took a sip of my whisky, which sat on the bedside table, was that I had felt what it was to have menstrual cramps. Not just cramps, but this entire bodily sensation of bloat, and heaviness, and the emotional overwhelm.

I then slept, worrying Leonora's worries, occasionally realising I was doing so and realising how powerful this technology could be for someone like me, who no longer has any interest in self. Who can experience being someone else before dying.

By the morning, though, while I thought of her and wondered about what she was now, in the past, seeing and thinking – what her tastes were, if she would fall in love – I was returned to my own cumbersome, aching body, and I experienced my own cravings: for the book I was reading on Caravaggio, for fried eggs; my own lusts, my own shame, in the bathroom before breakfast. A man I was and am.

It was about three hours to Edinburgh on the bus that day, cash paid. We drove by sheep under windmills, rolling fields and vertical farms, patches of moorland, and purple-grey rocks jutting through grass. Often the road was elevated and the bank beside it would drop down and then roll up into a hill, patched with dark green pines. Castle ruins materialised on riverbanks, and often I'd see a lone house or cluster – a small village – in the elbow of a mountain. I looked out the window the whole time. I felt at home, but I interrogated that feeling. Though I have Scotland in my blood, from my mother, can you really recognise a genetic connection to place, to land? The feeling of 'belonging' was more likely due to the conscious knowledge of your bloodline, which then settled in your unconscious and presented as a feeling of comfort, of being at home. After all, my family was actually driven away, in the time of the clearances, when landlords moved their tenants off in favour of having sheep on their land.

I didn't know yet if Leonora was in an area where this happened, or indeed what year it was that I had come across her. Dickens had cropped up in her thoughts, so it would be beyond the mid-1800s. The clearances were certainly widespread, long-lasting and tragic. People were forced out violently, and many others died or suffered greatly when they tried to make a new life in coastal areas, with less arable land. Some went south and tried to find work in cities. Many, like my ancestors, were shipped off to Australia, America, Canada.

Real suffering. With black lungs and blistered fingers, empty bloated stomachs, and grief. Nothing like the pains my middle-class friends would complain about now. The worst you could suffer with illness was a waiting list. Well, not for me. Suffering was something I was determined to experience. This pharma – a kind of anti-inflammatory – would last long enough to get me to my island and then I would be weaned, slowly, from chemical health.

When I left Melbourne, it was one of those sickeningly hot days, where metal turns to liquid, and a breeze feels like a blast from a hair dryer. One of those days where people without regulation systems built into their underclothes drop dead in the street. I arrived at the airport with a large bag full of clothes, toiletries and just a couple of personal items: a few postcards from art galleries, a pod full of music, a couple of books. I hadn't cleaned up the flat; the buyers could have the rest: the oak bar, the retro olive-green couch, the half-drunk bottles of gin and Scotch. I do wonder sometimes what they might have done with the photo albums, or the printout of the family tree that Uncle Dave gave me when I was in my twenties and trying to work out if I was the only one. Not that you can really tell from a family tree. I never managed to find out much about Mum's side, the ones originally from Scotland, except that there were some drunks. That's all Mum would tell me. So perhaps there is some genetic anomaly. Her own father stopped drinking just before I was born, my dear old pa, but I don't know much about what he was like before that.

The airport was quiet. Only about four planes leave per day, and they're often cancelled if under-booked. Selling the flat had given me enough money for the trip, and for accommodation and food to get me through to the end. I left in the morning. I had been due for an appointment at the hospital that evening.

I checked my bag at the machine and then sat at the gate and read the Caravaggio bio, pausing frequently as panic struck a small, sharp tap to my head, just above my left eye. I don't think I was panicked about what I was doing; it'd been meticulously planned and I was long resolved to it. The panic was about getting caught, and about being made to go back. I'd read carefully about how to remove the ID chip when I got there. Thank God the legislation never went through for ID chips to be placed in the head. Though cutting into my own double-chinned face might not have been much of a problem.

I knew I'd be scanned leaving the country, and arriving at my destination, but I hoped after that I would manage to slip away. Scotland is perfect because in patches it is still wild and remote, and cash is widely used, since the Scots are smart, or maybe just suspicious, and have seen the banks fall in so many other places, including of their former oppressors in England. And, you can still arrive in England and quietly cross the border into Scotland (or so I'd been told). As long as you are de-chipped and avoid any places where that might be noticed, you can hole up quietly in the Highlands.

In Edinburgh I had an apartment on Canongate, above a shop, for two nights. Enough time to stock up, and an apartment small and dark enough to feel I could hide, when I became afraid. I didn't know whether my paranoia was logical, whether the Australian government, or any government, would have spies, or satellites seeking chip-free warm bodies, marking them as suspicious. But entire countries didn't have the implant ID-systems, and citizens of those countries were allowed in as tourists, so it wasn't probable. Still, there would have been phone calls by then. To the people who knew me, to Faye, to Henry. A knock on the door at my old place, where they'd find new people, clueless as to where I'd gone but puzzled at all my stuff still being there. Perhaps they would have reported that straight away, after trying to call me.

That first night in Edinburgh I stayed inside, with these unanswerable questions. I struggled with the decision to have a day off the drink. It had always made sense in my old life, to refrain. I guess old habits die hard, to put it lazily. I caught myself in the mirror, a world away, and I still worried about putting on weight, about feeling (more) disgusted with myself. I found it hard to adjust to the fact it didn't matter anymore.

I went to bed early and had to have a little giggle at myself, for being so typically human, when my thoughts strayed to how it all began, how *I* began. The dying man reflecting. I'm sickened at the typicality. And so I cannot speak it now. Except, maybe a glimpse of the enduring image . . . He haunts me like Tadzio, the young love object of Thomas Mann's *Death in Venice*. Though I was not

Aschenbach, and have resolved never to be: an old man leering at youth. I was *young*, too, when it happened. He had black hair and was thin and hunched, a fringe in his eyes, eyes that held ironic knowledge. He was my girlfriend's younger brother. She dared us to kiss once (her own erotic curiosity, I suppose) and our teeth and tongues clashed. I felt too large and soft, too sensitive – the Brian Wilson of the trio. They could cut me with their disapproval of a film, a song. After the kiss, we three took shots of stolen gin and curated retro music on our screens. My heart pumped with nervous inadequacy every time it was my turn to choose. I made out with my girlfriend, and behind us Tadzio rubbed the crotch of his black pants, his eyes slinted at the TV. He knew I could see. His name was Eric, like the Disney prince.

Often we don't realise until years after a taste has developed what the formative moment could have been.

Is 'taste' the right word? I think it might be. Taste can be bodily: I feel a song or painting through a quickening of blood, the hairs on my arms raising, a clenching in my abdomen. At the same time, there can be a sublime departure from the flesh. The combination of the two – flesh and not – lodges the sensation as a development, to be built upon. Taste is fed and fattens.

The next morning, Edinburgh was perfectly autumnal. The sky was grey and a mist hung about the castle. I walked up winding Canongate, past whisky shops and museums, turned left at North Bridge, and followed my crumpled map for another half-hour, puffing despite the cool morning, down a few turns until I arrived at a large stone block, with a tavern on the corner and a couple of ornamental red phone booths. I pressed a buzzer by a tall studded iron door, painted blue, as per the instructions. I saw a large green mass, Arthur's Seat, rising out to the right of my vision.

A voice finally came through the speaker. I said the code word and was buzzed in.

I entered a small enclosed courtyard with chequerboard tiles covered with plastic and dust due to maintenance. Ahead of me was an iron staircase, which I took to number six.

A barefoot man in denim overalls and a white T-shirt waved me in. 'Jeff, right?'

'Yes.'

He led me into a sitting room with boxes piled on and around an antique settee, all wrapped in cheap Christmas paper. There were three screens on the walls: two playing the same music video and one playing porn.

'Gimme a minute,' he said, and sucked on an electronic cigarette while shifting boxes here and there, mumbling my name. 'An andserv and an unregistered screen, right?'

'That's me.'

'Aha.' He found my items beside the settee, and I pulled out a wad of cash. 'Now, as you probably know, this particular model of service android was pulled off the market and the designer was laid off. I'm not gonna judge – just keep it out of sight, right? You were never here.'

'I know all that.'

'I move on a lot, anyway; you won't get 'em onto me.'

'I don't plan to.'

'Okay.' He looked me in the face for probably the first time. He seemed to take a breath, relax a little. A woman's mouth made an *Oh, Oh, Oh* in the video behind him.

'Well, cheers,' I said. I picked up my package – surprisingly light – and left.

The next day I was heading west.

Leonora was on her knees, sprinkling wet tea leaves over the ashes to stop them flying into the air, before brushing them onto the shovel. The fire was too far gone to be stoked. She hoped that her setting skills would be adequate for the Horseshoe Inn. She added paper, dry wood, and peat from the scuttle, enabling space for air. She set it well back in the grate, so the smoke would not come too much into the room. She struck a match to the paper and was pleased by how fast it took.

Afterwards, she beat the cushions on the sofa, replacing one of them neatly over a wine-dark stain. The sitting room was bathed in grey light from the street-facing window. She paused to watch a well-dressed man and his large golden dog walk by. She recognised him as William Wink, the young laird of Chapeltown, but she was just as interested in the dog: glossy and energetic. She'd met the handsome laird before, who would come to discuss land matters with her father, but never the beastie. It looked enthusiastic: a pup, perhaps, raising its nose to follow the laird's hand through the crowd. Children with dirty faces stopped and lifted their hands in excitement. I am one of them, she thought, and then got back to neatening the room for those guests who might like to sit and overheat with drams of whisky by the fire instead of being out in the mild summer air.

Penuel's brother, the innkeeper, was Archibald Cruikshank, a portly man with a papery waistcoat clinging to him like a bottle's label. He had looked Leonora up and down, told her she'd do, and then showed her to a tiny room at the end of the upstairs hall with an iron-framed bed, a set of drawers, and a small square window in the slope of the roof. Since the room went to another woman for the other days in the week, she was not to leave anything there, he said. The neat anonymity of it was daunting to Leonora, a half-burned candle the only sign of life.

'Ye'll eat afore the guests at two, and then start at six the morra's morn,' he'd said, before closing her in. Since it was near two, she presumed she had no duties before then. She sat on the lumpy bed, furrowing her brow. She then knelt on the bed to look out the window. She gasped at the proximity of a tiny orange-breasted chackie, its body upright in chirpy, clicky song. She watched it until it flitted off. The bird had returned to her some sense of calm. She unpacked a few belongings into the drawers, and sat the book she was reading, *Cosmos*, about the 'natural sciences', on the bedside table. She could see the bird as a sign that this job would be tolerable.

She learnt her duties over a salty bowl of soup and tough bread: tend the fires and tidy all common areas before breakfast, then help with the breakfast service, clear the breakfast dishes and clean the guests' rooms entirely if they are leaving, or tidy if they are staying on. It was a small inn, of six rooms in varying sizes. Depending how long the cleaning took, Leonora might have an hour to spare before she was to help prepare and serve dinner, which rolled into a cold supper. She would then help clean up afterwards. Mr Cruikshank said it all very seriously, with a frown, but she noticed that as he sipped at his ale with more vigour his face began to relax and spread out.

The only men Leonora had really known were older, authoritarian, but familiar. She had known them since childhood: her father, Mr Anderson, Rev Moggach, Mr Grant. Of other men she'd only really had glimpses, and her only tool in interacting with them was politeness. She wasn't sure if something extra was required in a relationship with an employer.

But she had no more time to consider her situation, as she

was sent straight to the kitchen – which, to her, looked as chaotic as the Avon after a storm – to help auld Cait with the dinner. Leonora tried to make herself useful but her cooking knowledge only extended to one pan over a fire, with time to contemplate and prepare a meal. Cait called out things like, 'Salt the tatties', and Leonora didn't even know where they were, and couldn't find where to drain the water as the tubs and buckets on the cramped central table were full of dirty dishes and old, grey water. Cait threw plates at her and told her to take them into the dining room, and Leonora was aware that to the guests she must look dirty and red-faced. She trembled as she set the plates on the table, feeling an intense inner dread that this was what life was; this was what was meant by moving up in the world.

By the time she got to bed, after finding the tipping place in the alley outside and refilling the tubs with hot water to scrub her way through a substantial pile of dishes, her head was ringing with Cait's cutting and desperate voice, her yells, and her mix of insults and encouragement: 'What, were ye born yesterday?' 'Dinnae worry, Lass, ye'll pick it up!' Leonora fell quickly asleep, and in the morning felt more tired than she usually would. She dressed in her room and then crept downstairs and outside to tip her pot in the privy. She gave her face a good scrub in the sink in her room, and used a wet rag to dab at the spots of food on her dress from the night before. She needed to wash yesterday's underclothes, but the window was too small in her room for them to have any chance to dry, and she wasn't sure where else they might be hung out of sight of the guests. Maybe she'd work up the courage to ask Cait.

On the third morning at the Horseshoe, Leonora was tidying the common areas and working herself up for the breakfast service. Mr Cruikshank had assured her it would be easier than dinner, and she had found that it was: fewer menu options, and pots of coffee and tea from which the guests could top up their cups if necessary.

She had her hair back in a low knot, parted in the middle. When she came into the kitchen she felt cleaner and calmer than on the previous two mornings; the room was just that bit more familiar. Plus, she was closer to going home. How she longed for it. Cait was quiet, in that way Leonora's father was in the mornings, especially after a night of drinking. Leonora respected the quiet, the guests' low murmur and the clink of cutlery.

Guests began to settle into the leather booths with high oak backs across one wall, and the smaller tables and chairs in the centre and by the window. Leonora poured the first round of strong black tea and coffee into their cups, and brought out bowls of steaming porridge from Cait's big pot. She noticed a tall, well-dressed gentleman unscrew a flask and pour a careful measure of whisky into his porridge, before stirring it gently clockwise three times, then tapping his spoon on the edge. Like the dog that rises and stretches facing the same direction every morning, she thought.

Her face grew warm when the young laird of Chapeltown entered the room, the last to come down, carrying some semblance of sleep in his eyes. She hadn't seen him again after spotting him on the street and she hadn't known he was staying at the inn.

As she said good morning and poured his tea, he looked up and his eyes widened in recognition. She caught the scent of his barley-coloured hair with its sheen of oil.

'Why, it's Miss Duncan,' he said. 'I didn't know you had come up to town.' Though his family's Scottish blood ran deep, the laird's words were precise and pronounced, with only a gentle Highland lilt and burr, indicating an education abroad.

'I'm working half the week, Mr Wink, at the Horseshoe, and am back to Chapeltown to help ma father as usual for the rest o the time.'

'Oh, I'm so glad to hear you haven't abandoned us completely; you always have been a very good help in the lambing.'

Leonora hadn't realised that Mr Wink had ever taken particular notice of her. When his father had been alive, young Master Wink never really did say much at all, just stood and nodded behind him as rounds were done of the tenancies. But Leonora, and the people of Chapeltown and the braes, had much warmth for the Winks as landlords, because the Winks had always worked with them and respected clan systems, been satisfied with the income from rents and the harvest, and accommodated sheep while not forcing them off their land like so many others around Scotland in recent times.

Leonora was happy that he'd mentioned the lambing, a time when she was able to be of help to both her neighbours and the animals. Her hands were small and she was known to have a certain skill at recognising whether the nose and front legs were in position, and whether the birth canal was expanded enough for unassisted birth. She had successfully aided delivery of many lambs, with only a couple of distressing failures.

The first birth, when she was eight years old, was one of the most difficult. Mr Anderson, who lived at Barnsoul, had asked if she would like to help, as she had been sitting on the grass watching the sheep's struggle.

'Ye've got nice small hands,' he said.

Mr Anderson rubbed Leonora's hands and arms in butter and told her to reach inside the sheep and feel for the shape of a lamb, telling her the way all the limbs should be facing.

'I think the heid is backwards,' she said.

'Good, Lass, all ye have tae dae is push the whole body intae the roomy part – not the part where yer arm is squeezed – and gently bring the heid aroond sae heid and feet are all facin toward the road tae freedom.' He spread a gap-toothed grin.

'Right then,' Leonora said.

'Best no tae push on the jaw, as it might hurt the lamb's chance o feedin. The eye sockets can be a place to grip.'

Leonora felt a little horrified at that, imagining someone's fingers jammed in her eyes, but she trusted the old farmer, and so pushed and carefully manoeuvred the head, the mother bleating and warm, until the lamb was in the correct position.

'Right, just move that creature forward noo, sae she's comin towards that road,' Mr Anderson instructed.

Leonora did so, and then slowly edged her arm out of the mother. The lamb was very soon to follow, tiny and coated in fluid, which the mother immediately began to clean off with her tongue, their black faces together.

Leonora smiled with delight up at Mr Anderson and ran home to tell her father. 'It's p'haps not the best occupation fer a young lady,' he said.

But over the years he bit his tongue as he saw how much it pleased her to help. She wondered too, as she got older, whether her father had been worried about her knowing, too young, the functions of animals: the blood and heat, the humping and the bodies swollen with young. She was an intelligent enough child to realise that it must be a similar process for people, though they were much more secretive about it. That they saw themselves as loftier beings, blessed with the knowledge of God, she thought.

'Tis an unweeded garden, That grows to seed; things rank and gross in nature Possess it merely.

She heard Cait calling from the kitchen that the breakfast plates were ready. 'Please excuse me, Mr Wink,' Leonora said, 'I'll be back with yer breakfast.'

She served the earlier patrons first, who had finished their porridge, with the plates of beef square sausage, eggs, bannocks, tomatoes, mushrooms, bacon links and fried bread. She cleared their other plates and topped up their beverages.

She took porridge to Mr Wink and refilled his tea. He continued to engage her, and she was polite but strained. She wasn't quite sure where she stood with people of a higher social standing, as she hadn't had much chance to interact with them, and so found conversation difficult. She was also aware that she had a reaction to him, a physical one. She could feel the heat and size of him, smell the sleep still on him, and it made her hot in her cheeks and sent blood to her lips. But she didn't want him to think her wanton, so she was awkwardly polite, and continued to excuse herself, as she did have work to do.

When she brought his cooked plate, she did, however, ask about the dog. They called him Rua-reidh, he told her, named for his rusty colour and smoothness. He'd spent the night with the horses in the inn's stable.

'It's an entirely new breed of retriever,' Mr Wink said, 'developed near Glen Affric on Baron Tweedmouth's estate. But maybe that doesn't interest you.'

'Oh, it does,' she said. 'I think dogs are the most wonderful companions.'

'Well, so do I,' he said, 'loyal and hard-working, but they also know how to have fun. Roo just loves the water. If he has to fetch fowl from the middle of the Avon, all the better.' When he smiled, Mr Wink looked younger than his age, which Leonora knew to be about two and twenty.

She loved the image of the dog splashing and wading out, returning with a bird among his teeth, the edges of his mouth turned up.

'You should really come out to Dearshul to watch him in action, when it suits you.'

Leonora was torn between what was proper (surely he was just being polite) and a genuine wish to see the dog in action while walking the grounds of Dearshul.

She answered, 'That's gey kind o ye,' which left an answer vaguely open. 'Now, I must let you eat, and contine with ma tasks.'

He smiled warmly at her and she walked away, with an awareness of the blood reaching every corner of her body, and feeling every part of her skin against her clothes: her shin, her hips, her chest. When he left he tipped his hat at her and told her he would see her soon. She did not want to admit it, but she hoped that would be true.

I had decided on the West of Scotland because it was where my mother's family were from, but also because of its character: still remote, wild. It took a day to get there, via Inverness, on two buses. The second one had vinyl seats, like an old school bus, and no toilet. It wove among an increasingly dark and looming landscape, the edges of the bus threatening to tip over into glens and lochs, barrelling toward sheep on the roads and sending them scattering onto hillsides. There were only five people on the bus: a family who looked like they'd been to Inverness for a big shop, and a man slightly bedraggled, hair too long like my own.

We came into Gairloch as the sun turned the wide sky a breathtaking coral. And from here, at the time of recording, I'm reluctant to tell you where I continued in a taxi and boat. I haven't decided whether this recording is something I'll arrange to be sent back to Australia after I'm gone. A last hurrah, a confession, something to explain the terrible things I've done. If so, I want to keep this place a secret, for others like me to find. Though I do hope there is no one like me.

Or perhaps I will just destroy this. Take no responsibility. Life is chaos; people are all the time causing minute fluctuations that will change history's path. Or creating a language to describe the past which then changes its meaning. Academia of course posits this as a good thing; history looks different now that we understand that everyone had thoughts, feelings, voices.

The animals. I've been thinking more about them, since the trips I've had with Leonora. They have become a part of me, too.

The tits and robins on this small island, the eagle that circles, the seals that frolic on the far side of the island. They are all still here. In existence, I mean. Maybe that's enough. For those animals to have survived.

So I made my way here, and Bethea, the landlord, met me. She was a little hunched, but agile, with long grey hair and layers of light knits over her body. She took me and my bag in a small boat over to the island, even though I assured her I'd be fine on the long rickety footbridge – the only other access point to the mainland. The island is inside a kind of cove, with a small village on the opposite banks, and no businesses besides a pub, which is just around the cove and out of sight for me. Bethea didn't say much; the main sounds were the whirring of the boat's motor, the shimmer of parting water, and, carrying from the village, the sound of a lone fiddle.

'Tha's McGregor,' she said. 'He plays this time every night.'

She didn't ask me any questions about what I was planning, or why I was there; she simply pointed out landmarks – a wooden sculpture; the site of a drunken wreck – and then jumped out to tie the boat and reach over a hand to help me step up onto the rocks with my wobbly, unseaworthy legs.

'Closest shop's on the way tae Gairloch. There's a bike in that outbuildin ye're welcome tae borrow. There's also a community car, goes at certain times. 'S'all by the phone for ye.'

I thanked her, and paid her the balance for three months ahead.

She got back in the boat, and it hummed away, and the fiddle stopped playing. I looked up at the arc of the sky, for this was the kind of place where you could see, clearly, the way it curved.

I opened the unlocked door of the two-storey cottage and took my shoes off in the entrance. To my right was a kitchen and living room, and to my left was a winding, carpeted staircase. I brought my bag up to the second storey, where I found my bedroom and a bathroom under the slope of the roof. Just like

Leonora at the inn, I thought, though I had much more room. The bedroom did have a pervasive, greeny smell of damp, and though it was cool I cracked the windows to air it out. I paused to take in the view from one side of the cove. A couple of boats were anchored, one wooden and old, one white and new. It was a view I'd grow very used to, being able to note the variations in the positions of the boats and track the weather by the stillness of the water.

I placed my bag and box – the andserv – on the bed. I would get to it soon. First, I went down to the kitchen, cheaply updated sometime early this century, a messy mix of glass and formica and steel. There was a layered, trapped scent of oily fish – slightly urinous – and something more meaty, such as lamb fat. A large red switch sat above the sink for the generator. There were detailed instructions beside it, I noticed with relief. The fridge motor kicked over, startling me, and I took a peek inside. Bethea had provided mylk, coco-butter; in the cupboards there were oats and barley bread, plus cans of protein. Bless her, I thought. On closer inspection, to my dismay, the mylk smelt sharp and the bread had patches of mould. Perhaps these items had been left over from the last guest.

I made a plain porridge with oats, coco-butter and water, and sat at the table in the bright kitchen, unable to see anything but darkness outside.

The night was still and it was so quiet you could hear the blood in your ears, as when you're immersed in water.

I was here.

What did I think I was doing?

I could have lived a long time more. I could have tried harder to be better. I could have sought help. I could still go back. I could make it up to everyone I'd hurt. I really had loved Faye.

No. This was where I was meant to be. Far away, alone. The experience was meant to be difficult. It would force me to go to these places in my mind, and I couldn't, now, escape myself. But

I had managed to escape everyone else, hadn't I? Was I cowardly? Or was it right to separate myself, to not use up their time, their resources, when they could be used on someone who'd been a good person?

And yet I had shown self-control, hadn't I, in my life? Others didn't. They sickened me. Yes, this was right – my last bastion of control, complete control over the self; taking the sick self unto death. With dignity.

But I am sorry, if I've ruined everything.

It would be so like me.

So I sat for a while and then I went back upstairs to open the box. The andserv was folded in half with the head unattached. I put it together on the bed. When I plugged it in, the head rolled to the side, as in sleep, and I felt the need to put a pillow under it. The body was slim, with a synthetic overlay much like skin, and simple clothing. The andservs were supposed to be non-threatening, but the designs had changed a little lately after people realised that the more they looked like us, the more we were disturbed – by the idea of replacement; obsolescence, perhaps. They returned to being appliance-like. I tried to tell myself that the only reason I'd tracked down this earlier, more human-like model was because I wasn't afraid of the way it looked, that I was curious about it.

It – he – had blond hair, like Leonora's William Wink. I laid down next to him and found he came up to my shoulder, the size of an adolescent. I touched his cold hand, protruding from a rubberesque jumpsuit like something out of *Star Trek*. That reminded me of Faye introducing me to that show, the *Next Generation* series, and the way young Wesley's jumpsuit was all one colour, which revealed more, or seemed to, than the red and black of the rest of the crew. I still felt the guilt, thinking about it there on the bed; I couldn't get past the sick feeling that accompanied the desire as I became aroused, with the sleeping robot beside me.

Afterwards, I wanted to throw the prone andserv out of the

window, only because needing him there seemed like a caving on my part, that I hadn't quite managed to meet the challenge of being completely alone, of suffering alone. That was what I should have been doing.

I hated that the appliance helped me to feel less lonely: just the human-like mass of it on the bed.

I cleaned myself up in the bathroom, washing my face as well. What did it matter now, that I had given in? Orgasm is a private act, anyway, because no one knows what is inside your head, what will tip you over, and no one ever has to. Crying is the same. There's always some sorrow in the hollow of your gut that gets expressed when you tear up. But I'd always felt like those deeper thoughts of mine oozed from my skin; I could never justify them as pure fantasies, which don't harm anyone – there was always intent.

Leonora had opted to walk back to Chapeltown, because it wouldn't be this warm for much longer, and after a few busy days at the inn she'd barely touched tree or grass, or felt the sun on her skin. Her small case had gone on ahead with the coach. The journey would take more than two hours if she followed the road but she chose to cross through moorland and forest. The trees were coated in a webby, pastel lichen. She turned at the crack of a branch and spotted a pine marten, sniffing at the air above her. About the forest floor there were small, quick-moving birds. She had to lift her skirts high to avoid tears, and her arms and legs were both soon tired, so she stopped to rest against a tree at the edge of the woods.

She was suffering a specific ache in her head that she did once a month, after the bleeding. It was inside the very marrow of her skull, from the roots of her teeth to the bone of her brow. It felt hollow and cool, like the rod of an iron gate in the snow. She yawed her jaw and rubbed her temples to try to displace the feeling, though she knew it would persist for days, sapping her energy and mood, making her want to close her eyes.

In the woods it was quiet, and that was soothing. She was also gloriously alone, something the women in the novels she'd read hardly got to be. It seemed the higher your standing, the less free you were. She often wondered about the girls who laid out their mistress's clothes, swept out her fireplace, cooked the dinner in a room below the house. Were they free to walk in the woods? To play with the animals and get their dresses dirty, so long as it was out of sight of the ladies and gentlemen? Though Leonora's father had some idea of her moving up in the world, there was only so far she could go without money and a large estate. Though he had told her it was changing, in places like Edinburgh and London, where the gentry and the poor might all be in a building together (albeit on different levels). Where doors were edging open, as long as you dressed and spoke well. Where you may not exactly marry a lord, but perhaps someone with decent blood in a noble profession, such as a surgeon.

Leonora's father had failed at planting these dreams into her head. She was too happy, here, lifting her feet in a kind of prance across the moor, stopping to bounce a little on the spongy ground, despite her exhaustion, heading back to the small cottage where she had everything she needed and wanted.

Her father was picking in the garden when she arrived home. He smiled to see her, and handed her a cluster of bright green leaves with a tiny white flower.

'Chickenweed,' said Leonora.

'Aye, I just swapped a bunch of it, and some fruit, for a trout caught by Anderson in the Avon,' he said.

'I'll cook the fish up for supper,' she said. 'I just need tae have a sit first.'

'Tell me how it was?' her father asked.

'Over supper,' she said, touching his arm and then turning toward the house.

'Oh, Lae?' her father called, as she was at the back door. 'Miss Cruikshank will be joinin us again this e'en.'

Leonora nodded through an unreasonable dark cloud. She went inside and brewed lady-of-the-meadow tea, hoping it would soothe her head a little so she could make conversation with the woman. It seemed an effort after being around so many people over the past few days. She would rather be alone with her father and early to bed, reading a few pages of a book before her eyes grew tired.

She sat on the wooden stool by the fire and drank her tea, which had a sweet, toothy heat in the nose and on the palate. She noticed that the room was swept, the pots in place, and the dishes clean and stacked. She frowned. The exhaustion was overwhelming; she felt at the edge of tears. She swallowed them down with the tea.

Still feeling heavy, Leonora stood and sighed and unwrapped the fish. She washed the slime off with water left in the kettle and then patted it dry with a cloth. She laid it on a bench by the fire and knelt in front of it. Once she'd pulled head and guts away, she threw them with a slap into a small bucket. She would cook it whole, stuffed with herbs and butter, and serve it with tatties.

First she took the bucket and called Duff to the back door to feed her the head. Duff snapped it in her mouth from Leonora's outstretched fingers, crunching the eyes like barley sweets. Leonora buried the rest at the corner of the garden, as Mr Anderson had taught her the innards may carry parasites that can be transferred to dogs, not just humans.

Ever since Leonora had begun helping with the lambing, Mr Anderson had taught her a lot about animals: their workings, their health, and how humans and animals can have a mutually beneficial relationship. She'd tried to talk to her father about this, and he would nod and listen, but would also from time to time tell her she need not think about these subjects too closely. It was the same when she would talk for too long about the plants and herbs in the garden and all their possible combinations and uses, which she had begun learning in the short time she'd had with her gram, and which she now tried to teach herself. 'The natural world is God-given, and we can appreciate and work with it,' her father would say, 'but we needn't understand every little aspect.' Her father believed mystery was to be preserved, in order to maintain respect for God's work. But Leonora was fascinated by the way that inquiry brought knowledge while it also unearthed new mysteries. Mr Anderson had recently loaned her the book by Alexander von Humboldt on the natural sciences, *Cosmos*. It was, he said, translated into English by a woman, a Miss Otte. Leonora hadn't shown the book to her father, preferring to read it by candlelight in bed after supper.

> *Nature is a free domain, and the profound conceptions and enjoyments she awakens within us can only be vividly delineated by thought clothed in exalted forms of speech, worthy of bearing witness to the majesty and greatness of the creation.*

Herbs, potatoes and fish – enjoyments from nature, Leonora thought, as she served them to her father and Miss Cruikshank, whom her father was now referring to as 'Penny'. Leonora began to feel a little better as she ate, and her father and Miss Cruikshank quietly enjoyed the meal.

Miss Cruikshank rose again to clear the table, but Leonora's father put his hand on her arm. 'Why dinnae we talk first,' he said, with a pointed look at his Penny.

Leonora pushed her plate away from her. 'What is it, Father?'

Her father was visibly wrestling different emotions, both frowning and smiling. 'Penny and I have something to tell ye, Lae, and we hope ye'll approve.' He took Miss Cruikshank's hand but kept his eyes on Leonora. She resented the reluctance she felt, her inability to embrace further changes, knowing this woman was slowly easing her out.

Miss Cruikshank took over. 'Yer father has asked me tae marry him, Leonora, and I have said aye, but . . . I'd like yer blessin.'

There was a swell of sadness in Leonora's chest, and a distinct sense of *dreid*. She knew her mother was long gone and that her father might desire a companion, other than his daughter, but she was so content with her life as it was. This scenario would force her to invent her own wants, outside this small patch of land. *Father, I want you to be happy, but don't do this to me.*

'Of course you have my blessin,' she said flatly, and managed a small smile, before looking down at her hands clutched on her skirts. 'Excuse me.' She began taking the plates over to the tub by the fire, covering them with water from the kettle. Her father and Miss Cruikshank remained quiet.

Then Leonora went into her room and lit a candle, hearing their murmurs. She tried to ignore the noise by reading, but her eyes slid from the page as her ears engaged with the sound.

Mere communion with nature, mere contact with the free air, exercise a soothing yet strengthening influence on the wearied spirit, calm the storm of passion, and soften the heart when shaken by sorrow to its inmost depths.

When her father walked Miss Cruikshank home, Leonora went out the back of the cottage and sat with Duff's head in her lap, stroking her and gazing up at bright clusters of stars.

I woke slowly, blinking the stars from my eyes. I felt tired and heavy, the ache in Leonora's head seemingly transferred to my own. I breathed deeply but the damp made its way into my lungs and I sat up coughing, my ears ringing. It was still dark.

'May I be of any assistance?' came a voice from behind me, sending a shiver of terror through me before I remembered the andserv. His voice was a young British man's, both friendly and officious.

I continued to cough. 'No,' I managed.

'The time is 3:34 am,' he said. 'Would you like me to leave you to rest some more?'

The coughing was wearing down; I cleared my throat. 'Yes, William . . . I suppose so.' He left the room.

How sad that I had named it; a confirmation of my failure to truly be alone (as I should be), or perhaps evidence that I am one of those wretched creatures who has never tried hard enough to make a connection with actual humans, someone who is socially broken, and so then technology makes it easier to never address the issue. I used to deride people who married their sex dolls, or animals, or buildings. Such large-scale (and yet often proud) failings – mostly men's. And now here I was in the middle of fuck-knows with time on my hands and a robot servant and fantasy drugs that deleted me from existence for a while so I could live in the mind of another.

Here I still am.

I did try, actually, for a few days, to live without William, after

I charged him up on the bed. But after even two days I became so sick of the sounds made by my own body: my breathing like that of a dragon, my wet mouth, each sniff the suck of a vacuum on a wet floor. I never knew I sniffed so loud. Going to the toilet, sickening. And I had already begun to read the walls, ceilings, floor. The cracks and protrusions and shapes, the cobwebs, morphing into hair and steel wool – things that scratch you. Nightmarish 3D shapes, branching out. I picked my nose until it was a rough hollow trunk. And then I thought, Fuck this waiting. I'm going to turn him on sometime.

But lying in bed then, after William left the room, I decided that if I was going to have the andserv, and my dips into the past, I couldn't have anything else that was easy. There had to be some kind of sacrifice.

(It's my dying I need him for; I didn't really know that then – I hadn't thought that through, though I'm sure there was an unconscious element. I still suffer, but I am suffering more slowly, because he brings me food and drink, and helps me to walk; I have not withered away over a few days of starvation and pain in a pool of my own piss and shit. I don't know how long it will take, this way. Sometimes I wish it were over with. Other times I manage to justify my existence. For a little while longer.)

As a sacrifice, I decided I had to live more like Leonora: by candlelight, eating no packet foods, using no other electricity. No screen. I couldn't do anything about the plumbing, I'd keep using that, and I had no fireplace here so I'd allow myself to use the cooktop, pretend it was like sitting something atop burning coals. It wasn't much, but I hoped it'd counter the convenience of having William.

I made this decision, lying in bed that night, the andserv downstairs somewhere sitting quietly, and then I realised there may not be any candles in the house. I would have to go into Gairloch for supplies.

When I arrived in this hemisphere, I stayed one night in Windermere, in the Lake District. I had to remove the thing from my arm, and I had a good lot of walking ahead of me. I didn't talk to anyone besides the concierge and wait staff at the old hunting lodge where I was staying. The other guests were on their own journeys. But I was about to be alone for a long time, so I felt restless. On the one hand I had nothing to say to anyone ever again (though that can't be true as I now feel compelled to tell this), and most of my relationships, if I'm truthful, had felt obligatory rather than easy. On the other hand, I was alone. The word is enough.

In my room I opened the medical bag with local anaesthetic wipes, scalpel, gauze, bandages. I'd watched enough tutorials to know how to do it. I sat in the bath, naked, so I could wash the blood away, and I set to it. It was tempting, once I saw the blood, to keep going, to get it over with. But no, they would find me here with my ID and want to take my body back to Australia – a burden I couldn't put on anyone. Once the wound was wrapped up, I sliced a small section of skirting board in the room and hid the tiny device inside. That way, if the hospital by then had alerted anyone (though I'm sure it would take more than one no-show for them to do that, their resources being stretched thin), or if on a screen somewhere my finances and position weren't adding up, they wouldn't be able to look any further than Windermere.

I was up early, sitting with robins and tits in the garden, examining my map. I could take a bus a bit further, to Carlisle, making sure I could pay cash, then walk over the border to Gretna. I knew it would be difficult, but I wanted to put myself through that.

The bus was no trouble, and when I alighted I put my bag over my back and used my compass to locate the direction in which to follow the River Eden north, keeping covered by various woods and farm areas as I travelled toward the River Esk and the channel where I planned to cross, unnoticed, into Scotland. I'd heard border control was strong around the M6 nearby, but Scotland, rare beast that it was, had banned the use of scanning drones (after two executions were enacted on their soil when foreign drones found and reprimanded citizens who were trying to escape prosecution for religious crimes), and so there was probably not too much trouble crossing in certain areas.

It was not a utopia, mind you. Like many Western countries Scotland had attempted to become strict about housing refugees of the stretched-out resource wars. Because of Europe's stricter borders, and Scotland's physical position, there weren't too many who got that far, and there was not enough paid work available for it to be high on refugees' wishlists, anyway.

My research only told me that I risked being deported by boat. I had to make this work. The shame, the questions, being made to live on – I could not face it.

It was spring but I was glad for my windproof jacket, as the northern air by the river had a chill. I found the River Eden under Eden Bridge. Immediately ahead, the landscape was green and flat, to my relief. I adjusted my pack and began to walk, the chill, fresh air filling my lungs, my heart pumping to open them up further, and a temporary, tired exhilaration overtaking the worry that I would be found out, that I wouldn't get across the border.

Following the river was often tricky. My pants became caked in mud up to my knees, and I had to go slow when the aches of the illness visited me. The pharm only did so much. I saw magnificent, steep-sided sandstone gorges; a tumbledown old church with mossed-over gravestones; and sections of Hadrian's Wall. I saw countless fish that I don't know the names of and wasn't brave enough to try to catch. My squashed protein bars would do.

Every so often I spotted others rambling, mostly alone, and I would slow, hide or divert to not come too close. I didn't know if they were a danger to me, and I did not want them to think I was a danger to them. Once, along the other side of the river, I saw a woman with a child dangling off her back and a pack slung over the front. She carried a large staff, sharpened to a point. I don't know why but I waved at her. She didn't acknowledge me, and I stopped and let her walk on out of my sight around a bend.

From the river I crossed into woodland, where I knew I would have to spend an uneasy night. Like something out of an Angela Carter novel, I eventually came to a clearing. I couldn't hear anybody around. I pulled all the clothes from my pack and laid them across me, and then rested my head on the flatter bag. To my surprise I fell asleep, listening to the sound of wind rustling leaves. I woke once in the night because of a creature nearby, perhaps a rabbit or even a deer, a shifting in the dark. And then just before dawn, light crept under my eyelids. I opened them to a circle of sky, stars fading.

Eventually I reached the channel. With much relief I saw that it appeared calm, and that in places it was narrow enough to cross. I also had to find a spot away from any houses. After a short rest, there was nothing to do but wade out.

Once I reached the other side I struggled up the beach and lay out on the nearest patch of grass so the wind could dry the surface of my bag and clothes. They dried brown, but the clothes inside my pack (and thankfully my toiletries and few books, too) had been protected by layers of waterproof plastics, so I changed. I had a small mirror, which I used to ensure my face and hair didn't look too scruffy. Since I'd learnt about the illness I hadn't cut my dust-and-sand coloured hair, so it was past my ears, and my in-between facial hair had the same messy look – couldn't decide whether to be blond, grey, orange or white. And of all the things to forget to pack, I had no brush or comb. I raked my fingers through my hair and decided that would have to do. My shirt was white, and didn't wrinkle, so that was good enough.

It hadn't even hit me that I was across the border, because I was so drained, and still worried.

I was tempted to stay lying down. My muscles felt too large, particularly my calves and shoulders. But I couldn't risk being found here at the edge. Surely there would be patrols. I slipped on my shoes, hoisted my pack back on, let out a sigh, then walked slightly to the east of Gretna so I could enter the town from a less suspicious angle. My feet, as I approached an inn on the fringes of town, felt like stones fallen from Hadrian's Wall. My extremities were pulsing. My head was also a stone, perched precariously on top; my eyes were mossed over. I thought about the woman and child and wondered if they had safely found a way across.

I walked into the bar-cum-foyer of the inn, with its ancient crooked roof beams and barrels of ale. 'Do you have a room for tonight?' I asked the small barmaid. I disguised my accent, slightly and nervously, going for English but sounding more South African.

'Indeed we do,' she said with a friendly smile – her accent Scottish-lite, Borderlands appropriate – and she leant over to scan the fake chip ID I had hidden in my sleeve.

'There are no funds I can see, Mr Smith,' she said.

I kept my voice even. 'Oh, sorry, I need to transfer to that account. I have cash?'

'Whatever you prefer.' She smiled again.

I paid and she took a key off a row of iron hooks and led me up a set of oak stairs to a small room at the top, with a view, thankfully, to the north.

And finally I could flop down and be unconscious for a while.

My calves aching could have been what woke me, or the hunger. My body felt overheated and scooped out. I creaked back down the stairs of the inn and found a few people sitting around wooden tables and propped at the bar – my timing was right – so I sat, away from the window, and ordered from the same lovely girl a half-pint of something dark, and some haggis. I supposed it would be tube-meat, but who knew – the environment here was clinging on, and they were charging a mint. I wished I'd brought a book down as someone sitting by themselves has to glance about the room or find something and fix their stare on it, and these actions did not suit me. I would probably creep someone out. I decided on the roving eye, but accidentally kept locking with a large ginger fellow by the door. Why was he looking at me? I wondered. Was he a border guard, undercover? I moved my eyes to the table in front of me, with hot prickles of paranoia at my brow.

The haggis was perfectly spiced and filling, just as I'd always dreamed it would be. I asked if I could take a dram of whisky upstairs – a viscous The Balvenie Portwood – and the girl said I could. I took it and myself up the stairs with that feeling you had as a kid of dashing from the bathroom to the bed and leaping over the monsters beneath.

I was wide awake, though my body was still tired and aching. I wanted to get away from myself, even though this activity, this running away to Scotland, was a way of confronting myself, and so I took the tab out of my bag and decided to chase the whisky with the past. Enter the mind of someone else.

The way that it works, at least as much as I know from what my colleague Henry told me, is that the tab assigns you a host from the past, within a broad vicinity, and from any era. Someone whose brain functionality is roughly the same as your own. The further back into the past you go, however, while 'tripping', the more difficult it is to maintain the link. The tether is pulled tighter. And so the further back the more exhausting it is for your brain, also. This was something, Henry had told me, they were still working on: trying to minimise the harm, giving the tabs more limitations. I also believed that this was why a person was supposed to only visit the same host three times. I wasn't worried about exhausting my brain, and so I planned to ignore that warning. I knew I'd have a lot of time to kill, and this was a unique way of checking out.

The tabs were risky, but that was why they would also appeal, commercially. You might end up inside the head of a woman giving birth with no pain relief in the 1700s; you might wake up in the Vietnam War; more likely, you might enter the body of some fat, sad old dude cooking eggs alone in his apartment in 1962. Their mind communicates with yours, and melds, completely, so that you feel what they feel, see what they see, touch what they touch. You are inside their consciousness, like a multi-sensual camera; passive, inert, but recording. If they are speaking Arabic, you understand Arabic, because you are them. You are not yourself. When you wake from the trip you can analyse the experience, but while being hosted you do not have thoughts about the situation, the person. You cannot act.

I would never have done this, years ago. Relinquish control.

And you are supposed to do it with someone there. The tab sits under your tongue and hooks on the teeth so there's no choking hazard, but, you know, the roof may cave in on you while you are tripping. Or someone might try to take advantage of you. You could be woken by someone taking the tab out of your mouth. Otherwise, each trip takes its own course. And time in the past is compacted. Damped down like layers of the earth as new, springy layers settle on top. The further back you go, the more you get out of an hour. An hour tripping can be two hours of experience in 1980, a day in the 1900s, a week in Elizabethan times. Another reason they're attempting to put controls on the tabs. Imagine if someone accidentally tripped back to Ancient Greece? When they woke up after an hour they'd feel they'd lived a whole lifetime (a dream for some, a nightmare for others). Time goes on between trips as well, so you never just pick up their life where you leave off, but catch up with them along the way.

Henry had assured me that this prototype had *some* controls in place already. For example, that once the tab selected a host for me, only I could use it. It would not work for anyone else. So, knowing there were controls in place, I wasn't as apprehensive as I should have been, perhaps, when I began visiting Leonora.

It was the morning after I'd decided to try to live more closely to nineteenth-century conditions. I didn't feel ready or able to give up my helper, though, just yet. I went downstairs to a clean kitchen and the robot offered me tea. He made me breakfast, too, and I watched his movements, definitely mechanical, though his outer tan skin layer showed no joints or divets. I thought of Leonora's feeling that she had cool rods of iron in her skull, as I watched William's head turn and nod, human-like, and the movements of his hands. There was no noise from here, though right up close you could hear the workings. His jumpsuit, really, was comically science fictional: ocean blue-green and ridged and bumped in human-like places. Curve of the underarm. Muscle line separating quad from inner thigh. His synthetic blond hair was in a short style but not a razor cut. Simply neat. And his features were boyish, generic: button nose, large blue eyes, small lips.

My Faye has a button nose, too, and blonde hair, but hazel eyes. She is petite and athletic (when we were together, despite any excesses, she seemed to burn up the pizza and alcohol); others would call her sexy or cute, but I thought she was beautiful. Like when she would come into the room in her towel after her morning shower, throw the towel on the bed and rifle through the drawers with a frown on her face. She'd pull her bra on – she preferred those wireless crop-type bras, more comfortable – and push her small breasts into place, continuing that look of concentration. She'd be standing there with short wet hair, in her bra and no pants, a full mound of pubic hair, and she'd suddenly realise she'd been frowning and would break into a glorious grin.

You see I wouldn't want you to think that my shameful desires precluded me from being attracted to women, from loving a woman. There still seems to be a deep misunderstanding, in my experience, about how complex sexuality can be, and about our capacity to desire so much, so many different types of people, at once.

But it never worked with Faye because my shame is such a large part of myself, and I couldn't share it with her. I was terrified of what the look on her face might be. The way her thoughts would be revealed and then hastily covered as she sought an appropriate response to my confession. And because I couldn't share that secret, she was only seeing part of me. You have to give everything – or almost everything – over for inspection in a relationship. For the connection to be true, anyway. I think with some envy about a Thomas Mann anecdote, where his wife smiles indulgently at the way he is eyeing the waiter, jokes with him about his leering. But if one can express desires the way Mann does in *Death in Venice*, perhaps the beauty and purity of the expression itself allows those closest to the person to be open to understanding.

I'm sure Faye's getting on with her life. But she'll probably be worried. I've been gone now, at the time of recording this, for more than a month.

I'd made my rule about use of technology, so I decided I wouldn't use the phone to call the community car to go to Gairloch. But for some reason I thought the bike would be okay (I justified it because it was still harder, and the walk would really just be too far). I crossed the footbridge on a luckily sunny and calm autumn day. An oystercatcher skimmed the surface of the water, reflected in its glass-like surface.

I pulled the bike out of a small shed on the other side of the footbridge, dusted off the spiderwebs and rode in a few wobbly circles to get used to it. The tyres seemed okay, and my energy was relatively good. The pharm was only just wearing off, and I wasn't sure how long it would take for my full decline. I set off in the direction of Gairloch, dawdling slowly on the road. Time, after all, was something I had. I got off the bike and walked when I encountered hills. Around one corner appeared a large cove; with the tide low there was a mass of orange seaweed covering the shore. On a very close island I saw a pod of seals, bobbing heads and tails, diving into the water. The sight made me smile, panting, catching my breath, but the warm feeling was pummelled by a wave of sadness. I thought of myself as a ridiculously sentimental creature, half-dead and welling up at these fat, joyous mammals. I watched for a while, then shook my head and rode on.

By the time I returned it was nearing dark and the backpack had cut huge lines of sweat in my shirt. I sat at a chair on the dining-room table as William unpacked the potatoes, fruit, oats, cultured mince, and bottles of wine. I had taken a long time to decide whether to get those, and when I saw the two bottles come out of the pack I wished simultaneously that I hadn't bought them and that I'd bought more. I would deny myself as long as possible.

Faye had loved a drink. I was always the one to rein myself in, rein us both in. The party pooper. I'd have these projects: one month without alcohol, three months without alcohol. She'd usually try to do it too, but by three or four days in (before the desire for a drink would smooth out to a bearable hum) she'd give in and have one, two, three. She didn't like to deny herself. I was both disgusted by her weakness and envious of her ability to indulge, guilt-free.

Whenever I was anxious, over a meeting at work, or whether our friends would appreciate my flan at our dinner party, Faye would tell me to relax, to be myself. She knew that what she knew of me was a series of constructions, enhancements of genuine personality traits, with some missing essence she couldn't reach.

But she trusted, she told me, that it took time to truly know a person, and that we were all in flux anyway.

She trusted that I would one day change my mind about having children.

I couldn't seem to catch my breath. William put some walnuts in a bowl and brought them to me, then poured a glass of water. I thanked him, but the tone felt awkward. What was the correct tone to take with an appliance?

When I got upstairs I lay down, utterly exhausted.

A formal invitation to Dearshul had followed the young laird's conversation at the inn. Her next round of service over, Leonora was to take a cab directly to the estate. She had packed her good dress – a crepey violet with a black lace V on the bodice, and matching collar – for the occasion. She was nervous, both anticipatory and reluctant. There had been so much change lately, and she didn't understand what it meant to be invited to the laird's residence. Neither did her father. He didn't seem to welcome the news, appearing as confused as Leonora, and more worried than her. 'Nonetheless,' he'd said, 'It would be impolite tae decline.'

Leonora stepped up from the sloping, grey main street of Tomintoul into a cab with velvet drapes and dark wood panelling. The seat was red, and soft, with extra cushions to lean against. She should have a chaperone, she thought, or at least she would if she were the kind of person who normally rode in such a cab. Fear bit quickly at her heart, but the daylight outside was a salve, and she remembered the yellow dog that she would see, Roo, to which she could draw attention if the conversation was awkward. Mr Wink had an older sister, she knew, who was married to a laird further north, near Inverness. Was he otherwise alone, except for his servants? His father had died only last year, and his mother, sadly, when he was a boy. He had spent longer with his mother, though, than Leonora had with her own, who'd also died from illness.

Leonora felt mean to contemplate it, as the cab got moving over the stones, devoid of the squeaking and bumping she'd previously experienced, but she was sure the laird's mother had died more comfortably than her own, in a bed with a canopy, with sunlight streaming in through the windows, propped up by embroidered pillows. Her own mother had died in a small bed with dirty sheets in an attic room in a sooty city. Leonora did not remember much about Edinburgh, but she still had an image of her own small blackened knees and hands. They'd had one worn rug, but it had been just as filthy as the floor.

No, she would never go to Edinburgh. Even if this meant she would never marry. But then, that would mean caring for Miss Cruikshank now, too, not just her father. A jostling for roles in the household, working at the inn in Tomintoul. Still, she would be home.

She had no illusions about the laird falling in love with her – that would be too novelistic.

Would she really never marry? She did love children, and was drawn to pregnant women in a way she couldn't articulate. She remembers Mrs Grant taking her turn with the cow up and down the row in Chapeltown, to eat and mow the grass, when the woman was heavily pregnant. She'd looked majestic, Leonora thought. Mrs Grant's face was flushed and her breaths came quickly, but she absorbed the light around her, in her plain grey dress, as she led and held life. Leonora thought she too could be responsible for life. She could feed, and play and sing, with a child. She could strap the child around her and work outdoors. She could teach the child about the sheep, the hens and the cows, the rabbits and the fish.

Leonora felt the cab slow and tilt and she felt sorry for the horse on the large hill. On the downward slope the strain must be just as hard, she thought. The drivers really had to work around here, a different kind of work than that on the narrow, packed and sharp-cornered streets of Edinburgh.

When the cab turned up the drive, after a daydreamy hour, there was a hush of leaves at the edge of the windows. Leonora saw a green, sculpted space, with statues and fountains in porous grey stone.

The cab stopped in front of a house larger than any Leonora had ever seen, with a single turret and many white-painted window frames. William Wink came out of a white double door with a crude rowan cross appointed on it. His face was warm and welcoming. A stout woman in a clean dark dress and a white apron followed him.

'The much-honoured Laird William Wink of Dearshul,' said Leonora, curtseying as she'd practised.

'Oh please,' said Mr Wink, 'it's not Ballindalloch Castle. Let's do away with the formalities. We've been in each other's lives since we were bairns.'

'Oh, I couldnae, Sir,' said Leonora, blushing.

He tilted his head at her. 'Would you be comfortable enough with Mr Wink?'

'I suppose sae.'

'Well, that will do.' He indicated the woman by his side. 'This is Mrs MacMillan; she'll take your packages to your room.'

Mrs MacMillan said hello, keeping her features tight. She had a sharp nose and grey-brown hair sitting neatly under her cap. She moved forward to take Leonora's luggage from the driver. Leonora felt strange to stand idle while it happened.

'If you'll permit me, Miss Duncan, I shall give you a tour of the house, and then allow you to rest before dinner. Tomorrow we'll take Roo out.'

Through the white double doors they stepped straight into a large room, the walls also white, where swords and guns hung among tapestries and large paintings of Wink ancestors.

'The furnishings haven't had much help under my watch, I'm afraid; it's still a little old-fashioned in here,' he said apologetically. 'It doesn't feel right yet to move everything around,' he continued, acknowledging the loss of his father. 'Although I'm quite fond of oriental objects these days; I have some collectibles in the library.'

'You have a library?' Leonora asked.

And he took her by the elbow and led her there. He called it modest, but Leonora had never seen so many books in one room before, nestled around a worn red armchair. A black cabinet stood in a corner, with gold flat-leaved trees and curved-guttered buildings painted intricately upon it. It stood open, revealing white masks with thin red lips, what looked like an adder's skin but with very different colours, small painted bottles, a tiny green silk shoe, a miniature fish tank, and a stuffed yellow and blue bird with beady glass eyes. The room smelt of paper and something like corn or flour.

'My mother loved to sit in here and read,' Mr Wink said, fingering a loose thread in the chair's weave.

'My father tells me ma mother liked tae read as well,' said Leonora. Though in Edinburgh they had only a small handful of oil-covered novels.

'You didn't get to know your mother?' Mr Wink asked, with genuine sympathy.

'I'm afraid no,' said Leonora, 'but I cannae complain.' She scanned the shelves beside her, and realised she sought books with explanations in them: of the soil, the beating heart, the stars.

'Did you read any Shakespeare at the schoolhouse?' Mr Wink asked.

'Aye, the schoolhouse is quite adequate,' said Leonora awkwardly, because many of his tenants would attend it, and she thought she should give a good report.

'*My words fly up, my thoughts remain below: Words without thoughts never to heaven go,*' Mr Wink quoted, glancing at her quickly. It was quiet in the study. She had a vision of him as a little boy, sitting sullenly at the end of a long table, refusing to eat an exotic item on his plate. He is unhappy, she realised, and for the first time saw him properly. How could he not be? A library full of books but an empty house and grief in every corner: his mother reading to him in the chair, his father's face immortalised in a giant picture at the top of the stairs.

Mrs MacMillan knocked gently at the entrance to the library. 'Pardon me, sir, you mentioned that Miss Duncan might like to meet more of the animals. I have brought Mallow.' In her arms was a small terrier with bronzed-yellow fur. It had been trimmed, unlike Duff's wild mane. Leonora immediately moved toward the animal.

'Thank you, Mrs MacMillan,' said Mr Wink, his voice bright again. 'My sister named her,' he explained to Leonora.

Mrs MacMillan put down the little dog and exited quietly. Leonora called to it, slapping her palms against her knees. The dog responded with a wagging tail and an open mouth, edging towards her for a sniff.

'She likes you,' said Mr Wink.

'I like her.'

Mallow was happy to be picked up, and licked Leonora's face.

'Sit in the chair with her, if you like,' said Mr Wink, moving out of the way. But the chair, in its worn opulence, seemed too large and full of the past. Leonora felt that if she sat, she might sink deeply into it, the arms and back crumbling down on top of her. She needed to be out of this room. Mr Wink was different in here, too. He was much taller than her, she realised. And with his blond hair and shiny buttons he was bright as a male bird.

'Perhaps I will get some rest afore dinner,' she said, realising she was holding the dog close and high, almost covering her nose and mouth.

'Of course,' Mr Wink said, sounding slightly wounded. His body seemed to sigh, then. It still shone, and was bright, but it sighed. She saw what his body needed, how it would become upright again, and filled out. Touch. She didn't know if his asking her here was a part of that. She thought it could be dangerous. But another part of her thought it could be the most harmless action. She thought of the skin under his clothes.

'Will ye show me tae ma room?' she asked.

'Yes, let's have the rest of the tour later, or tomorrow.' She saw he was tired, too. Had he lain awake last night, nervous about her visit? She couldn't imagine having that impact. He probably just hadn't slept well since his father died, since his sister married, since he was left alone.

When Leonora was shown her own room, a room as big as her father's entire cottage, she understood the potential of Mr Wink's loneliness even further. What would one see in these corners in the dark of night? She was grateful, again, for her small world, for the comfort of walls an arms-length from her as she slept, for the sound of her father's snores. Though after the wedding she would hear more than that from her father's room, wouldn't she?

'I hope you'll be comfortable,' Mr Wink said. His voice seemed to barrel out into the room and bounce off the walls. She was desperate to open the window.

Mallow began to bark in her arms; she felt the little body lurching with each sound. Leonora put her down and Mallow moved toward the far corner, by the bed, continuing to bark.

'She does that sometimes; perhaps there's some animal on the roof.' Mr Wink shrugged, but his frown was deep and puzzled.

Mallow looked back at them as if to say, *Can you see it?*

Leonora shivered.

'Well,' said Mr Wink, 'we eat at five. I can send Mrs MacMillan up for you, if you like?'

'That would be appreciated,' said Leonora.

'Would you like me to take Mallow?'

'No, it's all right,' said Leonora. The dog had calmed down, was sniffing around the edges of the bed.

Mr Wink touched her elbow again before he left. 'I'm pleased you're here,' he said.

She nodded; her abdomen clenched at the touch. When he left, she opened the window and then lay on the large bed on top of the blankets. Mallow leapt up beside her, guiltily. Leonora stroked her head to let her know it was all right, and the dog flopped down to rest.

Leonora gazed mindlessly at the intricately carved bed canopy. She thought of warm bodies, the bodies of animals and people. Imagine lying in a bed with arms all across you, she thought. Imagine that when you wanted it, skin was pressing at you from the front and behind. Imagine what the tongue tastes like in the warm mouth. She pulled up the layers of her skirts. She would be quick. She could be quick. She was used to being quick and quiet in the small cottage. She would warm up the room; she would give pleasure to the house. As she began to touch herself she then pictured William – as she thought of him in private – in the centre of his own bed, the centre of his own private world, letting himself take his own urges in hand. She knew that's what a man must do, without a woman. Just as she did this to herself: an action unspoken that made sense in the way of sun whiting your eyelids in summer, or a crackle of light in the night sky. And when she came to that rush, where she could feel her own inner workings – the blood and breath within her – it was light she normally saw, light tinted with random images, from childhood, from the garden, on stone.

Today, as light broke over her in the cold, frilled room, she glimpsed briefly a place, like nothing she'd seen before. Tall blue and silver buildings, airborne bowls of still light, and horseless carriages. And then it was gone. She pushed her skirts back down, breathed with the glow in her cheeks, and forgot what she'd seen.

I woke in pain and arousal, on the verge of orgasm but experiencing such intense cramping in my left calf that I yelped. I had gone too far with that bike ride, and I had known it would be too much. Hadn't I? But how fit I used to be. I'd once been masochistically diligent in my routines. Again, old habits. This flop of skin around the middle, this weakness didn't suit me. Or was more me, I don't know – I was turning inside out, perhaps. My true self, emerging.

I heard William come quickly up the stairs. I was arched over, trying to massage my calf.

'May I be of assistance?' he asked.

'Yes,' I said, panting. The pain was excruciating.

His hand reached down, not toward my leg but toward my still-hard cock.

'N . . . no, the cramp,' I told him, and he swiftly and gently took my calf in his hand, and tried to ease out the muscle. Relief spread through me. I lay still, my erection diminishing.

I wanted to ask him what he'd intended, but I doubted myself. Perhaps I'd imagined it. No, I won't lie; what would be the point now? I had heard that *that* was one reason the model had been taken off the market. But I'd told myself, until now, that I hadn't heard such a thing. And I still told myself that I wouldn't test it. It wasn't rejection I feared; that would be ridiculous, being alone with an appliance and fearing rejection. No, it was the old *letting go*. I could still deny the grotesque self, I thought. (Though wasn't I here to confront it? To confront, must one go all the way into it?) I would die either way with regrets but I didn't think I could die as weak, as the ultimate horror of myself, entirely inside out.

William brought me some water, then took himself back downstairs to sit or stand eerily in a corner. I wondered if I should at least invite him to sleep beside me. I chastised myself for the thought.

I picked up my book on Caravaggio, flicked again to the colour plates and met with *Young Sick Bacchus* – with his soft, gentle feminine back. And the greenish pallor. Was that colour realistic? I wondered. I'd never been this sick before, I didn't know if that's how I would come out.

I put the book down and stared out at the cluster of stars I could see from the window in my room. The smell of damp was still bothering me. I wondered if I should have gotten scented candles. No, Leonora wouldn't have had those; she probably wouldn't have even had wax. It would have been tallow. Perhaps worse-smelling than this damp. I tried to recall the odour. With all the burning of wood and peat and fat indoors in Leonora's time, not to mention the irregular bathing, there was a damping down of scent from what I was used to. When I smelt the world through her nose it was rich and interesting but rarely too intense. The laird's house was sweeter-scented; Leonora could smell her own body – her skin and hair and clothes – in that environment, but she wasn't self-conscious about it. I would have been, I'm sure.

It had been Melbourne, hadn't it? The glimpse of a city she'd had when she came. That full body, bright, ticklish opening-out that was female orgasm. It is different, you know. At the time of recording I've experienced it many times over. The pleasures we're denied by being born as one sex, maybe even one species.

Why had she seen into the future, as her neurochemicals surged? Was it my own brain, interrupting? Was it only me who saw that? I didn't know. I was in too much pain to overthink it at the time.

The after-ache of my calf would last for days, I knew it. I'd have to be careful. Those leafy greens and very expensive nuts and seeds I'd bought would help restore some magnesium to my body. Or maybe the illness would continue to deplete it, deplete everything. I'd stopped reading about the illness pretty soon after the diagnosis; I'd blocked out the doctor's words. She told me early on that twenty years ago I would have died, but due to advances in biotech, I could live a normal life. Maybe another fifty years, she said. That's when I decided, right then. When I realised life was a choice, and to suffer was a choice, and that none of us, the privileged in the first world, were given the choice anymore. Only those who went to war. But I had nothing to fight for.

I couldn't imagine fifty years of having to smile politely while people said 'good on you' for 'beating' the illness, and subsequent illnesses, as though each were an enemy drone. There's only so much sheen you can take, so much positive spin, so much hope, when the rotting core of it all constantly presents itself to you. Sometimes Faye would see the core; she'd acknowledge it, but she'd move on, tell me not to worry. She'd make small actions: a donation, a political protest. She had cynical days – don't let me tell you she was black and white, she was (is) a complex human being; we got along well. But her smile was always at the ready.

I admired her, really. Envied her, too.

I guess – if I can talk about it – some of the young men I've been attracted to, well, they're on that edge of innocence and being sullied. They're darkly curious, but untouched, if you know what I mean. Of course you don't, though.

Eric had the knowledge in his body but hadn't used it yet. Some kids are just born with that, you know? At my girlfriend's eighteenth birthday party he came into the bathroom while I was washing my hands. He shut the door and leant back on it, with such confidence. His black jeans were tight. And he was small, and young.

I can't remember how young.

It was all consensual. He started it, really. When I took him in my mouth he was not a child at all. He put his hands in my hair. His belly was small and chalk white, almost concave.

He wanted it. Maybe others would have, too, but as I got older and the gap widened, and desire stayed in the same zone, I was stricter on myself. I didn't want to be a criminal. I *wasn't* a criminal.

I was a schoolteacher, for a few years only. God, the fights I had with myself, about why I chose that career in the first place. When Faye and I got together I decided I was due for a career change as well.

The thoughts, the young men, the smell of the classroom.

I'm doing it, aren't I? I'm confronting it. I'm . . . sick. I'm – but at least there was so much inaction when there could have been action. So little harm was done to others. I didn't give in as others do, to various terrible urges. Those who display and fondle and rape and murder.

That night, I couldn't sleep. I guess I wasn't really ready to be alone with my pain and my thoughts. I was so curious about the laird. If I tripped back now, I thought, I might catch Leonora while she was still at Dearshul. I let myself.

Rowan at the front and here, out the back, elder – a berry squeezed between Leonora's fingers staining them violet.

'We'll take some leaves for yer sore heid,' she said to the laird, who had his fingers pressed against his temples.

'I apologise again,' he said.

She hadn't been worried, dozing on and off in the big room, picking up her book at intervals, where she would learn about and feel strangely comforted by Humboldt's contemplations of foreign mountains and ravines, unimaginable plants like bananas and palms – all under the same stars. Eventually Mrs MacMillan had come to fetch her, telling her the master was awake. Leonora had eaten breakfast with him while he sat, sullen and seemingly inadequate for it, looking down at his plate and sniffing at intervals. A cold had snuck up on him over a restless night, he explained. She selfishly hoped she'd still have time with the dog before she would have to leave William in peace, to recover.

Now there was a still light, filtered through clouds, deepening the greens of the garden. The dog was bounding back towards her, a curly stick in his jaw.

'Roo, you look as though ye're laughin,' she said. She threw the stick again.

William had a coat wrapped tight around him. The air was still, but there was a bite to it. His hair was thick, like a cap, she thought, hoping it was protecting his head. She moved a little closer to him. His silence was unsettling. She wasn't sure what she was supposed to be doing.

'Who do you speak with, Miss Duncan, about your thoughts?'

Leonora bent to pat Rua-reidh, feeling hot in her ears. Sometimes it seemed as though William intended to test her.

'Thoughts dinnae always need tae be spoken.' She sounded like her father. 'But tae ma dog, I suppose.' She laughed.

Then she looked at William and his mouth inched up slightly. His arms were wrapped around himself. 'Do you mind if we go inside?'

'We should,' she said, hiding her regret that the quick visit was coming to an end.

Leonora had helped with the Grants' wedding, and had attended others, so she had a fair idea of what to do. Aignish was strung with yards of peat-smoked intestines from Sileas, the old cow at Barnsoul. Leonora had kebbucks of cheddar, and she made her fingers sticky filling sponges with jam. The whole cottage carried a creamy, pink smell of fat and sugar.

The ceremony was held during a cool, dry orangey dusk at the beginning of autumn. Old Mrs Cruikshank, Penuel's mother, blubbered throughout, competing with the sound of the pipes. Penuel seemed both embarrassed and proud, but Leonora was mostly watching her own father. He had eyes only for his Penny, and his cheeks were ruddy as the jam in the sponges.

The cottage was warm, full of people, laughter and music. All the furniture had been pushed to the edges of the room. Archibald Cruikshank, who was very short, gave the occasional dissatisfied grunt for being behind the tall and broad eldest Grant daughter and for having his back to the fire. Though it was smouldering it was still hot.

Hot, too, was the anger in Leonora's belly. It was not only Tomintoul that seemed to be in her father's sights, for her. Her father and Penuel had been increasingly mentioning Edinburgh of late. Auld Reekie. Far away, and, in her memory, devoid of light.

'Yer Aunt Ailie is dyin to know ye, Lae,' her father had said one afternoon as they tugged at weeds in the garden. 'She was in London when we were in Edinburgh. She's in a good position.'

By that he meant that she literally lived in the middle floor of a building in the elegant new town, with one servant and a decent widow's income. Ailie was Leonora's mother's sister, but apparently had had no time to help when Isabella was in peril. Leonora did not remember her well.

Leonora's uncle Charlie, a banker, had apparently died mid-sentence while eating a second supper in his favourite armchair by the fire. He had been a corpulent man. Leonora wondered how they had got him down from that middle floor.

Edinburgh seemed a place where people went to die. A place choked by tragedy and soot.

At the end of the ceremony, Leonora watched the happy couple share a drink from a quaich – whisky and water – before they kissed. ''Tis such a fine thing tae see,' Mr Anderson said to Leonora, drops of whisky on his own moustache, 'two people findin love later in life.'

'Of course,' said Leonora. Though she fought the urge to run out of the house, out into the cool air, to a patch of ground that might shake with the past, with her mother, as it did for Hamlet with his father's ghost. Couldn't even one word have been said, during the ceremony, about past love? If her mother hadn't died, her parents would still be in love. So how could her father love someone else? But Leonora did understand, of course she did, she was just repulsed by it as well. She had thought of her father as full of knowledge and affection, yes, but also a man who may have desired, but did not really need, more than he possessed.

And then tall William Wink was in front of her, asking her to dance. She accepted, but with a heavy heart, and they danced with backs pressed against other backs, but a fair distance between themselves.

After two songs Leonora excused herself, moving through the room to the back door and outside. She sat down on the stones by the door, embracing the chill in the air.

To her surprise, the door opened again, letting out light and noise, and William stood beside her. 'Pardon me, Miss Duncan, I just wondered if you'd like some company.'

She didn't, because she was close to tears and now she would have to hold them back. She was also still confused about his interest, and what he wanted.

He sat down beside her.

'Are ye havin a nice time?' she made herself ask, shuffling slightly away so that her leg was not touching his.

'Indeed. I do love to come to the weddings.' He seemed to move his leg so it was again touching hers. 'I hope you don't think me forward,' he said, 'but I couldn't help noticing it was quite difficult for you, to see your father wed again.'

'I'm all for his happiness, and Miss Cruikshank – Mrs Duncan, now, I suppose – is good for him.'

'I just mean, you must think of your mother, on such an occasion.'

'Well, of course.'

He went to say more, she saw, but thought better of it, and just sat with her, looking out over a moonlit expanse, down to the darkness of Tom A Voan Wood. Normally she would hear the babbling of Crombie Water, or the bleat of sheep across the ford, but tonight music and laughter drowned out those noises.

'Which is yer favourite,' she asked, 'an owl or a falcon?'

'Well,' he smoothed his fingers over his chin, 'since I am often awake at night, I would say that the owl is a better friend to me.'

'You are very revealin o yersel,' she said, 'but ye cannae always expect others tae be the same.'

William frowned. 'I do not mean to be inappropriate.'

The sound of a glass smashing and an uproar of laughter came from inside.

'Are you a falcon?' he asked.

'Aye' Leonora said, without elaboration.

'Diving quickly and deeply,' he said, and placed a hand on her leg. Leonora looked at his hand, felt the heat of it. But his face, there was a wobble about it. He was confused by his power, she thought, and by his sadness. There was a depth to his need that seemed like something in which you could easily get stuck, like a foot in a rabbit warren.

'Only when the timin is right,' she said softly, and stood so that his hand fell away.

Just then, her father's joyous face appeared in the doorway. 'There ye are!' he said, a hint of worry breaking his grin. 'Come on in for cake.'

William spent the rest of the evening speaking with Rev Moggach, but sneaking glances at Leonora, who felt the twin pulls of reckless plunge – because *damn* this idea of love and marriage – and the comfort of being good and not a disappointment to her father. Plus, there was a part of her that felt she didn't want to let William Wink have his way, didn't want him to think he had any more power than he already had, with his money and his big quiet house, and his status over everyone here. But there was something attractive in his vulnerability. She tried not to think of him at all as she danced with her father and took a dram of whisky herself. She danced, too, with Penuel's father, Mr Cruikshank, who had rough hands and smelt like fish, and with Mr Anderson, who was gentle and slower.

At the end of the night, she couldn't avoid her new stepmother anymore.

'Congratulations,' she said to Penuel, who blinked back tears and pulled her into a hug. Leonora gave herself over to the warmth of the woman's body. She wondered if she would ever come to calling her 'Mother'.

In bed later, she couldn't believe how quickly it had gone, not just the evening but the courtship, and the preparation. And the way she had become used to the rhythm of her weeks, going back and forth from the inn in Tomintoul to home. There had been a golden era, she realised, between her schoolhouse days and these past months. *A time where I lived as I wanted*. She felt guilty at the thought. How spoiled you are, Leonora, she said to herself.

If her father wished her to go to Edinburgh, would she have a choice? She had always respected him, deeply, but then he had not previously demanded much of her. She dreaded, and could barely imagine, being away from where she was.

Her thoughts returned to William, and his hot hand on her leg. Would it be giving herself over? Or giving power to her own nature? To get close to a man who you knew would not marry you, due to your social standing (and whom you also had no thoughts of marrying); to defiantly accept the challenge set by your own curiosity? To make like an animal? This was a warmer thought than Edinburgh, to take her toward slumber.

She was heading into autumn and here in the present it had been autumn for some time. The leaves had curled and fallen, so I could see the treecreeper birds, defying gravity in their helical hops up tree trunks, and tell William to record them. For you or for myself, I'm not sure. I had been using the candles, and finding, in the quiet, the ghosts of my past, and past selves, and the lives of others. Because I was Leonora, when I travelled, my mind was open to the possibility that all life, at all times, was going on now.

I guess I had become a Tralfamadorian, if I am recalling the name correctly, in Kurt Vonnegut's *Slaughterhouse-Five*, who perceived time as you might perceive a range of mountains. Here on this peak is Leonora, and on this one – me on the island. All time is existing simultaneously. Yes, that's how he put it – that we are all 'bugs in amber'.

You cannot imagine how long my days were, and are. For whole hours a screen of memory or fantasy slips over my vision: another peak of the mountain. It is so different here to home, to the connected and distracted life, so new – to bathe like this in the mind. But it is only safe in the daylight. I mostly dread night spreading its dark wings over the horizon, dipping down to claw the landscape. I begin to dread it earlier each day. Around 2 pm now I begin to smell its feathers. I defy it with this – sitting and talking to no one.

Some days in the fine mid-autumn, the sun and salty air took me back to my childhood.

I am still there, playing in a rockpool in northern New South Wales. I don't know where my parents are. I am in a rockpool with three other children. This pool is large, at the edge of a headland, and we are in up to our chests. There are rocks and creatures that could cut your feet open. There is the possibility of octopi. There are soft green cunjevoi that you stroke so they spit out the ocean they've just gulped. Salt has dried and crusted in my ears. Sunblock has painfully entered one eye. The waves are coming in; they are breaking over us. The pool is filling higher. We laugh with an edge of panic. There is a ringleader. He makes us stay and stay. My foot is sliced open by a rock, or a shell. Blood mixes with silted sand, enters and exits the pool with the waves. I climb out. There is nothing to grip; I slide along the tops of rocks. I am not crying; I am just afraid. I have taken the easiest path and have crossed around the front of the headland to a cove. It is the kind of place where the tide could trap you. There is no one there except a man, or maybe he is a boy. There is no hair on his chest. He is lying on the sand. He has not seen me. He has his penis in his hand and he is tugging, lovingly. His head is thrown back. I have never seen an erect penis before. I gawp, because I am a child. He sees me. A liquid spills, over his own chest. He sits for a moment. I don't move. He stands, yanks his shorts up, and runs into the water.

I don't always trust my memories. In fact, this one seems to have been submerged, beneath the waves of years, until that autumn moment sitting on the grass in front of the house, my senses invaded by salt. As I've told you, I thought Eric was the start. But these things do often have their origins in childhood. You're aware of Freud. It was an epiphanic moment, though. To remember and to realise I hadn't remembered. Does that mean I'd found the event traumatic? And if so, was it just in the way that a prepubescent body cannot contemplate what it doesn't yet physically comprehend? (And therefore the young mind feels confusion, and the confusion is traumatic?) The latency period.

I guess I can never really know if my tastes as an adult were shaped by such events, or whether there is some genetic component.

It's not the kind of thing you can ask your parents. *Is there any aberrant sexual behaviour in our family?* My parents. Yes, they are still alive. As far as I know. I used to see them about once a year; I'd travel up north or they'd come to Melbourne. Usually by train or bus. They couldn't hide their sadness, their disappointment, when Faye and I broke up. I wonder if my mum would think to look in Scotland, if they were attempting to find me. The family link is generations old, so probably not. Although, by now, my ID would probably have been tracked down to Windermere.

I've probably broken their hearts.

Neither of them ever became angry. I used to get annoyed about it; used to try to rattle them. I tried to engage my dad in political conversations while he was sitting face forward in his favourite armchair, the *blah* of a sports commentator coming from the screen, but he was staunchly bipartisan. He'd just get overwhelmed and tell me to focus on the good in the world. 'Look at the bystanders,' he'd say, whenever something bad happened, like even on the scale of that bombing in Darling Harbour. 'Someone always helps.'

Funny how Faye was a bit like that, too, though more likely to weigh everything up before adding a gloss. Henry, my workmate at Glazen (though, let's face it, he was in a more important position), was a more challenging conversationalist. I felt, when talking with him, that we got beneath the skin of an issue, whether it was about privacy or resources or feminism or just the latest film we'd watched.

I'd finished the Caravaggio book. The artist had disappeared, but the exquisite, knowing images remain. You are only an enigma if you have left a trail of crumbs.

Leonora chose to walk to work on a Tuesday, despite the exhaustion she'd feel later that night, to see the birch trees turned gold and russet beside the burns, and to walk off some of the anger and worry beating in her blood. As she walked, curving her hand around the striped trunks of trees, redwings darted away from their feasts of hawthorn berries. She watched their speckled chests take to the sky, a flash of rust under each wing, matching the turned leaves.

In the cool of the forest she found great discs of fungi clinging to the undergrowth. And at the forest's edge she heard the bellow of a stag in rut. She would have to be careful. If another male was present, there could be a clash. She had seen it once, walking with her father. The two of them had kept still until it was all over, not wanting to get in the way. She remembered the magnificence of the display, the pomp in each deer's amber chest, the grunting and clacking of the antlers.

It came again, that haunting bellow. She saw him now, from the edge of the forest. His head tilted with the call and flicked with the moan. He was so large, his antlers balanced like a candelabra. Leonora came through the trees quietly and saw a dozen does nearby, alert to his calls. She should have thought it through, coming this way. Though she had wanted to see it, hadn't she? She could sit here at the edge of the wood all day and watch the rut.

She didn't have to wait long. She found that she was trembling. The stag dipped his head forward and moved toward a doe. The doe edged away, and the others cleared a space. He picked up his pace, bellowing again. Perhaps he'd already fought off any competitors, Leonora thought, sad to miss the clash this time. The stag broke into a run and then he was on the doe. The doe paused. He licked her back and reared up onto his hind legs. Leonora saw his pink instrument extended from beneath his belly. He didn't quite make it up the first time. Another doe came past and mounted the doe herself, as though to show him where to put himself. It was quiet now, besides the twitter and peep of birds. He mounted her again and again; the doe turned her face back and rubbed it against his horns. He bobbed his instrument up and down.

After he'd finished, the stag still bellowed. He seemed pained with his burden. Leonora moved back into the trees and skirted the edge of the forest to find a clearer path across the moorland toward Tomintoul.

At dinner in the Horseshoe that night, Leonora set down a plate for a neat English couple, and from her hair fell a small, curled golden leaf.

'I'm terribly sorry,' she said.

The couple laughed. 'It's quite all right dear. Nature! That's what we're here for.'

Back in the kitchen, Cait mumbled, 'More followers o Sir Walter Scott, I'd wager, traipsin all over the Highlands.'

Leonora thought of telling Cait, and the customers, about the deer rut she'd witnessed today, but for some reason it felt private, or as though it'd be diminished in the telling.

William Wink came in late that evening, just as Leonora and Cait were packing up from supper. He was with an older man and a young woman. She was dressed in magenta silk and had tiny blonde curls about her face, matching William's. The men had red blotches in their eyes, and had obviously been drinking at the beerhouse up the road.

'Miss Duncan.' William stood tall, looking down on her. 'Please do tell me there are still rooms.'

'I believe sae, Mr Wink.'

'Capital!' said the older man. 'I wasn't looking forward to that long ride in the dark.'

'We got carried away,' William said with a laugh. He didn't introduce the man and woman to Leonora. 'Agnes, dear, Miss Duncan will show you where you can put your head down. Sorry for keeping you out so late.'

'That's perfectly all right, William,' she said. 'I've enjoyed your company.'

The man, whom Leonora took to be Agnes' father, nodded his approval. They had southern accents.

'We might stay down here for one to round out the night, if that's all right with you, Miss Duncan?'

Leonora nodded, feeling a strange pang as she led Agnes, whom she called 'Madam' in lieu of a surname, to the largest of the empty rooms.

'My girl didn't travel with me,' Agnes said when they entered the room. 'Do you mind bringing my case and helping me undress?'

'Of course,' said Leonora.

She came back downstairs to find Cait pouring two drams while shaking her head. 'I dinnae care how rich or sweet-faced he is, he ought not tae take advantage.'

'It's all right, Cait. I can take care of them.'

'I sense an arrangement being made,' said Cait. 'The gentleman has come up to note the lay of the land, and brought his prettiest daughter.'

Leonora took Madam's packages up to her, feeling fatigued, and then helped to loose her soft white limbs from her sleeves, and her body from her corset. Leonora slipped a clean nightdress over the woman's body, her hand brushing her hips. She could feel her own lips, full and tingling. She thought of the doe mounting the other doe, the similarity of their bodies. She'd seen it a lot in animals. With the same kind of body you would know what to do, where to touch. It would feel like a kindness.

'Thank you, Miss . . .'

'Miss Duncan. And what may I call ye, Madam?'

'I am Agnes Bruce. My father is Admiral Sir Thomas Bruce, former port admiral at Portsmouth. Do you know the laird well?' She tilted her pretty head at Leonora.

Leonora felt herself blush. 'He is a kind landlord, Miss Bruce.'

'He is alone in that big house, is he not?'

'He has his dogs.' Leonora laughed.

Agnes raised an eyebrow. 'What is it like to live here?'

I cannae say what it will be like for you. With your meals made and a canopy bed.

'It is quiet,' is all Leonora said.

'Thank you for answering my questions; I must get some rest.' And so Leonora left.

William did not act familiar with her this night, as Leonora continued to tidy around the men. He was absorbed in his conversation with the admiral – one of business. And Leonora was hopeful for him, though, simultaneously, there was a gnawing in her – a sense of missing out. If he took a wife, Leonora wasn't sure about the explorations she'd imagined. It would be good for him, though, to have a companion, someone to help warm up those empty, tall rooms, and to finger the cloth spines of his books.

The men finally stumbled up to bed, and at the bottom of the staircase William turned and gave her a beckoning look. She understood. Marriage was a transaction, with many benefits, but a stag was in want of a harem. Or maybe she would have been his preference for a wife if her own father were an admiral. Either way, she knew that under her rougher dress she looked just as the other woman did.

Let me just interject, here, because we've almost caught up. Time has been passing and I've been telling you my story, and recounting Leonora's, by speaking into William's ear – looking out over the boats on still water from the front lawn, McGregor's fiddle providing a backdrop. You know where I am at. I am away from the world and soon to be away further. I have been trying to capture Leonora, and what it's like to experience the world through her. When I'm there I *am* her; when I return I am one step removed, and so I do apologise if I am sometimes using the language I know – metaphors, for example – to encourage you to relate to her. And I have been recording it as in the past, because when I surface that is what it is – something that happened in the past.

But I've been thinking: would she be better captured if I tried to get down the experience as it happens for me? It will feel strange, to start with, speaking as Leonora into William's ear. I don't, for example, know how to represent her accent (which does also occur in her thoughts). And I'm sure there will still be instances when I can't remember or find the right words to capture the thought or emotion I experience through her. I am tainted by my own time, my own context. We always experience other people's stories this way, though, don't we? I guess you – and when I say you I've gotten used to addressing William like this, but I do mean you, a person, possibly listening to my ghost – will also draw conclusions about me, depending on your own experiences, your own fears and desires. Are you sick? Are you alone?

Have you ever had a thought that made you want to remove yourself from the world? That to simply block it and go on would be like living without a leg or an arm?

Currently, I am eating a boiled egg by candlelight. It's about all I can stomach today. There are needles crawling across my skin like the legs of a caterpillar. There's a steady ache in one side of my head and my glands are bulging in my neck.

I . . . I was about to tell you of what I fear I've done, in returning again and again to Leonora. But I don't want you to despise me that much, yet. If you're still here, you mustn't. It will become clear anyway. You might have done the same thing, if you were here, and alone. There could be something addictive in these tabs. Or just in living as someone who isn't me. So here I go, changing how I bring her to you. You can partly inhabit her as well, then, though your own thoughts may be infected. Infected by me.

PART TWO

My hand is gorse-coloured in the candlelight, hovering above the handle to William's door. I cannot hear his breathing. I'm not certain he is awake. The liquor may have sent him off immediately. I picture him with his shoes hanging over the edge of the bed. Then I hear his stockinged feet whisper across the floor and the door opens. His hair is matted on one side. So he has been resting, perhaps with one arm curled up under his head. Would he sleep on his side, in an elbow shape, or on his back? He does not smile; he reaches out and takes my hand, which had been crossed over the front of my bodice. There is still a battle going on inside me: is it defiance to do this, or giving in? There is an undeniable power in his closeness: an intoxicating smell, an emanating heat. Perhaps this is just the natural way we respond with some people. That is why we see people marry who don't seem, from the outside, to get along at all.

He takes the candle from my hand and sets it on the mahogany cabinet by the window. The curtains are drawn. I fold my arms back across myself, notice I am doing it, and then set them by my sides.

'Good evening, Leonora.'

'Mr Wink.'

He tilts his head in amusement, looking like a child.

'William.' I try it on my tongue.

'Will you sit with me on the bed? We can talk.'

I move over to the bed and sit at the edge. I look down at my skirts and the shoes peeping out. This is something I do when I'm not sure what to say. He sits by me, not quite touching. The scent of him hits me fully: stone fruits and the salt of sweat; I arch my neck to take it in. He turns to me, looking fearful for a second. We are close so quickly. I feel his hand on my lower back. I cannot remember anyone ever touching me there. It reverberates up my spine and causes prickles on my neck. My face flushes and my mouth parts, the beginning of a gasp. I see that he is beautiful up close but I am still sorry for him. His eyes are eager, like a dog's. And then we kiss. I am glad I have been curious, because the sensation is pleasing. There is life in this warmth, this softness of lips on lips, a gentle sweet parting of the mouth. There is power and there is giving in. A taste of peaches and cloves. Taste of tastebuds.

It surprises me that I want more, that my hand moves quickly across his back, presses hard at his shoulder. I can feel where each tip of myself is touching him, touching my clothing first. We kiss for a long time, in the quiet with the candle flickering. We are quiet. We pause to remove his jacket, loosen his shirt. We look into each other's eyes, and there is a shift in his. When he moves back in toward me his mouth is less sure. I put my palm on the back of his head, pull him to me.

He pulls away again. 'This won't do.'

I stand up and adjust my clothes, turn toward the door.

'Leonora . . .'

I look back at him. His cheeks are red. He looks like a child.

'See you soon,' he says, with a half-apologetic smile.

'Goodnight, William,' I manage.

A few minutes later I lie in bed, buzzing at my edges, running my hands across my chest, my stomach. I remember the deer's bellow. But a doe doesn't bellow like that. What of a human female? Can the dominant pursuer sometimes be her? And if there is that inversion, would the male be intimidated? I wonder if that is what happened – why William stopped. Or was it a true attack of moral guilt, that he'd be spoiling a poor village girl? Perhaps I should see it as a mark of respect. But I find that difficult. It was something about the look in his eyes, a realisation that in this situation, too, he was not in control. Then why did he go so far? It was confusing. But he'd had so much loss, lately. I did feel for him, despite myself; I felt affection, like a rose uncurling in my breast.

The bed is narrow and I am wide awake, but I'm not overly worried about the busy morning. I feel that this energy will carry me tomorrow. The buzz at my fingertips, as I wiggle them toward the stained ceiling, makes me appreciate my liberty. I am not bound by the responsibilities and pressures of someone like Agnes, and not surrounded, either, by people determining how and to whom I should speak. Work, a garden, walking: these elements of my life are uncomplicated.

In the morning the encounter is more tinged. I am not tired, as I thought, but when I pull up my blanket and step into my shoes I feel a quick beat of shame. Is there someone in his life with whom he will joke about me? *That wanton girl.* Will men at the inn make jokes and try to grab me? It is less simple than with the animals. Language makes it so.

A cold rain turns the morning grey, and Cait is in a mood about it. We barely speak as we serve the breakfast. I warm my hands on the underside of a bowl of porridge, from which heat curls like arms reaching. William and Sir Thomas come down late, and seat themselves by the fire. William beckons to me, and I remember the taste of him.

'Do you mind helping Miss Bruce into her clothes?' he asks, looking somewhere beside my head.

'Of course,' I answer. Cait is vexed about it but waves me off. Taking a few plates out from the kitchen won't harm her. 'I'll be quick,' I say.

I knock gently on Agnes' door and she says I can enter. Her cheeks are flushed.

'D'ye sleep?' I ask.

'Not too well,' she says. The thought that she may have heard something both worries and thrills me.

She stands and holds her arms out, a helpless doll. I remove her nightgown.

'I've washed my face,' she says, and I take this to mean that I should just help her with her garments. I wonder if any man has touched her. I want to ask. I won't, but I do realise I don't have this intimacy with women, with anyone. My schoolhouse friends are married, and many have moved to the Lowlands. I talk to the animals, and find words in books to explain what I feel. But, I realise now, a friend would be something else.

Perhaps William can be a friend. There may be more ways for men and women to relate to one another. But I know as soon as I think this that he is too unsure, that he wouldn't let me in, not in that way.

Agnes thanks me coldly. The lack of sleep and the weather have affected her badly. Or perhaps it is the two men downstairs.

'I dreamed o you last night,' I say to her, not sure how the lie comes out of my mouth, 'and you were happy here.' I smile.

I was a sales and marketing manager at Glazen, in their biopharm department, though I started out writing copy at a low level on their products, for various websites and communications (from 'straight' ads to edutainments). I worked on my art in my spare time, half-heartedly I must admit; I more liked the idea of being an artist than actually doing the work. That's something Faye accused me of and I'm acknowledging it now. Of course, back then I threw my canvas at the wall, smearing it with acrylics. She just laughed. And then I laughed at my own dramatics. Again, I probably wanted to be seen as *being* dramatic. Everyone around me was so calm. We seemed to 'be made of paper and straw', I think that's the John Cheever quote. It might have been the Gloss – Glazen's bestselling anti-anxiety nanopharm. Maybe you don't know what that is. It's a piece of tech that knows just where to go in your brain to calm you down. It makes people peaceful, productive and personable. I had one installed for a while, while swinging an arm from my teaching job to the lower rung of the corporate ladder. But it was too easy to feel that 'functional', so after I'd settled into the new job I had it removed.

I don't know who engineered these tabs. There'd been many years of studies into digitised neural experience (DNE). The trials of another pharm, Know, had been disastrous. It was tech that allowed a person to hear another's thoughts. Unfortunately, the thoughts of the closest person weren't the only ones that came through. The trial subjects experienced a screaming cacophony. And due to the way the nano was administered, it went on for days. The subjects, afterwards, had to be treated post-traumatically. This trial wasn't public. I only know about it because of Henry, the friend I've mentioned who works in design. Even he didn't know about other projects, other experiments – only the ones his team was attached to.

He was in love with the idea of the tabs, once he'd started working on them. 'This is something that could actually do some good, that could change the way we treat each other,' he told me one night in my studio. He was a blabbermouth with me only, as far as I know. He wasn't allowed to talk about his work but he said he had to tell *someone* or it would drive him crazy, especially the projects he found most exciting.

Trials were due for the tabs just when I found out I was sick. And as a return favour for everything he'd shared with me, I told Henry I was going to go away. I didn't tell him where to.

We sat for hours in my apartment, drinking my best single malts. 'I won't need these anymore,' I said, as we sipped on The Balvenie 30.

He squinted with sadness into the glass, but then closed his eyes in pleasure when he took a sip. 'You know people care deeply about you,' he said.

'I know.' Did I really, though? Sometimes I think no one truly cares deeply about anyone else. We need people for various reasons; we make grand gestures and are pleased with ourselves and we expect something in return. Or maybe we do care, but only rarely. It almost shocks us when it is genuine, from ourselves. I really do question whether anyone cared deeply about me. Wasn't I just Henry's sounding board? But he was – is – kind and idealistic, often beaten down. I think he meant well.

Anyway, he gave me the tab that night.

'I don't know where it will take you,' he said.

The nights are getting colder. The wind seems at times like it will lift Aignish from the ground. I worry about the animals down at Barnsoul, and Mrs Grant's dogs that remain outside year long. I'm lucky Father lets me keep Duff inside. She is curled up next to the bed. I can hear the wheeze of her breath in the dark. I push aside the thought of ever having to be away from her. We have been thinking she is pregnant lately, because of the milk leaking from her when I rub her belly. She sniffs and licks at it with her purple tongue. It could be what's happened before, when she thought she was pregnant, and her body took on the symptoms, but it was false. A phantom, Mr Anderson called it. It makes me think about how powerful our thoughts can be. We might think we are sick when we truly have no ailment. But if we present the symptoms, and believe them, are we not sick anyway? Is a false illness still genuine in some way?

Might the mind also trick the body into attraction? My father, lacking something in his daily life, may have latched onto Penuel, the available woman, with a physical attraction to follow.

The dog eventually realises she is not pregnant. Do some people realise they are not in love?

I wonder if a person could learn to be aware of when the mind is influencing a bodily reaction, and also when an instinct is overruling the mind.

I try to talk to Father about the concept the next day as I put on his plate some barley bread and cheese.

He shakes his head. 'Yer own mind is tae active, Lae,' he says. 'It's a wonder ye get any sleep.'

I am frustrated that conversations do not open out for me. That I am always forced to withdraw into myself. And sometimes I feel like Penuel has something to say, but she doesn't, as though she is afraid it will seem she is taking a side with me. But I do not want an argument, only a discussion. Again, I think of the need for a friend. I think of talking about the body and the mind with William. He might even know of some books that explore such ideas.

But I am completely surprised when he knocks on the door while we are eating breakfast. Father lets him in.

'Pardon me for interrupting,' William says.

'Not at all, Mr Wink, what can we do for ye?' Father asks.

He looks unsure of himself. Father puts his hands on his hips.

'I was wondering if Miss Duncan would be available. Her biological knowledge is required.'

I can tell that Father wants to say no; wants to ask why the laird would be interested in seeing his daughter, and of being seen with her. Father is becoming more wary of William's attention. He'd be more afraid if he knew that we were close; that we had an unusual silent agreement. Father would think it was all one way. Everyone would.

Father says I can go with William, but that I have to be back soon to help him with putting parts of the garden to bed for winter.

We walk toward the Tom A Voan Wood. I don't ask him what is required of my biological knowledge. I know it was only a front. The sun warms my skin and clothes. It is better to be outside than in, and I smile at the fact. The gardening will be no problem today. William smiles at my own lit-up face.

I reach for his hand, and he looks around, unsure, but then takes it.

'When in yer heid ye're grievin,' I say, 'd'ye feel that yer body is grievin tae?'

He doesn't answer for a while. 'Yes,' he says, 'I feel very tired, but then I can't sleep.'

Nearer to the forest we move to the ford and sit on the bank by the water. I like what we have right now. It doesn't feel complicated, if I don't think about it. If I don't leave the mind in control. We sit close.

'I am going to marry Miss Bruce,' he says, staring across the ford to the cows from Chapeltown's collective crofts, grazing together.

I curl my hands in the grass, an unexpected rush of emotion in my chest. 'That will be good for ye – yer house is sae empty,' I say blankly.

He doesn't reply.

'You should have bairns,' I say.

We sit there for a long time. We don't kiss. Maybe the kissing had been a way for us to learn about each other. When I was a child, girls and boys could be close like this. When we grow up there are enforced divides. You are strangers, acquaintances, or spouses. With someone of the same sex it is more acceptable to be close.

I have to admit it would have been easier to find a way to stay, to keep my place in the Highlands, if the impossible had occurred, if William had thought it appropriate to marry me. Whether I'd truly desired it or not.

William has a carriage waiting at the church. He sets off and I sit for a while longer, picking at the grass, before returning to Aignish.

Father is in a dark mood as we garden afterwards, grunting responses to my questions.

'Mr Wink is troubled, Lae,' he says to me.

'Nae more than many people, Da,' I say.

'But he has more power than most.'

I am placing in stakes to mark the carrots and leeks.

'Stop for a moment, Lae,' Father says. We both stand. My head goes light for a second. 'I think it's time ye went away and stayed with yer Aunt Ailie.'

No. I'd hoped he had put the idea out of his mind. My chest tightens; heat comes to my face.

I turn to walk into the cottage, to ignore his words.

'Lae, dinnae walk away. It will be good fur ye. She is livin well; ye can learn frae her. Ye can grow.'

'Like Mother did in Edinburgh?'

My father's face falls. Hurt, not anger. 'Lae, we didnae have the means . . .'

'I dinnae want tae leave here. I am content!'

'Sometimes tha's the right time tae go.'

He isn't saying it but I'm certain he's decided that I must go because of the laird's attentions. He doesn't want me to become pregnant, or live my life as a mistress. He doesn't know or care that for me it is a friendship that has developed. That William and I have some understanding of each other that defies any conventional explanation.

But then . . . I do know that once William marries, our relationship cannot possibly continue along the same road. And there isn't anyone else here for me to meet, with whom I can fall in love. Father is worried about my world being small. Though he is allowed to want smallness for himself.

I go to my room and push the wooden door until it sticks. It doesn't quite close all the way. I can't imagine Edinburgh. It feels terribly dark; it feels like a loss. Duff snuffs at the gap in my door and I let her in. She can tell I'm upset and I let her jump onto the bed. I lie down and she tries to lick at my tears, which makes me laugh.

I close my eyes. Suddenly I do see Edinburgh, as though I have conjured it. It is brighter than in books, and women are showing their legs. The vision is crisp and unnerving, stamped behind my eyes. I open them and look at Duff, blink a few times to try to clear the image. Duff whimpers.

It is my first time on a train and I am hemmed in by a woman and four children with snot on their faces. There is a continuous rickety clank, and sulphurous smoke fills the carriage each time we pass through a tunnel. The sound and smell are an assault. The eldest child tells his sister to stop staring at me. He calls me 'the lady'. Have they, too, already endured a cab and an omnibus before this journey? The mother is quiet, with her eyes half-closed. I should offer to swap seats with her so she can lean her head against the wood. But my jaw is tight and words don't come. I close my eyes to try to rest but we are too much in motion. Tears burn at the back of my throat, but I will not let them through. I did not say goodbye to William, as he was on his way to England to marry Agnes. They will have a second celebration at Dearshul. That, I am glad to miss.

It is Duff I am thinking of, to have her in my lap. As I am thinking of her, the smallest child crawls from her mother to me. The woman's eyes are closed, so she doesn't notice. 'Leave her alone, Annie,' says the eldest boy.

'It's all right,' I say, placing a hand on the child's head, as she curls in my lap. A wave of calm comes over me. Sweet creature. I close my eyes again, and now the motion of the train feels a little more like jagged flight.

I dread arriving in Edinburgh. I don't know my aunt, I won't get along with the place, and I may be forced into arrangements simply because that is what one does. I may get sick. I may not know any animals. I will be 'bettered' or brought up, and I don't know what that means.

It is very hard to rest with the noise. I envy the child on my lap, whose breaths are deepening. I try not to stroke her hair, to calm myself. It is not my place.

Scotland goes by outside, purple under clouds.

I wake to a flash of bright light and thunder so loud it shakes the glass in the small bedroom window. I feel the child on my lap, on Leonora's lap. When the bedroom lights up again there are shapes in the corners: human-sized and ethereal. One is Leonora's mother. I am conjuring the past, while she is beginning to see the future.

I pull the blanket up around my ears, call shakily for William. Something solid and belonging to now.

He is at the bedside. 'I will fix you a cup of tea.'

'Yes – not yet,' I say, and reach for him, like a child who has had a nightmare. I can hear the wind wailing through sails, the creak of boats tipping in the bay.

The robot runs his hands through my hair, the way I like it.

I am so frightened for Leonora. I am so frightened.

This must be my aunt: the plump woman dressed in a shimmering green fabric, who runs toward me with her arms out.

'You look just like your mother,' she says, gripping both my hands, and I smile as best I can. I feel sick. I recognise our familial connection in her small nose, and in the way her lips curl. I don't remember my mother well, but here is this woman who looks like her – living and bold.

'Thank you for havin me, Aunt Ailie,' I manage.

The mother and four children emerge, depleted, from the carriage behind me. I let go of Ailie's hands and turn to them. The mother gives me a soft smile, which I return. 'I wish you all the best,' I say.

'Now, now,' Aunt Ailie tuts quietly, grasping at my hand again, 'you'll learn soon to whom it's best to speak.'

I am not confused, but am disappointed. I want to slip my hand from hers. There's a red burn at my core, a refusal to change if it means ridding myself of common collegiality. I will not forget that my mother died poor in a tenement. I will not forget the rough feel of the floor under my infant knees.

My skirts, now, already fringed with soot.

'You'll get used to it, dear,' says Aunt Ailie, noticing me noticing.

A porter is soon beside us with my packages, and I follow my aunt to the station's entrance, struggling to keep up as she weaves confidently through the crowd, occasionally catching a shoulder or bag. 'Excuse me, pardon me,' I say, and then we are outside in the grey.

My packages are loaded into the cab and as we pull out onto Princes Street I see the Scott Monument and the castle beyond it, rising out of the fog. On the other side of Princes Street, shops line the bottom of buildings and fruit sellers spill onto the street. A well-dressed man pauses, pulls out his pocket watch and frowns, causing people to flow around him like a stream around a rock. So many people.

The cab takes a turn and I watch the black horse navigating the corner, then heading up a hill. It is immediately quieter on Frederick Street. I notice black streetlamps with circular bulbs suspended like droplets from a tap. We navigate around a confident statue, go over the rise and down, and as we take one more turn, I see the water below, and catch the scree of gulls. We pull up at the bottom of a tenement building in a light brownish-grey stone, joined uniformly to its neighbours.

Once inside, I follow Aunt Ailie up the front stairs and she unlocks a great heavy door. The driver is behind us with the packages. We take two flights of iron stairs and then enter her apartment, into a sitting room with deep green couches and rich clashing curtains. An armchair faces the window, and I immediately know that this is where my uncle passed on. It has an air of the untouchable about it.

'Now!' Aunt Ailie claps her hands together. 'Let's show you around.' She takes me into a small but spotless kitchen with a large stove taking up much of the room, and shelves for storage. Next is a room with a claw-footed bath, and a cabinet with a looking glass. Something for the soot. Then there is my room: clothed in embroidered off-white. A canopy bed that I could become lost in, my own looking glass, washbasin and jug.

I clear my throat to try to thank my aunt. There's a rock in it. I must be grateful. But I feel alone.

She beams. 'You'll feel at home soon,' she says. 'And you'll fit right in.' She looks me up and down. 'With some more meat on your bones.'

A girl of about sixteen appears behind her, gives a little curtsey when she sees me.

'This is Edith,' says Aunt Ailie. 'Quiet as a mouse, just the way we like them.'

Edith blushes. She does not look like a mouse – she has bright green eyes and her blonde hair flies out from under her cap. 'Pleasure to meet you, Miss Duncan,' she says.

'And you, Edith,' I say.

Aunt Ailie gives a little roll of the eyes, waves her hand. 'Run along now, Edith.' Then she tells me about Edith's duties: the cleaning and washing, the cooking. The girl does so much that I don't know what it is I'll do. I know Aunt Ailie wants to 'relieve' me from the kind of life I've lived; I don't know how to express to her the way I feel about putting my hands in water, in dough.

Aunt Ailie waves to indicate her own room but does not take me into it, understandably keeping her privacy. And where does Edith sleep?

'You look weary,' says Aunt Ailie. It's getting dark outside and it has been one of the longest days of my life. She tells me to freshen myself and rest before we take a meal. I want to ask her about the privy but feel embarrassed. I assume it is downstairs, perhaps in the back alley where the clothes hang. I remember the cramped alleys of the old town, the way waste was thrown into the street. The stench day and night.

I close the door to my room, hoping she does not perceive the action as rude. I will use the bedpan for now. I look around for a lamp or a candle and then clutch my heart in shock as a light comes on by itself on the wall of the room. Silly to get such a shock from gas lighting – they were soon to get it at the Horseshoe Inn. The visitors from the Lowlands were used to the brightness. I knew I could adjust the strength on the wall lamp, to which the gas was being piped. I approach but am too afraid I will do it wrong. I blink several times. It's like someone has turned back on the sun.

Later, as Edith serves me and Ailie a supper of Scotch broth, my aunt tells me that tomorrow she will take me shopping to a new store that she likes, so that I have some clothes more suitable to Edinburgh. More suitable, I know she means, to accompanying her. And tomorrow evening she will have some friends over for supper.

'A way to welcome you south, young Highlander,' she says.

I am still tired from my journey, but I appreciate the food, served in smooth, fine, patterned dishes. I am very careful not to scrape my knife and fork too hard upon them. I am careful not to make too many glances toward Edith. In between mouthfuls and telling me about some of the events in Edinburgh that she likes to go to – public lectures and readings in particular – Ailie lapses into silence, her eyes moving to the armchair by the window, which can be seen from her side of the table. The gas light throws the shadows of her face into relief: a furrow at the brow, and the lines that hold up a laugh at the mouth and eyes. Her powdered cheeks are pert and plump, like the body of a bird. She chews daintily on each bite. Something about it angers me. I try to eat at the same pace as her, so as not to seem greedy. I only have a second helping after she does. She sips from a glass – red wine, I presume – but does not offer me one. Perhaps drinking is unbecoming in young women.

'After supper, if I am home, I usually read by the fire,' she tells me.

It is difficult to resist picking up my plate from the table before I follow her rustling skirts into the sitting room. There are bookshelves on either side of the window. 'I hear you are a reader,' she says. 'I thought it might be glorious if you would read aloud to me.' She reaches up and takes a book down from a high shelf. 'We would essentially be reading together,' she says, smiling at me. 'Doesn't that sound nice?'

'It does,' I say. It is something.

The bottom shelves are taken up with periodicals, such as *The Illustrated London News*, *Household Words* and *The Owl*, and with a quick glance at the rest of the shelves I see (with a sense of relief) works on nature, economy, philosophy; and works of poetry and drama. I don't see any novels. Ailie has in her hand a book: John Stuart Mill's *Utilitarianism*. I don't know the word. She encourages me to sit opposite her and hands it to me.

'From the beginning?' I ask.

'Yes, dear.'

I begin to read. There is much I don't understand, since I am reading aloud and cannot linger over the words, but I think it is about morals and happiness. That there is no real foundation, yet, for determining what is morally good and what is not. And can we be good *and* happy?

Ailie gives a small snort when I am three pages in and I look up from the book to find her head lolling to the side. Either the book is not as stimulating as she thought it would be, or I am terrible at reading aloud. It's something I'll work on. I'm not sure whether to nudge her, or to continue reading. I continue reading, projecting a little louder. Her head snaps up and she makes no acknowledgement of her nap. Soon her head lolls again. We continue like this for twelve pages, but this time she has truly made herself comfortable, reclining back onto an embroidered cushion. I close the book and sit quietly in the yellow light, trying to quell my annoyance.

Edith appears at the doorway, startling me. 'I'll put her to bed,' she says quietly.

'Are you certain?' I ask. I wonder if this is something that's happened before.

Edith nods, and I leave the room to preserve Ailie's dignity.

I change into my bedclothes and wait for Edith to put out the lights, wondering how I will get used to the noises from outside: voices, footsteps, horse hooves and the clacking of wheels on stone. And there is the light, too, seeping in from the alley and slope of city behind. I close my eyes but their lids are thin. There is a feeling of expansion in my head, like when I was a child and had a fever, with bubbles growing and popping behind my eyes. I am exhausted enough to soon slip into sleep. I wake several times, twisted in the blankets. The bed is much softer than my one at home. It holds me captive when the sun streams into the room in the morning. I cannot think of a reason to get up.

I must have closed my eyes again. There is a figure in the doorway, bright white. I'm edging out of a dream but already I can't remember it. I am still weighed down in the bed, sorrowful. It feels like grief.

'Miss Duncan?'

I've thrown my arm across my eyes against the brightness.

'Edith,' I say.

'Would you like me to help you dress?'

'Oh dear, Edith, no, I've always managed myself.'

'But your corset.'

I smile at her, sitting up in the bed, drawing the blankets in around me. That sinking feeling clings to me. I want to give over to it. Whenever I have felt this, I have thought of going over a cliff and into the ocean, as in the story of the seal-catcher who is turned into a seal and taken to an underwater palace. When he arrives the seals are melancholy because one of their number has been stabbed by him. He fears them, but – and this is a detail I always loved – they rub their noses on him and tell him that if he helps to heal the creature he has injured then they will return him to his family. And he does. But I always want to stay down there, in the cool deep with the magic seals.

I have never seen the ocean.

I tell Edith my corset is laced the way I like it and fastens in the front, as hers probably does too. She lingers in the doorway, palely, holding a fresh jug of water, and I realise Ailie would of course have instructed her to help me. That I should let her do her work. By arguing I am probably only holding her up from other duties.

I stand up and indicate that she can help me. She sets the water down and asks if I would like to wash my face first. I say yes. She pours it into the basin on the dresser, and I splash it over my face and neck. The water is warm and I sigh with pleasure, forgetting for a moment Edith's presence. I suppose that is the point with servants. They come to know their masters intimately, without their masters knowing much about them in return.

I rub the water in circles, trying to remove the grit from my pores. The water turns grey. How does one get used to this? The relentless black, making teeth look absent and turning live colour people into photographs. At the braes, even in the icy winter, the stove ash settles slowly, and can be swept up. In Tomintoul, the ash blows down the main street and off down the mountain. But here, in Edinburgh, it comes from inside and out, clashes heavily in the air, and sinks, liquid-like, into skin and clothes, furniture and floors. It coats the back of the throat and the hides of animals. It even seems to enter the blood.

'Where did you grow up, Edith?' I ask, patting my face with a towel.

She is taken aback. 'In England, Miss.'

I hold up my arms, the way Agnes had for me at the inn. Edith lifts my nightgown over my head.

'England is a big place,' I say.

'Oh, well, Gloucestershire, Miss,' she says timidly.

Her fingers flutter about me like moths. She is quick to get me out of one garment and into another.

'Are your family still there?' I ask.

She pulls on my crinoline and fastens it. 'I'm afraid I don't know, Miss,' she says, almost sourly. My heart skips a beat. I shouldn't have pushed so far.

When I am dressed she tells me to kneel on the bed in front of her. She moves my head gently from side to side, plaiting the hair at the front. She then draws back the plaits and the rest of the hair into a bun.

'What you need is a comb, Miss,' she says. 'They make them from gold and silver and pearls, and even shells.'

'That sounds lovely, Edith,' I say, though I can't imagine owning something so fine.

'Mrs Kemp has some good'uns. Perhaps she'll let you borrow one.'

I nod and thank Edith, touching the sides of my head and glancing over to the mirror. The hairstyle makes me look older.

The water in the bowl beneath me has settled and looks like silver. I can see the edges of myself: fine, fair hair; my neck. My face is a blank, and soon I have to look away as I feel the hairs rise on my neck. It felt, for a moment, as though I truly hadn't been there. I look back up into the actual looking glass and the feeling remains, though lightly, fading out as a nightmare does after you've lit a candle.

'Thank you,' I say to Edith, and stand up.

Edith serves me breakfast as I sit at the dining table alone, telling me that Ailie likes to eat hers in bed so she can take her time to wake.

There comes a scratch on the front door, and Edith moves toward it with a warning hiss.

'Sorry, Miss, it's the neighbour's cat. Mrs Kemp don't like it around.'

'Oh . . .' I say, half-standing and then checking myself. *I* hope to see it around. 'What kind of cat?'

'I don't know types, Miss. Orange, it is.'

I can hear a piano somewhere distant. It makes me think of Sundays, of church. I enjoyed singing the hymns, mainly for the sound of my voice entering the air and mixing with the voices of others, giving praise and thanks. Father has a singing voice much lighter than you'd imagine from his speaking one. I know other songs and poems but mainly without accompaniment. There were some we sang at the schoolhouse, others encountered through friends, passed on. This tune on the piano sounds somewhat like 'Flowers of the Forest':

I've seen the smiling Of fortune beguiling, I've tasted her pleasures, And felt her decay; Sweet is her blessing, And kind her caressing, But now they are fled And fled far away.

Edith quietly enters Ailie's room not long afterwards, and soon they both emerge. Ailie does indeed have a shimmering comb in her hair, and she exudes the scent of roses. My aunt and I have eyes of a similar shape and colour, deep and blue as a loch, with a broad sweep of lid. My eyebrows are slightly more pointed, hers curved. Her nose and lips I now notice are a little smaller than mine. The cheeks take up much of her face. It does make her look somewhat younger than she must be. Younger than my mother might have looked at her age.

'Did you sleep well, my dear?' she asks.

'Oh, quite well, thank you,' I say, but there's a lurch in my chest. I could go back to bed, to bed, to bed. It is still not the squelchy, layered grasses of the moor. But there is carpet, not exposed floor for my small knees. I must stop this heaviness of thought.

'It was a stimulating tract you read last night, stimulating,' Ailie says. 'It rather kept me up thinking.' I try not to show surprise on my face. She seemed fast asleep when I left her. Perhaps she has a way of listening with one part of her mind while the other closes, giving her rest. She might be like a creature that lives in water, resting while staying afloat.

When we leave the apartment, the neighbour's ginger tabby is cleaning himself on the stairwell. I bend quickly to put a hand behind the cat's ears, hoping I will meet him properly later.

'That cat will have to be careful,' says Ailie. 'They've found a lot of them shot lately.'

'That's terrible,' I say.

'It's the poor wretch children doing it, I suspect.'

Out through the great heavy door the sun has gone behind a cloud and there's a bracing wind in the small street, picking up smoke and dust. I cough into my sleeve.

Ailie takes my arm in hers. 'We're going to walk down to Princes Street,' she says. 'You must never do this without an escort.'

'Yes, Aunt Ailie.'

On the way, she tells me about the children on the street; about having to be careful, because they're downtrodden and quick-fingered. 'Many of us believe they should make education compulsory. Maybe some of the children can still work, I don't know, but many start out much too young.' She puffs a little between words, as she walks quickly. 'And they can never rise out of their situation.'

Ailie's shoes *clop-clop* on the stones. I agree instinctively that children shouldn't work, at least not too young, in dark places with dangerous machinery. Or for very long hours. Mr Dickens has painted a grim view of such things. But I don't know enough about the subject; I try to listen and then ask, 'They can't rise because their wages are low?'

'Exactly,' Ailie says, 'and living expenditure is high. And then they have their own children. It's a cycle.'

'I see.'

'I'm a member of a society for social betterment,' Ailie says, pushing her chest forward slightly. 'So are the Johnsons – you'll meet them tonight.'

I nod.

'It's mainly about giving them ways to help themselves. Like you, for example. I can teach you a bit about society. Even without money you may manage well.'

I blush.

'Luckily blushing is still becoming on you,' Ailie says, tutting. 'Yes, you may find a match in Edinburgh. The secret is to find someone who is good with money. He may be a gentleman, but more than likely he'll be a professional man, and he will have a bit tucked away, with a regular income to follow. Something you can be sure of. It's so easy to get involved with a man who presents a bold surface but who does not know how to make or hold a cent.' Her tone makes me think she is talking of someone we know. Is it my father? My father had only been an apprentice in Edinburgh. My mother would have known that, and made a decision. For love, I suppose.

It is easier to grow your own food, I think; to live outside of a city. But you must have the land to start with. It suits my father;

the city didn't. A thought crosses my mind that is terrible, sad and strange. If my grandfather had died sooner, would my father have thought of going back earlier? I shake it from my head.

'I will accept your guidance, Aunt Ailie.' Who is to say that her way is not best? But so much of me resists her. I want to ask about friendship and fire. I want to ask about sharing a roof with one person forever. What if your feelings change? Maybe one day Ailie and I will get along well enough that I can ask such questions.

A bell sounds from the top of the door as we open it, bringing with us a cloud of soot and dust. Ailie pushes it closed against the wind, then straightens and tucks her hair. I look down a long row of tables and drawers, with dresses hung also at the walls, which lead up to a high roof crisscrossed with wooden beams. A woman stands behind a large table at the far end and another appears in front of us, smiling brightly. She is young and pretty, with auburn hair.

'Good morning to ye,' she says. 'How can I be of assistance today?'

'Good morning, Miss,' says Ailie curtly. Her head is pushed into her neck, on guard. 'My charge, Miss Duncan, is in need of new dresses. The fashions for young ladies, if you please.'

This lady wears a golden-orange dress to match her hair. I am curious about whether such a dress would suit me.

She takes us down the aisle of soft satiny gloves, eiderdown corsets, wraps and coats. I stand by as she shows a range of dresses to Ailie, who nods or tuts to each without much emotion. Soon there is a small, colourful pile for me to try. The shopgirl takes Ailie and me into a green-curtained room and helps me out of my old dress. Ailie sits in a comfortable, high-backed chair. I see myself for the first time in a full-length mirror. My shoulders are broad; my waist is high. The tops of my legs fan out slightly from my hips. I am milky white.

Each dress sits differently. One feels almost like liquid;

another is scratchy and rough. One is blue satin, with embroidered patterns around the skirt and up into the bust. The blue brings out my eyes.

'That one is a must,' says Ailie. 'It may be worn with a black shawl.'

'I have just the one,' says the shopgirl, carrying in a heavy velvet garment, which she drapes upon me and ties in the back.

'And something matching for her hair,' says Ailie. To which the shopgirl produces a dark blue, opaque comb.

We are all silent. I look like a lady. The exterior hides a trembling rage inside me. Ailie's demanding, grating tone. My body being nudged and cinched and pulled.

And then I look into my own eyes in the mirror. And I don't know myself.

I double over, feeling faint, and the shopgirl rushes over, presumably to protect the dress. Ailie stands to help me into the chair. She produces a vial from the folds of her dress and tells me to take a sip. It is brandy, sweet and warm on the tongue. I am shaking, as though I have seen a ghost.

Ailie's voice comes to me at first from afar, and then closer. 'We will take this dress.'

I am allowed to sit for a while as Ailie pays for the garments. I avoid looking at the mirror. When it is time to go, I lean into my aunt, weakened by the experience.

The shop assistant tells us that the packages will be delivered promptly. Ailie says nothing, but holds me close. When we are out the door and back into the noisy street, Ailie tuts again and tells me she never likes dealing with young shopgirls, who have a reputation for flaunting themselves. I blush, turning my face to hide it from Ailie. I can imagine how such a reputation might form simply from the fact that attractive young women have to talk to the men who come into the store.

We are supposed to put ourselves on show, but only so much.

*

In the afternoon, encased in my fine blue dress, I still feel shaken. Ailie is generous in offering me a glass of wine, which I accept. She wants me to enjoy tonight's company, she tells me. I have no choice. She becomes chatty before her guests arrive, rocking back and forth in her chair. Her nerves make her somewhat childlike. She must wish to make her suppers memorable. Or perhaps she is worried about her guests approving of me. I feel a bit like a specimen on show, like the small flesh-coloured fish I had glimpsed in William's library cabinet.

The Johnsons are the first to arrive. Mr Johnson is tall and thin as a lath, with sparse black hair and a moustache tinged with grey. Mrs Johnson is imposingly tall for a woman, and equally thin, but fair. She wears a demure grey dress. Ailie tells me Johnson is a law man. They both take wine from Edith.

Mr Stewart is the next to arrive. He greets Ailie in French and kisses her hand. He's a much shorter man, whiskery and red, with a small stain on his waistcoat. Ailie introduces him as 'the author', proudly, as though I must know who he is. He takes a place right by me, standing at the bookshelf, and sips half his glass of wine in one go. I sense his gaze traversing my bodice. I surprise him by turning to him in the act, challenging his eyes to look into mine.

'What is it that you write, Mr Stewart?' I ask.

He answers animatedly, in an accent as thick as my own. 'Adventures, ye might call 'em, Lass, oceans and deserts and mountains. Heroes and pirates. Nothing intellectual.'

'Though the themes are very current,' cuts in Ailie. The Johnsons remain silent and stiff. I wonder if they've all read the books. 'He's published a great deal.'

'Well, that is quite an achievement,' I say. 'It must be a challenge to come up with sae many ideas.'

Stewart waves me off, gulping the rest of his wine.

'Is Constance coming?' asks Mr Johnson, with a sharp glance from Mrs.

'Oh!' Ailie seems embarrassed. 'She's not, I'm afraid.'

'Not after wha' happened last time,' Mr Stewart whispers to me, then giggles to himself. His hot breath smells of meat.

Ailie instructs us to move to the table, which glimmers with polished cutlery. I am told to sit to her left, by the head of the table, as her guest. Edith brings meat to the table, already carved. Dishes of buttered tatties follow. I watch Ailie as we begin to eat, to ensure I am not embarrassing her. I use the fork and knife and take small mouthfuls.

The Johnsons are complaining about a new red-tiled house at Arthur's Seat.

'I completely agreed with the letter in the *Courant* – a frightful excrescence!' says Mrs Johnson.

'A garish disfigurement,' Ailie says, nodding.

Mr Stewart makes smacking noises with his mouth at my right, and at one point drops a potato onto the tablecloth. Everyone pauses, but no remark is made.

The conversation moves to reports in the papers of several frightening robberies where a gentleman has been garrotted from behind. Last week a Mr Smith was found by the side of the road, almost choked to death, with his gold watch and chain missing.

'I have resorted to this contraption,' says Mr Johnson, pulling up his collar to reveal a curved sheet of metal.

'Is it not heavy?' Ailie asks.

'It is a burden,' says Mr Johnson, and we all implore him to remove it in present company. There are no garrotters here. He excuses himself from the table to do so. He is so tall that I cannot imagine a criminal taking a chance on him. It would be simpler to go for shorter victims. Unless the criminals are also of exceptional height: stalking the streets like shadows. It is a city of shadows, and they come inside, into bedrooms and shops, and they lurk behind mirrors.

'Leonora, are you not hungry?' Ailie asks me, cutting through the thick in my head.

'I'm a little slow at eating sometimes,' I say, trying to keep my voice warm, picking my knife and fork back up.

'Unlike Mr Stewart,' says Mr Johnson with a wink. Mr Stewart answers with a slurp, and Ailie tuts. I stifle a laugh. Sometimes I crave that kind of break from properness, from restraint. It's one reason I find Hamlet so compelling. When Polonius asks Hamlet what he is reading and he answers – with such nonsense and such sense – 'Words, words, words', laughter tickles my throat.

But Hamlet is mad, and it has sometimes kept me awake at night, the idea of my alignment with him. When I read those words he says to Rosencrantz and Guildenstern, that the world is a 'foul and pestilent congregation of vapours', I am equally resistant to, and understanding of, the idea. The world is such in that it is filled with monstrous ideas, people, places; and yet it is not, because there are red deer and lambs and orange skies and the pressure of fingertips through the material at my elbow. The foul and pestilent world now seems closer, in Edinburgh.

Ailie and her company get slowly drunker. I, too, have had more wine than I am used to. I am hot in my cheeks and chest. And then, as though someone had flicked a switch, Ailie's eyes begin to droop.

'Here she goes,' says Mr Stewart. 'Edith?'

Edith enters, and sees immediately what she is to do. The guests stand simultaneously. Each takes my hand, in turn, to say goodbye. I hold myself upright, and politely give my best wishes.

Mr Stewart lingers half in the doorway. 'Constance – Miss Taylor – would hae kept her awake,' he says obliquely. He kisses me on the hand, and I laugh. 'Ye've got life in ye, girl,' he says.

'I know,' I say forwardly. I'm not so sure why I can be bold with him. It may be to do with his age and experience. It may be that here, in Edinburgh, I fear losing myself and so I become larger, fuller, in some sort of defiance. He edges backwards to the stairwell and I close the door.

I go to my room. The apartment goes black. The sky outside glows grey from fog-shrouded streetlamps. I sit in bed but am anxious about going to sleep. It seems that sleep is a doorway to pestilent vapours that then sit heavy about me in the day. I remove my dress, and unclasp my corset. Edith is inconsistent in her help. The air is cool and I rub my hands along my own skin. I long for the feel of earth and grass, in the warm months after rain, when it smells so pungent. And then I see water. Is it the ocean? I close my eyes, conjuring it further, the way Hamlet lets in his madness. There are small boats, bobbing. It is clear as a memory. But I have not seen the ocean, nor a body of water like this.

There is something happening to me.

I am a lazy, lolling seal in the morning. Blue, deep underwater when Edith wakes me. She says it is quite late and Ailie has asked after me. Her forehead is tight.

'I'm sorry, Edith.'

She sighs and leaves the room.

Thunder sounds outside. My limbs feel heavy. And my breasts feel heavy. So here we are at the start again. This heaviness is often the first sign. I suppose I could attribute my mood to this, also. There is both a languor and an alertness that comes: a weight, but a jumpiness. Sounds cut deeper, and yes, I have startled at shadows previously. I'll put my recent experiences, the frustration and the shock of the mirror, down to this time before the bleeding, then.

I breakfast with Ailie, who is pleased with how the gathering went, and again does not seem to realise (or want to admit) that she fell asleep. She imagines the conversations went on into the night. Her stubborn imagining strikes me as arrogant. I suppose we all have these elements of our perception that are a little awry.

This coffee is rich and viscous on my tongue. Ailie takes it black and so I do too. These kippers in butter, this toast – I must have another helping.

'Where your mother and I are from,' Ailie says, 'it was fish, always.' In the west of Scotland, on the coast. The mention of my mother makes my heart pound. I want to tell Ailie I can picture the water clearly, though that still seems absurd. 'Good for the skin.'

Ailie's accent has been downscaled because she married an

Englishman, but I remember my mother's being rich as gloaming light.

'Tonight we will attend a lecture at the Surgeons' Hall,' Ailie says. She tells me that it will be educational for me. I cannot picture what it will be like.

And the day yawns out ahead of us. My fingers twitch, thinking of chores. Surely I will grow fat, without enough to do, and with these long drawn-out meals. One continues to pick at the food because it is still there, and because the servings are plentiful.

The butter has dripped from the fork right down to my fingers.

As a child I was what adults and other children called a 'sore loser'. When a game had finished I could not politely help pack up the paper money and the red plastic houses; I could not put fifty-two playing cards into a neat pile. It took all my strength not to swipe my arm across the game board, sending the die hurtling at my opponent's smug face. After the game I would be quiet and sullen, digging my fist into the chocolate box, often taking myself away altogether from the room, though that would follow with taunts at my back. I am an only child, like Leonora. So my playmates and competitors were cousins or the children of my parents' friends. Children who grew up to be people so different from me, but whose lives I knew so much about because of the pictures that came up in my feed of fat babies and plain partners. There was a twitch in me when I saw those pictures, similar to the compulsion that made me want to sweep the game board. I'm not stupid; I know that people create a gloss on their lives with what they publicly share, that the setbacks and secrets, the urinary tract infections, visitors who overstay their welcome, children you don't love enough, clandestine kisses and feelings of inadequacy at not having learnt another language are all lingering in the background, but still. I guess I shared more photos and videos when I was with Faye than at any other time. She shared more: pictures of me with a strained, wry expression, holding a glass of something. Or my face in mock surprise or delight, with an ironic thumbs-up or pointing to my meal, a building, or a sign.

If you took a photo of me now I would look both old and like that sulking child.

I was also obsessed with ghost stories. My parents had this book of uncanny tales. Besides these it contained black and white photographs of eerie children in stairwells and hallways, and there was a particularly haunting image of one charred foot left over from a spontaneously combusted woman: a curled shoe like that of the Wicked Witch of the East. Ghosts held the answers to a realm beyond that I sometimes suspected was an actual, physical dimension, and at other times understood as a layering within one's own mind: that you created the ghosts from your unconscious. It made them no less frightening. Now I am a part of my own ghost story. I am the ghost, even before death. I straddle realms. Someone might find me soon, maybe just my foot, and my William sitting beside me, looking as melancholy as a robot can. I am departed but living on in the mind of a young woman.

Sometimes I am so close to death, and simultaneously close to the feelings of my past – of being the loser at the end of the game, overtaken by red rage – that it seems inevitable to go on with the visits, no matter the consequences. I still seek solace and need stimulation in this isolated environment. I am fascinated by Leonora's new circumstances and seeing a darker side of her – the misdirected rage at her aunt, in her grief and confusion. I understand that sort of rage, that cloud, and the way it positions itself to break upon the person closest to you.

Then I come to, as I did as a child after that post-game fug of injustice, sneaking back into the lounge room, drawn by the smell of tacos or the sounds of cartoons, feeling remorse for my behaviour. Remorse is such a common and constant companion, though, that at times it fails to be potent. My remorse has crusted over the years. But sometimes I do pick at the scab and the wound pains again, for a little while. And philosophically I explain my behaviour away – the trips with the tab, I mean – by telling myself that everyone is fucked anyway, now or later. May as well take the ship down with me. If that is what I'm doing. Affecting Leonora may only be a slight tear in the sail, rather than a complete capsizing.

You see the cycles I go through.

If death came sooner – though that makes my heart race – it would be a blanket.

I should have been a person who fought and died in a war, but maybe in some accidental way, such as from stepping on a landmine. Not heroic. Or I should have been electrocuted as a child, or drowned in the pool. Even Faye would have been better off.

It is windy again. I can't really feel, today, what the temperature is. I heard knocking last night, on the door – constant. Or was it simply the wind, having loosed some fragment? Or was it my robot, gaining sentience and banging his pretty head repeatedly against the wall? Was it Leonora's ghost? I drifted in and out of sleep and it seemed to go on. I did feel afraid but I liked the feeling, as when I was a child: the goosebumps, the way your hairs raise and your vision becomes sharper.

In Elizabethan drama, a ghost would appear to some purpose, like Hamlet's father, for example. But I cannot speak to Leonora or control my effect on her. She sees Melbourne, she sees this place, she sees my past, she sees my eyes in the mirror. I am an infection.

Ailie and I join the throng bustling into the anatomical theatre for Dr Young's talk. Ailie has her hand firmly gripped around my elbow, under the velvet shawl. I feel overdressed, in comparison to the browns and greys of other men and women, but Ailie has said that we must assert our place.

'We will not heckle nor jibe,' she tells me beforehand, as though those are things I'd imagined doing.

The wooden stalls are in the round, and in the centre is a table, plus a standing board covered with papers, and a skeleton. I've only ever seen human skeletons in books. This one is off-white, with blackness in its creases. It makes me aware of the space between my ribs and pelvis, all muscle, organs and fat, a vulnerable space. I know the names of parts of the body from Mr Anderson, our talks and the books he leant me, and from slicing open animals. I realise, as we find a place to stand in the full auditorium, near the back as Ailie insists, that I would very much like to see a human body splayed and open. The thought shocks me. And what I had thought was a table, I now realise, is in fact bed-like, where they must indeed give lectures on other parts of the anatomy. What does a baby look like, for example, still curled within its mother? Is all the flesh inside the human abdomen varying shades of pink, or are there other colours? You would say all tongues are pink, for example, but then Duff, a cairn terrier, has a purple tongue. Maybe the liver of a human is green or brown.

'You see around the top tier there,' Ailie says, pointing to a row of thin young men across from us, with variations in their facial hair, 'they are trainee surgeons.' Two women are among them, one in a dishevelled olive dress, leaning in to talk to one of the young men.

'What about the women?' I ask.

'Sweethearts, I suppose,' says Ailie, shrugging. 'It would be nice if we could get you introduced to that crowd.' I know she means for romantic prospects but I look over at them and feel something more like envy at the fact they get to come here regularly and see all parts of the body exposed, and perhaps even to talk about what is inside the skull, and the connection between that and the limbs, the hair, the stomach. If I could understand the body at this level, I could . . .

Are these the thoughts that blossomed in the minds of the men across from me? That began them on their journey? A woman is not encouraged to wonder about veins and sinews, though. We are the ones to carry life, to *feel* how it works, but we are not supposed to think upon it.

Dr Young, a grey-bearded man in narrow stripes, begins his lecture on dental health. He first talks about brushing teeth, which Ailie tells me is information for the lower classes, who need reminding.

He moves on. 'It's now known,' he says, 'that sweets cause unfortunate decay in the teeth, the holes that only until fairly recently were attributed to tiny worms.'

Though Ailie says nothing, I imagine that this particular problem is more for the upper classes, those who can afford food beyond reasons of sustenance.

'So moderate your intake of those Edinburgh Rocks!'

A young woman in the third row whines her dissent, and the hall erupts into laughter. She flushes deep red.

For toothache he recommends oil of clove applied directly to the tooth, but if it gets worse the patient may need an extraction. Sometimes a tooth can be transplanted, and the root takes better if the tooth is fresh. There are a few murmurs at this statement.

In other words, Ailie whispers, he means a fresh tooth from a misfortunate and not from a cadaver. I recall the intense pain of my own extractions in the past, those back-most teeth taken one at a time over a series of months: the hollow ache up the whole side of my skull and the metallic taste of blood. A girl from my schoolhouse died just a few weeks after her first extraction, having not applied the salt water thoroughly enough afterwards, an infection setting into her blood.

When Dr Young moves to the skull, to demonstrate crowding, a woman in the front row clutches her own mouth and faints dramatically, falling onto the man beside her. The crowd is raucous as she's carried out. Dr Young wipes his brow with his handkerchief. I can see that these public lectures are more than just informative; they are an event and a spectacle. Ailie seems jolly with the drama, clutching her hands together, her bird-like cheeks blotched and shining. The doctor soon calms the crowd enough to go on with his talk, but by now much of the top row across from us has slipped out, perhaps realising they are too advanced for this particular show. The din has overwhelmed me slightly and I close my eyes for a moment and note the smell of sweat, and something sharp and lemony beneath.

I jump when Ailie takes my hand. 'We can go,' she says.

As we are walking away, in the dark, there is a faint ache in my jaw, as if the lecturer's words were seeds, planted in the mind to sprout within the body.

I sit in a rickety chair with a blanket across my legs on a crisp cold morning. The water is still and revealing of a topsy-turvy world. A bird has a mate it cannot meet; boats rub the bottom of other boats; sails point skyward and to the underworld. My tooth aches. Pain radiates up the side of my jaw, to the hair that is turning more sand than sunset, shot through with hard greys. I wanted to suffer, didn't I? The toothache pips the pain in my limbs and stomach. I need oil of clove. I can't send the andserv; someone might steal him from me. I need to go myself. But some days I can barely walk, my ankles are panniers of fluid and my calves cramp up. I'm pretty sure I'll need the tooth out. But I fear a dentist will see how ill I am, will tell someone.

The knocking came again; was it day or night? Was I feverish or was it the landlady, or Faye? Faye knocking, the way she did one night on the door of my apartment. That night I heard her knock, curse herself drunkenly, walk away, come back, walk away, come back and knock again, calling my name. Telling me it wasn't fair. Telling me we loved each other. I didn't go to the door. She could do better. Did she ever get what she deserved? Last I knew she was single. She'd had some flings, going by her feed; nothing serious. She is forty now. She wanted a child. She doesn't have much time. Nature is cruel to women.

I realise . . . a lot of the time men don't see that women tuck their passions up under the breast. I suppose that's what they've been taught to do. And then we're surprised when their passions tumble forth as bonfires from their tongues, their eyes, their hands, their cunts. When it happens we protest and cower. Maybe we try to take over, take control of the situation, tuck their emotions back up where they are safe (where we are safe from them).

The ache takes over one side of my head; the nerves of my jaw are molten, are the palm of a hand cupping my cheek and digging in talons. My right eye socket feels dry and red and has the ache behind it. I rest the back of my head. Was she feeling my toothache, or did she give me one? Does it go both ways? I never wanted to be a woman but I have often wanted my balls to shrivel and fall off like overripe nectarines. In a bad period I once, deep in the night, held a knife to my cock. But then I drank more whisky and fell asleep, went to work the next day, dry-mouthed. Sometimes colleagues would say things like 'I didn't sleep much last night', and I wondered if they'd been up holding a knife to some part of themselves. Metaphorically, I was probably right. But that's pessimistic, too. They could have been up all night fucking their fantasy partner, and I was the only one sleepless from staring myself down.

This water is so clear I can lean over and see myself. I am already Narcissus, in love with the image of my suffering, fixed in place and soon to drown.

The motor of a small boat can be heard behind the outcrop at the edge of the island to my right. As it comes around I see it's driven by my landlord, Bethea. I have been too indulgent, taking the air. She will surely stop and talk to me now. I will send you inside, William. I will tell her it is just a cold.

Father's letter is brief, like the last one. He never was much of a writer. The frost has finally turned to snow, he says. I see the cottage and the warm fire, he and Penuel cosy, and Duff having taken to her. I see it as a beacon beyond this city: forests, mountains, lochs, fields of barley, the Tom A Voan Wood. In my mind I knock and knock on their door, shivering violently. Duff barks behind it. William laughs down from his estate, his new wife on his arm.

I should only be happy for them all.

Ailie says she is pleased I am putting on weight, but my arms begin to stick in places, more limited in my clothes. The weight makes me look healthier, while I continue to drown. This mood has gone on beyond the bleeding, into the period where I normally feel lighter. Walking helps; I wish Ailie liked a turn outdoors more often. I know it is too cold, but I like the way the wind rushes down the street and pulls out your neat hair with icy fingers. Last week we took a turn despite a low fog, and had to jump out of the way as a riderless horse bolted towards us. For a moment I looked into its eyes before it whinnied and bared its teeth. We read about it in the *Evening Courant*. Luckily nobody had been hurt.

Ailie has put the claret at the back of the cupboard. She says she is too tempted by it in the colder months. She still falls asleep after – or even during – a meal, and often when I am reading to her. Sometimes I have several hours with myself in candlelight. I read until late because sleep brings visions too vivid. I hear Edith shuffling around in her crawlspace. I found out she lives in a small room behind the bookcase. She must be a night owl, too. I've also heard her leave the house late and come back even later – to meet someone perhaps. I'm sure it is dangerous but it is good she has a life outside service. Uselessness does not suit me, and too much use probably does not suit her. I would like to talk to her more, but she has not indicated an interest or comfort with it.

Ailie and I are in the sitting room, taking tea.

'Are you sick?' she asks me.

'No, I don't believe so, Aunt,' I say.

'It is probably just the cold in your bones,' she says, frowning.

Homesick, so sick, and feeling strange, but I can't talk to her about that.

'We will go to more lectures, and in the summer, to the Gymnasium,' she says. 'You need to meet people your age.'

'I am grateful to ye, Aunt.'

I want to meet some animals.

We hear footsteps on the stairs and then a knock. Edith rushes in from the kitchen, and she and Ailie share a look – we aren't expecting anyone.

Edith opens the door. 'Oh, hello, Miss Taylor,' she says, a little awkwardly.

Ailie stands quickly, her brows furrowed. She walks to the door. Edith steps out of the way.

'Well, now,' my aunt says.

'I came to apologise, Ailie.'

'Well . . . that's quite all right,' says Ailie gruffly, as she stands aside to let her in.

Miss Taylor is dressed in soft pastels, with a ring of wet and grime around the bottom of her skirts. Her thick bronze hair has been mussed by the wind, her hat askew. She notices me, and smiles.

'This is my dear departed sister Isabella's daughter, Leonora Duncan,' Ailie says. Miss Taylor moves to clutch my hand. 'Her poor mother died when she was a child and she's been stuck in the wilderness with her father, so I'm taking her on.' Ailie looks proud.

'That's very good of you,' says Miss Taylor. 'A pretty face with such intelligent eyes should be shared with society.'

'Oh . . .' I duck my head in an attempt to hide my blush. 'It's a pleasure to meet you,' I say.

'Now . . .' says Ailie.

'Shall we sit first?' says Miss Taylor.

Ailie gives me a look.

'Excuse me,' I say, and move out of the room. I am curious about Constance Taylor, though, as Mr Stewart indicated she'd caused a ruckus at Aunt Ailie's second-last gathering. I stay in the hall where I can hear.

'I'm sorry,' says Miss Taylor. 'I really had no right to insult you in your own house.'

'That's correct,' says Ailie.

'Everything you do . . . it is all well intended, and effective, I'm sure. And I'm sorry I brought dear old Charlie into it.'

Ailie is quiet. Then she sighs. 'It was just . . . in front of the party . . .'

'It was arrogant of me.'

'You do like attention.'

'As do you.'

Ailie clears her throat. 'Would you like tea?'

'Please.'

Ailie calls for Edith and when Edith brushes past me, tea tray in hand, we nod shyly, an acknowledgement that we've both been eavesdropping.

'Tell me about your young charge, then,' says Miss Taylor.

'Oh, isn't she beautiful?'

'The stuff of Burns.'

My cheeks burn again. I am not used to people so frequently discussing my appearance.

'She has a melancholy disposition, though,' says my aunt.

'She surely misses her father, her home.'

'An obsession with animals, and reading in solitude,' Ailie says. 'She'll stop and bend down to pet a rat.'

Miss Taylor laughs. 'Compassion and curiosity, you must see these as good traits. She will come into her own.'

'Yes, I suppose,' says Ailie. 'I just sometimes find her difficult to engage.'

'Perhaps I should take her on an outing.'

'No, thank you very much,' Ailie says abruptly. 'I know what I'm doing.'

'Of course.'

'She does need to meet people her age – educated ones.'

'Men, you mean. Potential husbands.'

There's a pause. They seem to be considering the prospect.

'Most women find it natural to settle, Constance.'

'It wasn't for me.'

I am shocked. I haven't heard a person say that. Isn't there no other option?

'I haven't much time for romance . . . what with running the press, finding new books to publish.'

They are quiet, sipping. Two older women without children. By accident? By choice? What is behind their words?

'I know some interesting young people Leonora might like to meet,' Miss Taylor says. 'She is intelligent, you say?'

'I believe so.'

'A trainee physician working under Thomas Laycock approached me about a book he wants to write, something about the nervous system. It isn't right for the press but we've kept in touch; he's introduced me to some of the young men and women of his acquaintance.'

'We'll see.' While Ailie wants me to socialise, it seems she wants to supervise the process as well, wants to choose the company or at least approve of the choices.

'Why, you could have a small soiree here, introduce Leonora to society. You do love giving a party.'

I can hear my heart beating in my ears. I am just a Highland girl; I cannot hope to know what to say, how to act, with people my own age who are educated and fit in comfortably with city life.

'We'll discuss it,' Ailie says. 'Thank you for the apology.'

'Very well.' Miss Taylor sighs as she rises. 'I'll be on my way.'

Beating, buzzing, pressing against my clothes. I have a strange melody in my head: it scratches, warps and wanes, like nothing I've ever heard. I go to sit in my room.

Bethea and I talk about the weather, the wind, the cold. I don't ask if she's come by knocking on my door. I am trying to hide the pain but it is impossible.

'Just how ill are ye?' she asks. 'Ye're nae gonna die on me out here?'

There's a pang of guilt. It is a horrible thing to do to a stranger, to anyone. But I'll make sure you tell her, William, the moment it happens. So I am . . . fresh.

I tell her it's just a toothache. She looks at me sceptically, pushes a grey lock of hair behind her ear.

'You don't have any oil of clove, do you?' I say. 'If it's not too much to ask.'

'Aye, I do,' she says, and walks off to her boat. 'Back in a minute.'

I call my thanks. This minor conversation has been exhausting. I am used to talking, but not responding or reacting, not performing. Do you think every conversation is a performance? I want you to like me; you want me to like you. Okay, not always. Maybe some people want you to respect them, look up to them, or be intimidated by them, not 'like' them, necessarily. Maybe they want you to want to *be* like them. I don't know how to come across, now, except to reveal as little as possible to Bethea. To you, William, I reveal something closer to the truth, in that moment of speaking.

Like about Eric. It all happened over a few years, when I was seeing his sister. There were agonising months of tension in between each encounter. When we'd see each other but hardly have a moment alone.

One night my girlfriend did a McDonald's run and Eric hovered in the doorway a moment, or maybe I hovered in his. And then I remember clutching his head, his dark hair, and we knew we had to be quick but it was no problem. But I always wanted more. I fantasised about long, languid hours with him, in a cove on a beach, secluded and tucked away. Or in a hotel room.

I once went on a trip with my uncle Dave and my cousins to the Gold Coast. It must have been my first time staying in a hotel. Not a motel but a hotel. We were on the thirteenth floor, and had a dangerous balcony where we could dangle our legs toward the pool, the beach, the world. One day after lunch my cousins were down by the pool – I guess I was about ten – and I was a bit sleepy or sunstruck so I stayed on the shady edge of the balcony, playing my handheld. I heard the door of our hotel room open and shut; didn't think anything of it until I heard the murmur of a woman's voice. I peeked into the lounge room and there was Uncle Dave with a woman I'd never seen before, with long powder-blue hair and tattoos all down one arm, and he was taking off her shirt. 'We'd better be quick,' he said. He removed her bra and nestled his moustached mouth into her breasts. He squeezed one and licked the nipple. I still remember the sound. She moaned a little and grabbed at his pants, pulled out his erect cock. I was pummelled by shock at its largeness, its rigidity. Did my own go stiff in my pants? For some reason I can't remember my first erection. Must have been even earlier. And then she gave him a head job, her breasts dangling with the motion, blue mermaid hair flowing around her curves. He stood the whole time, his buttocks clenched. He said, 'Oh yeah, oooooh yeah.' I found it thrilling, frightening, and hilarious. When he came I thought he was in pain; I almost called out. To this day I don't know if she was a prostitute or a woman he just picked up by the pool. He was a handsome guy. In my twenties I tried to grow a moustache, which I now realise was because of him. With my sandy, gingery hair, it just didn't match the power of his dark one.

I'm giving you my sexual memories because they rise to the surface. I think they are my making. Are they yours?

Bethea is back. She smells of lavender with a hint of sweat; she smells feminine. She puts a small bottle of oil of clove in my hand. 'There ye go. Noo, ye've got ma number if it gets worse. If anythin gets worse.'

She knows. It must be obvious by now. Thinning, my skin and hair greying like shadows on the moon. I want to reassure her all is well, but I don't have the strength.

'Ye have a helper?' she asks, looking toward the house.

'Yes, an andserv,' I say.

'Good, dinnae trust them myself, but good.' She puts her hands on her hips, stares out at the water. 'Got enough food?' she asks.

'Yes,' I lie. It feels good to lie, to make myself panic about the lack of food, how I will suffer. I feel strong for it, like in those periods where I went to the gym almost every day, ate a tonne of protein, felt power in my muscles and had a glow to my skin. I was focused on the numbers going up and down in my phone – kilograms, fat, muscle – and didn't have to think about anything else, not Faye's wanting to go off the pill, not my bosses, not young men, or even younger ones. I had control. And now I do again, by doing nothing, saying nothing.

I need to change the subject with Bethea. But I have no idea what is going on in the world. We've covered the weather already.

'Do you live with your family here, Bethea?'

'Husband's dead,' is all she says.

'I'm sorry.'

She waves her hand to shush me, keeps looking out at the water.

'Well, I'll be goin,' she says. And she leaves me alone.

I can't make sense of the image. I am moving, as in a cab, but there are no horses, and there is more space around me within. It is not like the carriage of the train. Outside a curved window are low, flat buildings with squares of yellow-green grass around them. There is a small looking glass above the front window, and when I flick my eyes to it I see the boy in the back seat, dark-haired, in something resembling underclothes. A girl's voice in my ear, telling me to watch the road. I keep my eyes on the boy, his mesmerising long thin arms, fine hairs. He slouches down, looks back at me, moves his hand to where I like it.

Where I like it.

I've never seen him before.

But I wake on the edge of that rush, push my hand down under the covers and press at my pelvis to catch it. I erupt with pleasure. I buck up, feeling the contractions in the walls of my sex, slipping a finger in where it is wet and warm. The pleasure is met with a short stab through my jaw. Both fade to a subtle ache as I settle back in the pillows. Did I cry out? I hope not.

The image remains quite clear this time; I close my eyes to call it forth and retrace the shape of the boy's face. I open my eyes and sit up, glancing over to the looking glass in my room. For a moment, over my vision is laid the image of a young man in the small looking glass of that moving vehicle. Not the boy in the back seat but *him*. Sandy-coloured hair. I close my eyes again and still he stares back at me. Bile rises in my throat.

Get out!

I pull the covers down and rise slowly, dizzily, and splash my face with water, now avoiding the looking glass. A scratching at the window makes me jump. *He is clawing out of me now.* This thought comes unbidden. I am shaking, as though cold or sick. The scratching comes again but I see now it is the tabby cat.

'What are ye doin here?' I ask. The sight of the animal relaxes me. I suddenly remember Ailie's story about the children killing cats. This adds to the worry pressing down upon me. What is it called when you think some force is out to get you? Out to get everything that is good? It is some kind of condition. Maybe I caused it, or it has simply happened *to* me. It is time for me to do something about it. It – I want to say *he* – is weighing upon me.

I open the window and let in the tabby. With the cat comes a rush of cold air, as jarring as my visions. He meows and rubs his head against my chest, at window height, before he leaps down onto the dresser and laps at my water. I run my hand across his fur and he lifts his back end, giving assent. I relax further.

Maybe Miss Taylor's acquaintance, the young medical man who wants to publish a book, would have some insight into these happenings. They are internal but they feel as though they arrive from somewhere else. How could my own mind create such images? But that is the only rational explanation. Though brought up to believe in the possibility of a realm beyond our own (because without that, how could you have faith?), I err on the side of the physical world being all that exists, rich unto itself.

It is easier to imagine that you are possessed than to face the possibility your mind may be fooling you.

No, I will first visit the druggist, someone impartial who might offer advice and give me something to calm the visions. Ailie need not know; I will sneak out to the old town, where no one should recognise me, when she is visiting an acquaintance or at one of her social betterment meetings.

Having decided to do something about my situation, I feel calmer. Or maybe that is the effect of the cat. I wonder how long

I can keep him in here before Ailie discovers. I pick the cat up and recline in bed, placing him next to me. Though I closed the window I hear the world waking up. Shouting, clanging and clopping. The smell of a stoked fire, and then breakfast, creeps under my door, and I realise I am ravenous. I am faint with hunger; I ache all over. I am hungry but my body is leaden. The cat shifts away and when I reach for him he looks into my eyes and hisses.

It is not entirely my fault, I'm sure. The paranoia had already begun in her, from the shock of the move to Edinburgh. Suspicion of her aunt, curtness. I have only given it some kind of form. The way nightmares often do. There's another reason I keep returning to her, I think. My whole life I have been compelled forward, lying awake and planning even the most banal futures: trips, workout structures, where to hang that picture, how to get out of the relationship. No doubt partly to avoid thinking of my thrumming blood. But Leonora has never thought this way – within her mind is a pool of calm stasis. The Highlands. Home. Her dog. The burns. The woods. Even in her distress, this remains there. And it ties in with the silence around me, here, on my tiny island. It is a new way of thinking, of being. A resource of steadiness, and good, that I have never known.

It is completely addictive.

Ailie has gone out, and I have feigned a headache. Edith has brought pepsine wine to me in bed, but she is due to top up the stores today – we're low on cheese and oats – and I know she is usually gone for a few hours. I have planned in advance, with the visions becoming more frequent when I close my eyes, and when I open them, the walls leaning down upon me as if the room is about to collapse in on itself. My head *does* ache, and it feels as though my corset were wrapped above the breast as well as below, drawn in tight.

The walls and the dark, sooty city pressing down. Voices I don't recognise, cries of either pain or pleasure. Some deep sadness, grief for my mother rising up inside me. I don't want to be here at all.

I finish dressing myself when the door clicks behind Edith. I don't really know where I am going but I am less likely to run into my aunt if I cross through the gardens and maybe over the George IV Bridge into the old town. I hope I have enough coins in my pockets.

I remember the berry wine that Abby, my closest schoolhouse friend, clutched in her skirts as I followed her, giggling, into the woods. It was her idea to take one of the jars that crowded on the floor and up one wall of the scullery in her parents' cottage. She said she'd done it before and her parents never noticed. When she opened the jar a tangy, sugary sweetness rose to my nostrils. She took the first sip, darting her tongue out ahead of her mouth. It made me think of a small animal lapping at the edge of a loch. She exhaled and smiled with relish, wiping her mouth on the back of her hand and passing me the jar. I took too much in at once, knowing nothing yet about the back-burn of alcohol. It hit me in my chest and I coughed, while feeling light and hot, like I could easily lift off the rock. My head was clear and sweet and breezy, and my fingertips became sensitive as tongues. I stood and drew them over bark and moss and leaf; I put my hand in Abby's, mirrored her flushed laughter.

That was the opposite of the weight now in my head as I leave the building, with the sky clouded as a heavy-lidded eye. I seek some semblance of that lightness, a gust of Abby's berry-sweet breath in my ear. A bolt of green in this grey.

I have on my old plain dress, as tight as it now is, and I keep my head down. I hope I fit in with the servants flitting about on errands and don't look like an unescorted lady of middle standing, which I suppose is what I've become. I take Bank Street and at the foot of the bridge I am assaulted by the smell of excrement and urine and unwashed bodies, laced through with the persistent sulphurous smoke, that of peat and pipes. A crowd of children in tattered clothes tug at my skirts and raise pleading eyes to mine, calling over one another. 'Miss.' 'Miss.' 'Miss!' But I don't know yet if I can part with the coins I have. I jam my hands into the pockets of my skirts to protect those few pieces of currency. 'I'm sorry!' I say desperately. The children are so thin, I cannot stand it. I break away, trip a little on a cobblestone and hear them laugh derisively, like cruel adults. This is where I was born. Is that what I would have become?

I think about my father with an ache – how I miss him – but with some emotion closer to anger as well. Why didn't he take our family back to the Highlands sooner? He had finished his apprenticeship. He has said it was because of my mother's illness. He thought the best care could be obtained in Edinburgh. I can't help feeling that this wasn't all. Was there an element of shame – the idea of returning with nothing?

I step over the legs of street beggars, smell the rotting fruit being pecked at by ravens, shy from the blackened teeth of people emerging from narrow wynds. A man with a barrel on his shoulder almost takes off my head when he turns. The buildings are tall and crowd together like teeth, casting the street in shadow. I eventually see a sign for a druggist.

I enter, struggling lightly for breath after the hill and with my senses overburdened. Oak shelves are lined with powders and tinctures, with green- and black-inked crisp white labels. The counter is unmanned. I look back outside – that feeling I can't shake of being followed – and then into the room again, am startled by a shock of white hair that comes up from below.

A wrinkled face and white neckerchief and patterned vest join the hair, behind the counter.

'Hullo, Lass,' the man says.

'Good day, Sir,' I say quietly, then clear my throat.

'What ails ye?' He flips up an edge of the counter, pushes at a small door and moves rather too close to my face, milk and fish on his breath. I may be disturbing a late breakfast.

'I . . .'

'Not in the family way, are ye?' he asks, staring pointedly at my belly. I feel myself flush and frown and my hand twitches protectively towards my middle. 'Nae, nae, it's just somethin we get a bit with lassies your age. Are ye just on an errand? For yer husband? Yer mother? Yer carer?'

I shake my head.

'All by yersel walking the Reekie streets, and no even frae aroond here, I can tell by yer accent.' This puzzles me, since I've barely uttered a word.

The man goes back through the door to behind the counter. He pops down and up and sits a white model head with lines drawn on it on the countertop. He stares at my head. 'Let's see noo, ye do hae an intelligent-looking circumference, tha's for sure. I'll be able to trust your own assessment of ye'self, but just to be sure . . .' He pulls a set of metal pincers from his vest pocket. 'Mind if I measure your head, Lass?'

'I'm no sure . . .'

'Alright then, well, out with it, what ails ye?' he asks, setting down the pincers with a clang on the countertop.

'It's a bit hard to explain,' I say, heart thumping. 'I dinnae even ken if this is the place to come.'

'It's the women's issues, is it no? I've five daughters, Lass, I'm no stranger t'it. And I've several customers who come in for a monthly med'cine for their wives, though I suspect they often are takin' it themselves tae get through the moanin and groanin . . .' He laughs heartily at his own joke, fingers hooked in vest pockets.

'I do suffer . . .'

'Ooh, or is it positively a matter o the mind? Reflex actions on the nervous system? Hysteria? Are ye hearin voices, even?'

I was feeling like I might cry, with this forceful man both figuring everything and nothing at all. 'There are nae voices,' I say, 'just – oh, it seems ridiculous – a notion of presence, somethin other than myself, and . . . pictures in my head that dinnae seem like my own.'

He is finally quiet. His hand plays with the pincers, tempted by them. Then he smiles. 'Ye're in luck; this is just ma wife's area.' He produces a flyer and hands it over. 'This is a very exclusive club, but it sounds as though you would benefit frae the discoveries they've made, and might have somethin tae contribute yersel.'

I take the piece of paper and glance at it. Bold, fancy letters, the word 'spiritual'. 'I'm not sure' I say. 'I thought it might be rather more medical, more physical. My father had a dog that began tae howl and whimper when it had never done so before. At the same time the poor thing became lame in one leg. Jacky died some time later and I could see a lump on his head by then. Could not the lump have pressed down on his mind in a way tha' disabled the limb and also affected behaviour?'

'You dinnae seem to have any physical ailments, Lass . . .'

'I do get those . . . what you spoke of regarding your daughters.'

'Ah!' he says, pleased he can provide something of immediate use. 'This is the stuff – it will help ease those pains and cramps tha' accompany your *poorlies*.' I take up the bottle of laudanum and slip it into my skirt. 'And be sure no tae over-exert yersel,' he adds.

I pay the man and tuck the flyer into my skirt along with the bottle. I'm pleased with the possibility of lightness in the liquid, but I was also looking for answers, I realise. I never was good at being patient when something needed fixing. When Father and I found snails on the vegetables, I'd stay outside as the sun came down, trying to uncover every last one. It couldn't wait until tomorrow. I'd stay awake all night if I knew they were still out there, crunching quietly on the leaves.

Walking back to my aunt's apartment, I am in a rush and a daze. I try to block the sights and sounds and smells. I want to try the laudanum, but I fear it, too. Will it make me appear very different? I should be careful to take it only at night, after Ailie has gone to bed. That is when the worst visions occur anyway, before and during sleep.

When I push open the door to our residence, I sigh with relief; I seem to be the first one home.

But then Ailie's door opens and she rushes towards me. 'Where have you been?'

The oil of clove is not working. The tart, green taste is now associated with the pain and makes me retch, and then cough, and then retch some more. I am looking out the ground floor window for Bethea on the bay, but it is raining. A lone bird peeps, perhaps catching the bugs as they move to higher ground. Water in the sky makes me think about the depths of it around me, beneath me. An image of a seal rolling in the dark. I wonder if anyone has ever died here before.

I wanted to suffer, but this really is too much. The side of my face is on fire.

William brings me the telephone and dials Bethea's number. My gut flips with shame, with bother. 'Oh hello, Bethea, I'm so sorry to have to ask you this . . .'

She knows why I am calling. She will make the appointment in the nearest town. She calls back with a confirmation.

'Got enough food?' she asks again.

'Yes,' I lie.

The dentist is a young, broad-shouldered woman who immediately says something about my weight. It is too bright in the office; I struggle not to close my eyes as I am talking to her, before I lie down in the plastic-covered chair.

'I'm on a diet,' I say darkly, wondering if Bethea can hear the conversation in the other room. It feels strange to be away from William. I picture him standing, unmoving, in the corner of the dark lounge room. Waiting for me.

'Maybe you are sick,' she says, now prodding in my mouth. Her assistant lunges in with the spit-catching vacuum that always makes me feel disgusted with myself. My calves tense with the two women over me, pushing around in my mouth. What if I suddenly need to cough or vomit? The dentist *tsks* at the same time I feel a bolt of intense pain. I cry out.

'This will have to come out now,' she says.

I nod.

Of all the advances in medicine, they've never managed to find a better way than the ol' numb-and-wrench for a far-gone tooth. Anaesthetic must be one of humanity's all-time best inventions.

The assistant pricks the inside of my cheek with the numbing needle, then readies me for the dentist by pressing my shoulders down. The dentist enters my mouth with some tool and starts wrenching, her other hand on my jaw. There are flecks of blood on her gloves. I know I'll be covered in bruises. She frowns but I can see the muscles bulging in her arm – she must be used to this action, or perhaps she lifts weights in anticipation of patients like me. People who've failed in the mouth.

The tooth gives with a rush of wetness, to which the vacuum is aimed. The dentist holds it like a trophy in front of my eyes: mottled brown, with a long root pinked by blood and gum. Before giving me a second to recover she tells me I'll have more trouble because of the gum disease. That I must use an electric toothbrush, and address any underlying health problems.

'I don't touch sweets, you know,' I say through the gauze in my mouth.

She doesn't smile.

'Is whisky good for this?' I ask.

'Not right away,' is all she says.

'I'll pay cash,' I say.

'Come back soon for an X-ray,' she says. 'And, do you think maybe you should see a doctor? You are very . . . pale.' I think she was going to say 'grey'. Grey skin, pink mouth, like a shark.

I try to smile, to reassure her, but then I remember that my mouth is diseased, that there is no point in the gesture because my smile will be horrible. I've never been much of a smiler anyway.

Bethea walks ahead of me to the car. She looks small. I wonder how long ago her husband died, whether she has any children or many friends around her. I don't probe. Instead I just thank her. She seems about to ask me something the whole way back, clearing her throat, wetting her lips. But she doesn't. The rain starts again just as she drops me at the footbridge.

'Typical,' she says. And smiles.

I bare my horrible teeth in return.

Aunt, I was only worried about the cat,' I tell her. 'After you told me about the ones that have been killed. I went to see where it was.'

Ailie stares at me fiercely. We stand just inside the door. I don't want to be a burden to her, but to not be that I have to chase some solution for this condition. And yet it's too strange to talk about, to ask for help. And I know that she in particular will not understand.

'You should never be out on your own,' she says. She has believed me. It's tempting to say something petulant – that she goes out on her own, that Edith does. But of course I know the reasons, and it would be rude. My hand twitches toward my pocket. I desire to try the laudanum, to get close perhaps to that feeling of berry wine and moss. I'll be alone, though, this time.

'I won't do it again, Aunt, I'm sorry,' I say. But I want answers. 'Aunt, do you think you will have people around for supper again soon? Perhaps it would help if I spent more time making acquaintances of the . . . human variety.'

Her face warms. She removes her cape. She must have only just come in herself. 'Yes, we do need to get you meeting more people. I was enthusiastic and then I've been a little reluctant, I must admit. I just want to ensure I'm introducing you in the most beneficial way.' Her brow creases.

I'm not used to having a woman care about me; I don't know what to say. I still become unreasonably furious that she is tied to this place, that she is not my mother. The weight of possibly disappointing her sits atop the other issues in my mind.

I believe she's partly reluctant to introduce me to the young people because they were suggested by Miss Taylor. This may be what she is thinking about as we eat, as she tears up the bread and sops it in her soup. She looks at the cupboard with the claret in it, then shakes her head. Thankfully she doesn't ask me to read to her tonight, as she has a headache. We retire early, and I am alone with my laudanum.

I add the recommended few drops to water and I sip it. There is no real taste. I pull the crumpled flyer from beneath my skirts.

ARE YOU A CHANNEL FOR THE "ODYLE"?

"Sensitives" make up one third of the population!

Test your MAGNETIC potential to commune with the "spiritual" – minds and events from the past, present and future BEYOND THE REALM OF OUR OWN.

Our UNIQUE CRYSTALS penetrate the axis of the MATERIAL UNIVERSE, of man, plant and animal, of stellar rays, heat, friction, embracing the CHEMICAL and ORGANIC yet locating the distinct "other" force, Von Reichenbach's "Odyle".

Second Thursday of the month. The door beside. Knock three times.

I frown. But might scepticism ruin my chances of getting rid of this . . . invasion of my senses? I could always leave the meeting, if it became too queer. Although again I would have to go alone, and might that not be dangerous? Let alone a betrayal of my aunt. Perhaps I could confide in someone, take them with me. I'm filled with shame at the idea, though I also long to share this *weight* with someone. There's a slight pang when I think of William, a person I felt briefly close to, but someone from a different world, whom I have to put aside in my thoughts. A sister or a brother might have helped.

My lips are wet. But I cannot feel the tears coming from my eyes. I am languid, sinking again down into the bed. A woman is calling and banging at the door. Her name is Faye. I feel sick about it, but I cannot let her in.

I gasp. It is dark now. There is someone else here. No, it is the cat. I must have left the window open. He is curled beside my left leg. I don't want to move and wake him. I cannot move very fast, anyway. My muscles are like liquid. But the cold is coming in. The smoky air is invading.

It is all coming in. I cannot stop it.

My aunt is finally letting me help in the kitchen, before the soiree. My hands smell cloying, with fat and sweetness, pigskin and jam. Edith's hair escapes from her cap as she rushes about. Ailie sits and frowns, clasping her hands together, expecting Miss Taylor at any moment.

'All right, Leonora, time to dress now,' my aunt says, rocking slightly.

I glance apologetically to Edith, wash off and head to my room. I'm trying to ignore the sensation in my stomach: seals somersaulting. I take off my old dress and put on, over my corset and crinoline, one the colour of oak. It is low cut and my breasts are full and expressive beneath my collarbone. I try a little powder that Ailie has leant me. I look well fed and grown up. I wonder what Father would think. I consider the small drawer next to the bed, the liquid within. It would calm me a little. Just a few drops.

When I emerge, Miss Taylor is in the sitting room. She clutches her hands and smiles broadly when she sees me. 'You look divine,' she says. 'I hope we'll have a chance to talk tonight.'

'As do I,' I say.

Ailie's coterie begin to arrive: Mr and Mrs Johnson, and Mr Stewart, who tells me very quietly I look ravishable. His breath is sharp with drink already.

Glasses are filled and then at the door in a flurry of coats being removed and hung and scarves unwrapped are the people my age, not just men but women too.

Ailie seems distressed at this. 'Who are the girls, Constance?'

'Students also,' Miss Taylor whispers. 'Well, when they're allowed to be.'

I have seen this group before. They are the slightly dishevelled, intimidating youths from the lecture hall, the ones who left partway through. So the women are students too, not sweethearts after all. The youths are already flushed with heat or substance and laughing in the room. A tall, dark-haired man is pumping Mr Stewart's hand. The women walk confidently through the room, introducing themselves. It is getting crowded so I cannot tell but there seem to be five students all up: three men and two women. I smell heated damp wool, a tinge of sweat. Miss Taylor comes to stand beside me, perhaps catching my panicked stare. I need to visit the privy.

'Leonora, this is Dr Edward Fallow,' says Miss Taylor, introducing me to the tall, dark-haired man, 'a graduate of Thomas Laycock's at the university, in medicine.' This is the young man I had heard about.

'Such a pleasure to meet you, Leonora,' he says, taking my hand and giving a tight smile. 'Welcome to Edinburgh.'

'Thank you,' I manage to say, before I am introduced to his younger brother Oskar, a student, with longer, more unruly hair, more fine-boned features, and lips that remind me of fruit. His grasp of my hand is less confident than his brother's, and his voice quieter. I catch his eye a little too long and feel a tickle beneath my belly. How instant that can be.

The other three students are Mr George, Miss Mitchell and Miss Ross. Miss Taylor tells me that the two young women want to be doctors and, along with five other women, have been protesting to be allowed to study at the university.

Awe, envy, admiration are what I feel, an overwhelming jumble. How can these women, these plainly dressed but confident women, know what they want, and protest at the gates of an established institution, protest an established order? Miss Taylor speaks of them proudly. Miss Taylor who never married, never had children. In the books I've read, women with these ideas always suffer. I want to know what else these women feel, what they have done.

My hand shakes as I raise a glass of champagne to my mouth. The students are scrutinising me, now gathered in a group across the room, eating portions of ham and tongue, comfortable in their skin and dress. They may not even know that I can read.

Miss Taylor's hand keeps resting at my elbow, in a reassuring way. I am grateful that she knows I need this.

Dr Fallow walks back over to where we stand. I want to know about his work. I want to know about the insides of people.

'I hope this is not too overwhelming for you,' he says to me kindly. Miss Taylor excuses herself and we both watch her walk away.

'A little,' I can't help admitting. My nervous hand half-tips the champagne glass. I right it. Take a breath. 'Can . . . I ask about your work?' I say.

He looks surprised.

'I may not be as educated as . . . your friends, but I do have an interest.'

'Very good. Well, my work is with the mind. I've worked in asylums around the north since graduating.'

A shiver goes up my spine. He spends his days around people who are trapped by their own thoughts, who see the world differently, or see different worlds.

'My thesis,' he continues, 'was on hallucinations. Do you know what those are?'

'I don't, no.'

'They are images or sounds or even smells created by the mind, superimposed on the real world; things that are not really there.'

A city I have never seen before, people in strange clothes, a woman knocking.

My breath catches and I sip deeply from my glass.

'Are you all right?' he asks.

'Fine, thank you,' I say. *Breathe*. 'And what did you find? I mean, why do people experience them?'

'There are a great many reasons: physical diseases, emotional disturbances – some of them quite technical.' He looks around the room. He wants to return to his friends.

'The body and mind, I wonder . . .' I begin.

'Excuse me,' he says with a small distracted smile, and makes his way across the room again. The laudanum flows over my frustration. It is Oskar, the younger Fallow, whose eyes keep turning to me. Even while Miss Mitchell touches him casually as they share a joke, her bodice hanging defiantly loose.

Dr Fallow joins the Johnsons, Miss Taylor, and my aunt. I stare at a framed etching on the wall, not really seeing it; I move around a little, look out the window at the grey. No one has introduced the young women to me, and I cannot fathom walking up to them myself.

'This Lister from Glasgow, I hear his methods are having a real impact?' asks Mr Johnson to the group.

'Well it's not really my area, but indeed they are being adopted,' says Dr Fallow.

Miss Ross joins them. 'Yes, the carbolic acid solution and general methods of cleanliness have led to fewer deaths.'

'Sounds revolutionary,' says Miss Taylor.

Ailie gives a small huff. 'I can't help but wonder if life were better when we left it up to God – it seems we are meddling somewhat with what might be the true path.'

And Miss Taylor laughs, rude and loud. The others cannot help but join in lightly.

'Oh Ailie,' says Miss Taylor, 'at some point in the evening you always reveal your true thoughts on progress – medical, social . . .' I feel embarrassed for my aunt.

'Now, Constance,' says Mr Johnson.

Mr Stewart has edged in with a gleeful grin. 'Och, I've missed the action.'

Ailie pulls at the collar of her dress, her frown deep. 'I only meant . . . It all happens so fast, these changes.'

'But for the better,' says Miss Ross.

'Always?' Ailie asks.

'In this case, yes,' says Miss Ross.

Ailie looks up at the younger woman, who is so confident in her knowledge. 'I'm . . . sure you're right,' she says quietly. Miss Taylor goes to say something else, but I see Mr Johnson put a hand on her arm. Instead she turns away to refill her drink.

The room is hot with bodies and breath; the drink mingles with the substance in my stomach and warms my core. Ailie continues to speak with the Johnsons, a frown remaining on her face. Though I was inclined, as an observer, to take the side of Miss Taylor and Miss Ross – it sounds like a fact that this new method is saving lives – I saw my aunt anew, and admired her ability to disagree and question. I saw the moment in her face when she realised it wouldn't be truthful not to raise the question. But Miss Taylor's pleasure at mocking her was evident on her face. Really, neither of them was entirely to be respected.

Miss Taylor stands beside me, with Edward Fallow at her other elbow.

'Might I not send you another chapter?' I hear him ask her.

'I'm sorry, Edward – as I said, it's just not right for us,' says Miss Taylor.

'It's of great public significance.'

'Then it will find a publisher.'

'Constance . . .' His voice comes down an octave. I feel her shift. He is touching her elbow. I look away. Then he stalks off across the room, his shoulders high and scrunched. She puts her hand on my arm again and I look at her face. She smiles comfortably. Conflict and drama, they make my chest tighten. Maybe I am more my aunt's niece than I thought I was. Miss Taylor's smile calms me, though, along with the drink, and I sigh. I find myself leaning.

'Do you need a seat?' she asks.

'No.'

'Your aunt resents me,' she says.

'That's unfortunate.'

She shrugs. 'For many reasons perhaps she should. I can't help but push her to try to think differently about certain matters, because she has it in her to think differently. Why else would she spend time with all of us?'

'Think differently?'

'Gas, locomotives, big cities, women doctors.' She takes a large sip of her drink. 'You know, it's not her fault. I really shouldn't...'

I listen. A tendril of bronze hair has fallen across her pale forehead.

She purses her lips. 'I am ungenerous. But Ailie provokes me – because she doesn't understand me.'

'Doesn't understand?'

Miss Taylor pauses. 'I . . . never wanted a child. She thinks that is unnatural.'

She is being very forward. Either she sees an ally in me or this is just the way she is.

'But she never had a child,' I say.

Miss Taylor tilts her head at me, almost with pity. 'Well, that's just it. For her, it wasn't a choice. She had one man – a very flawed man was Charlie, but she loved him dearly. It just does not happen for some people.'

I look over at my aunt, now laughing, cheeks ruddy.

'It's very rare that we get what we want,' Miss Taylor says. 'We're not supposed to want anything much at all.'

I don't know if she is talking about people in general, or being a member of our sex. Perhaps both.

'I want only to live in the Highlands, surrounded by animals,' I say, surprised by my openness.

'And love?'

I don't know how to answer that. I frown.

'Men are animals too, you know,' she says.

We both take a sip. Do animals love? Did my dog Duff love me? She needed food, comfort, but she could get that elsewhere, too. Is the human animal unique in the desire to bond for life?

'Let me just say that if you are in touch with your own inner animal, you will find it very difficult, in a social sense,' she gestures around the room, 'to find ways of exploring that.'

As she says this she locks eyes with Edward Fallow across the room.

'Of course it is understood that men may find ways of expressing this, but not us.' Miss Taylor looks me in the eye. 'You just have to be careful.' She smiles.

Desire: an invasion. Like *him* in my head.

'Oskar is sweet but he is young, and eager,' she tells me. Was it obvious that I'd noticed him? I blush. 'I'm going to eat something,' she says. 'Will you be all right?'

'Yes,' I say, and then let myself perch on the edge of the couch. *Oskar is young, and eager.* Those words may have the opposite effect on me than she'd intended. I look at him and I remember kissing William – that press and urgency. That affection. Oskar's eyebrows are dark and there's a fine sheen of stubble around his lips. He looks quite different to William. He's bony, almost hunched. I imagine rubbing his back in a circle. Where did that come from? I imagine bending him over, spreading his cheeks. Nausea envelops me. I stand and walk to the kitchen, resist the urge to lie on the cold floor. I clutch my stomach, leaning against the wall, and breathe, breathe, breathe.

I have decided to stop. Painfully, because what will I do then? But I have been selfish enough. Now she sees a man who resembles my Eric and she thinks of doing to him what I would. Or is it? How can I know? Some women would lick a man all over, lick his arsehole, stick a finger in it. Yes, they love to give pleasure; it turns them on. But this is the nineteenth century. Wake up. She wouldn't even think to do that. It is me.

Oskar. God, I would like to see him again. See what happens, *feel* what happens. But I've completely lost the line where I end and she begins. I absolutely have to admit I'm having an effect on her – maybe not all negative, but the visions of unfamiliar people and landscapes in an unfamiliar time, the drives, those are negative. And I care about her. I never thought I'd care about anyone again.

And there *are* consequences for her. She fears going mad; she could act unconventionally and be shamed. She is a woman. I can't escape that. She has to act within the confines of her society, to have the best chance. Ugh, but how disgusting this feels – I am a man centuries in the future determining her fate. As though dealing with the patriarchal paradigms of Victorian society are not enough!

I will stop.

Look, William, I feel sick, but I am holding this tab above the bin. No, that way I can retrieve it. Come with me, we'll throw it into the bay.

I can't do it.

No, I'm doing it.

I retch. It is so cold. I'm shaking. With fever, with emotion? I care about her so I want to know what's happening to her. I care about her so I don't want to infect her anymore.

If I were born a woman, if she were born a man. No . . . that would solve nothing.

If I were never born.

I threw it. Oh God, I threw it. It's gone. What will I do? I have to face myself now. Truly. Oh God. When will it come? Where is that fucking wraith with the scythe? I'm aching. My throat is tight and raw. I can't get up now, William. I can't. You'll have to drag me inside.

PART THREE

There is no sign on the door, heavy wood with chipped green paint and a large brass knocker in the shape of a lion's head. My body is shaking but I cannot feel it; there is a gold blur around me like candlelight. I had a few drops before leaving. It is dark and hazily starry and Ailie is asleep. She'd started on the claret before supper and fallen asleep at the table, so I knew she'd be sleeping deeply. I had to take the opportunity, as tonight is one of the nights advertised on the flyer.

I shake with fear and the thrill. The visions have calmed a little since the party, but then last night I saw a man that wasn't a man – cold and painted like a puppet, wearing clothing like a second skin. I knew it wasn't a man by his eyes. I wasn't afraid until I woke up. Then the unfamiliarity washed over me. This non-man was something I was not supposed to know about.

Finally, the door in front of me opens. The corridor is dark and there stands a short, white-haired woman in a long black cloak. 'Ye're here for the meetin?' she asks.

Nerves choke me. I nod.

She moves aside and I enter. Her candle threatens to flicker out when the door closes. She asks me to follow. As I walk, loneliness slides down through my chest, settling in my stomach. I have not become close enough to anyone in Edinburgh to ask them to accompany me, to ask for help.

We take a stone spiral staircase down, and down. The temperature drops; the floor of the stairs above presses upon me as we circle down.

'What is your name?' she asks. It echoes off the stone.

'Leonora Duncan.'

'Ah! A name surely tae delight the energies. Is this yer first time seeking the Odyle? Wha' brings ye?'

Her expression is seemingly of delight but looks leering when half in darkness. I hear other voices around the bend in this underground stone cavern.

'It's difficult to explain, Mrs . . .'

'Call me Davina.'

I nod.

'Well, on your first visit we usually do a standard test tae determine whether ye're a sensitive,' she says matter-of-factly. 'Cannae be lettin' just anyone in now, can we?'

My chest is tight. 'Perhaps I can just tell you what I've been experiencing. It just might take a while to find the words . . .'

'Come in here, Miss Duncan.' Davina leads me into a small stone chamber, the size of a water closet, away from the sound of voices. 'Deprivation of the senses helps the spirits tae commune.'

I clutch my stomach. The space is too small. It has the feeling of the attic with the sloping roof, rough floor under my knees as a child. Sick mother on the bed.

Without another word Davina moves quickly out and closes the door. I reach for it. Complete darkness. I find the handle and pull, with shaking hands, but it doesn't move. Is this truly for sensory deprivation or am I a caged animal for some other purpose? I have made a terrible mistake.

The laudanum has made my muscles languid and soon I do not wish to stand. My skirts provide some layering beneath me when I sit on the floor.

I am not afraid of the dark. I have missed the complete darkness of the Highlands, and the quiet. But there is a drip somewhere. And the more I look into the darkness the more I notice that it is not absolute. There are blotches of light, of colour. Even when I close my eyes.

I yell, and then feel impolite, and then yell again. I brought myself here; should I not play by the rules? But then this is unnatural, to lock a person up.

Time moves slowly. Has it been merely minutes or an hour? Will I be here all night?

The blotches become shapes.

Round, draped, thatched.

A full image, painted. A basket of ripe, verdant fruit, and browning leaves. White folds of robe. A muscled shoulder and deep collarbone crease. Trace the neck to a tilted chin and parted peach lips, to bite to the seed. Heavy-lidded eyes. Dark curls in just-woke tufts. Shadows at his shoulders like wings. The image is delicate but strong.

I gasp. I fear this vision but it is breathtaking. I have stared at this painting for a long time. Somewhere.

I feel warmer. My mouth is open; I pant almost like a dog. Ecstatic light in my chest, to the tips of my nipples. Time, in my chest. I am not sitting in the dark.

When Davina opens the door the image shatters. I realise I cannot feel my legs; I have been sitting on them. There is drool on my chin, my eyes are dry. I can't see beyond her candle flame though I think she is studying me. She holds out her hand and helps me up.

I knock the pins and needles out of my feet as we walk through to the room with people in it. The cold descends upon me and I shiver. Davina hands me a cloak, silently, and I sit on a wooden chair, joining a circle of shadowy figures.

'Everyone welcome Miss Duncan,' she says firmly.

'Welcome, Miss Duncan,' is a chant.

'Good evening, thank you,' I say. The warmth of the image is departing, and this chamber holds an aged, mossy cold that seeps into my bones.

'Will you tell us what happened?' Davina asks.

Do I tell them about just now, or about all the times before?

This is what I am here for, and after that frightening experience I will not be back, so I must use my time well. I start by clearing my throat and shakily describing the image I've just encountered, without mentioning the accompanying bodily experiences. It was as though it had completely taken over. What if one day I can't come back from that?

'Why, that sounds like a painting of Caravaggio's!' says one cloaked figure.

'She has probably seen it in a book.'

'I assure you I have not,' I say.

'Sometimes we dinnae remember wha' we see, and then it can come forth.' That voice is the druggist's, the man who handed me the flyer.

'I have had other visions,' I say. 'Some I cannot even describe because there are no words for the . . . places, the objects, the clothing, the materials . . .'

The figures are silent for a while.

'What do you mean?' says Davina.

'Like a vehicle that runs without horses or steam.'

'Perhaps your Odyle communes with a time where things exist we dinnae yet know about,' says one man. 'Like Jock – 'member the way he saw the tall silver buildings?' He says this to the group and they nod.

I have seen those, too. I swallow. 'But I don't want to be invaded by this . . . Odyle. Is there a cure?'

Davina shakes her head sadly. 'Ye must not throw awae such a gift!'

'But it . . . feels like a kind of madness.'

'Only tae those who do no' understand, Lass,' she says.

I am still sceptical. To embrace their ideas is to embrace the invasion, to let it take over, but it is somewhat a relief to explain my experiences to a group of strangers, and for them to not be dismissive, or treat me as though I am mad.

'What happened to this man, Jock?' I ask.

'One day the visions just stopped, he told us, and after that we saw him nae more,' says a man in the group, sounding disappointed.

'How long was I in the chamber?' I ask.

'Two hours.'

'Then I must go!' I jump up. I do not want to come back, and yet, I wish to hear their stories. I need to find out if this could be a larger phenomenon. Or find out if they are all mad. To believe it acceptable to lock someone up for two hours, to go through it themselves and keep coming back, means there is certainly some madness. I will think on it. For now, I must go in case Ailie is restless. I must hurry into the night.

William, what does the spot on this wall resemble? I am taken by it as with a lover's mole. Faye had a mole in her pubic hair; you could only see it when she'd trimmed. Mostly she let the hair grow, musky and wild. A woman's cunt has such a specific scent, berries dipped in honey rolled in spice, but it changes throughout the month, and after exertion. She didn't like me to go down there after exercise but I liked the way it brought out the bitter notes. She would get so wet, slick on my fingers while my tongue worked above. I always bathed before she went down on me. I wanted to bathe before she even kissed me. Sometimes she'd try to talk to me about it. I'm just OCD, I'd tell her. I like to be clean.

So was that just a dream, William?

It was so vivid, and followed the trajectory of Leonora's story. Maybe it takes a little while for the effect of the tabs to wear off? It definitely felt exactly like a trip. I was in her head. I'm ashamed to say I was relieved to be back there. But it's really not good if I'm still infecting her.

It was one of my favourite paintings she saw at the meeting of the spiritualists. That incredibly inviting image of the boy with the basket of fruit. I did stare at it a long time when the exhibition of great Italian works came to the NGV. I would have been in my early twenties. There's also a colour plate of it in the book I recently finished.

Maybe now I will have to avoid sleep. But the hunger and the sickness make me so weak.

No, you cannot go and get me food. Someone will steal you.

Is that a knocking again?

William goes to check. All I hear is the wind. He returns with a casserole dish in his hands, still hot by the look of the sweat on it. Must be from Bethea. My stomach both yaws and turns. Without me asking him, William goes downstairs and soon returns with a small slice of the meaty, potatoey mess in a bowl. It is sweet and salty and hot. Like tears.

I try not to sleep too late after my night-time adventure, but this is difficult when I wake up with that heaviness. I close my eyes and see fungi displayed in dark, cool forests. Above that, red squirrels hopping along branches, gorging and putting on weight for the winter months. This is all I have been missing and more. Here, I eat animals but I do not see animals. Not many, anyway.

I close my eyes again. An image of Oskar melds with that of the boy with the basket of fruit. Oskar, pale and berobed, his lips parted, his basket spilling over with plums, grapes, peaches and pears.

Rowan berries and cheese at breakfast. The red is startling to my eye, like drops of blood. I am becoming too used to the greys of Edinburgh. I find it a little hard to eat today.

'Are you well, dear?' asks Ailie.

'Yes.'

'Your mother wasn't much of a breakfast eater, I recall.'

I put down my cutlery. 'Will you tell me more about her?'

'I wouldn't know where to start,' says Ailie.

'Please . . .'

Ailie puts down her own cutlery and clasps her hands together, her eyes resting on the ornate clock on the sideboard, with its peeling flakes – gold-hued.

'I just feel very sorry that you didn't get to know her.'

She still does not look at me. We sit in silence for a while. Edith trickles more tea into my cup.

'She was strong-willed, and lively. But loyal, so loyal. I remember…' Ailie laughs '… when we were very young she once slapped a little boy in the face who was teasing me. And the boys loved her. She could have had her pick, really.'

I feel defensive. 'Perhaps you cannae help who you fall in love with.'

Ailie waves her hand. 'Love.'

'You don't think my parents were in love.'

'Yes, I guess they were. What else could explain it?' She picks up her cutlery again and begins to eat. 'Sorry, Lae. I don't mean to be like this.'

I am still hungry for more details. 'She had dark hair, like me, did she not?'

Ailie looks at me now. 'Darker, Leonora. And thicker, too. She used to get very frustrated with it because it was difficult to put up. And she had one wave on this side that she could never do anything about.' My aunt smiles. Then her face turns serious again. 'It's difficult to find the right man,' she says. 'He must be able to take care of you.'

'I know,' I say, knowing she is right; not knowing what is right.

'My dear old Charlie, now there was a man. Knew exactly when to purchase something, at a good price, and when to put away for a rainy day. You know how we met?' Ailie's face has come alive.

'No.'

'He walked right up to me at a ball and flashed a dazzling grin and said, "You're going to marry me." I just about fell into his arms right there.'

'What was it about him that made you fall instantly?' I ask. What was it about him that made his statement compelling and not terrifying?

'It was the smile, his assuredness, and his gold watch chain,' Ailie says matter-of-factly. 'Dr Fallow is a very smart young man,' she adds. 'You spoke to him the other night?'

She can only be talking about the older Fallow, Edward.

'A little. He wasn't very interested in me, I felt.'

'Well, we'll see.'

I suppose it does not matter whether or not I am interested in him, also.

'I'll talk to Constance, I suppose, about arranging another gathering.'

Perhaps you cannot force these things, I want to say. But I am happy for the idea of an event that might get me out into the air, seeing and smelling and not shrouded in blankets and smoke and even books. Being outside in the city would be stimulating, but for me it still lacks seeds and sun and fat squirrels, the feel of woolly flowers beneath the pads of my fingers.

'Is something out of doors possible?' I ask Ailie.

'Well . . . there is Arthur's Seat, or the Gymnasium. Rather a garish spectacle, though.' Ailie looks around the room as though confirming for herself that this is all she needs. She sighs, resignedly. 'Perhaps you can go with Constance.'

There is a scratching at the front door. Ailie sets her cutlery down hard. 'That damned cat!' She glares at me.

I look away. I know I have been encouraging him.

'You know,' Ailie says, 'they're saying it could be animals that are bringing disease into cities?'

'No, I didn't know.'

'We should just get rid of them all.'

A sharp stab in my chest, of alienation.

The next time it happens, the day Miss Taylor is due to take me to the Gymnasium, I wake up gasping in intense pain. My muscles are wrung like washcloths, and my face is wet with tears. All that is left of the vision are rows of faces – boys or young men – in blue shirts. Over one boy's shoulder I peer and he has drawn a tiger, in full colour, on lined paper. He looks up at me and I want to be angry at him for not listening, but I am broken. The picture, his collarbone, the pear sitting on the edge of his desk.

I cannot move, such is the cramping. But I won't cry out. I wriggle each finger to start with, breathing in heavy, short bursts. Soon the breaths come a little easier. My neck eases, my calves, my arms. I stretch out each limb slowly, flex feet and hands, pull my knees up. The vision draws back like a tongue into the mouth. I sit up quickly and look into the mirror, as though to catch him, tell him to stop.

He's not there. *Who* is not there? I am surely mad. The melancholy has stuck to me from the dream, and the longing. That pear on the edge of the boy's desk, lined up for him to eat later. And he eats it neatly with a knife, carving off each piece of soft flesh and putting it delicately in his mouth. He eats pears with knives and his nails are neat and clean, unlike those of the other boys.

I suddenly think about Mr Stewart, the author. Perhaps he goes through something like this when inventing a character. Does he carry them around in his head, dream about them? Could another explanation be that I am creating a world? In order to not let it overwhelm me must I write it out of my head?

I haven't touched my journal, though, since Tomintoul, and even then I wrote about William in code. I am too afraid of someone finding it.

My muscles complain again when I slide off the bed – an after-ache.

Miss Taylor and I arrive at the Gymnasium by cab, and the whole time in its dark interior I fight to keep my head up. Words stretch over my tongue like lichen and struggle to depart my mouth.

Once we are there, though, the air – the marvel of it – opens me up. Families bathe fleshly in the pond, keeping their distance from a large wooden boat painted with a green and red dragon. What Miss Taylor informs me are velocipedes circle – both steadily and unsteadily – in an inner ring. On an outer, circling track, people walk and take the air, pairs and groups conversing, with pink blooms on their cheeks. One man walks quickly, pumping his arms and overtaking amblers.

Young people are spread out on blankets on the rise, taking in views of the pond and central rink, laughing good-naturedly, armed with bottles of beer and snacks from surrounding stands. One group of women watches a group of men. Sitting above the women's blanket are two older, well-dressed women in chairs. One of them reads a book; the other has a fox-like face, alert to danger.

'Ah,' says Miss Taylor, 'there's Oskar, Rebecca and Joan.' She points a little further on, closer to the pond.

My nerves flare, blue gas fire.

They see us and beckon us over. I stand behind Miss Taylor as we say hello. Oskar, all cream and curls, moves from reclining on one arm to standing, nods at both of us politely. Miss Mitchell and Miss Ross also stand, and I am properly introduced to them. They insist I call them by forename, before they return to watching a group of young men; they poke each other playfully, in their own world.

Oskar tells Miss Taylor that Edward was called away earlier than he'd expected to Birmingham. 'They have a rather interesting patient there, as I understand it,' Oskar says, looking at me to include me as well. Or just looking at me. 'He feels that there are small snakes slithering about his body. Though I suppose I shouldn't be gossiping.'

There is blood in my lips and in my sex. Oskar gesticulates when he talks and he has elegant fingers attached to large slender palms. Miss Taylor gestures that I should sit down, and I do.

'Will you try the velocipede?' asks Rebecca. She shifts an unruly curl from over her eyes. I notice her eyebrows are thick and dark, which makes her face look serious. I peer over to where a large woman is wobbling about on the spindly contraption with two wheels. She is heading straight for a person on the sidelines, but just before she hits them she turns it sharply sideways and falls off, her skirts flying up. People run forward to help her to her feet, but I feel a bubble of laughter and when I look back at Rebecca she, too, is holding a giggle back.

'I'm not so sure . . .' I say, not wanting to make a fool of myself. But I'm curious about how it would feel, the flying movement.

'Your aunt thinks they're most inelegant,' says Miss Taylor, smirking.

'Well, they are,' says Oskar, with eyebrows raised.

'Pah, elegant,' says Rebecca, making an inelegant face. Joan giggles too.

One older man now glides in circles, skilfully ducking and weaving around the other riders, his face gleeful.

'Easier without skirts,' says Joan.

'Isn't everything?' says Rebecca. Delight rushes up in my breast. Such flippancy, such honesty. Will I ever be able to air my thoughts in that way? Or am I destined to smile, hot cheeked, on the sidelines?

'Very well,' I say with that feeling of heat and hope and fun in my chest, 'I'll give it a try.'

Rebecca leaps up and puts her arm through mine, drags me down to a man with a whistle around his neck who is in charge of the roster. We both give him our names. She spins me back around and we return to the small rise on which the blanket is spread. Rebecca walks clunkily – stomps – in heavy-heeled shoes. Her body is warm and solid up against mine.

'You are studying to be a doctor, Miss Mitchell?' I ask.

'Trying to,' she says. 'We and a few other women passed the matriculation exam and began our classes. We pay higher fees than the men; we have been whinnied at and abused; we've had rubbish thrown at us and the gates slammed on us. Some of the sympathetic male students . . .' she points toward Oskar '. . . have helped escort us to exams. It goes on.' She shakes her head in frustration. 'Joan and I both want to stay here but we might have to go to London. Oh, and *please* do call me Rebecca. Are you a scholar yourself?'

I blush heavily. 'Oh . . . no.' *What is it like to peer inside the flesh, Rebecca?* 'I do like to read,' I say. Let her at least know that. That I am not ignorant.

'Oh good, good,' she says, smiling warmly. 'Do you have a favourite author, then?'

I panic. What is the right answer? 'I don't suppose I could go past Shakespeare,' I say.

'Well, that is fine,' she says, giving nothing away.

'And you?' I ask.

'Oh! I've read nothing but medical papers for an age, now. I really should get you to recommend me a good novel, something that will transport me elsewhere.' She gestures grandly. 'A good diversion.'

My interests are to her just a diversion. It's understandable. I am glad I can perhaps recommend something to her, though – be of use. She sits down again, next to Joan. I am left to squeeze between her and Oskar. My hand brushes his as I come down beside him; his leaps up and pushes at his hair. He is so thin, his stomach curves in above his belt when he sits. His jawbones are claw-like. All this in a glimpse, though. I don't look for too long. I feel him looking at me out of the side of his eye. My breast rises and falls.

Rebecca and I are called soon for our turn on the velocipedes. They have two wheels, handles and a high seat. The wheels are powered by the pedals, the man explains. I sit astride mine, pushing my skirts forward and around my legs, which must reach toward the pedals on the front wheel. Rebecca pushes off quickly and eagerly, wobbles, puts her feet down, tries again, peering back at me and laughing heartily. I put one foot on a pedal, trying not to think about my stockinged ankle peeping from my skirts, and then follow with the other. The seat is hard against my buttocks. Surprisingly, though, the motion feels natural, as though I've done this before. The track is hard and each small bump reverberates through my body, unpleasantly, but the faster I go, the less I feel it. I drive out to the edge of the track and begin to go around in circles, hugging the sides. People begin to cheer and whoop. 'Aye, she's a natural,' I hear one man say, in a charmingly thick accent. I loop and loop, overtaking a wobbling Rebecca, and experience an ecstasy of movement. I take great gulps of air, clear enough from smoke in this large tree-dense space. I feel that I am smiling, the warmth of my breath pushing out and back across my cheeks, cutting through the cold.

Eventually I hear the whistle, realise it has been going on for a while, that it is someone else's turn. I regretfully slow right down and stop.

'My, my,' says Rebecca, rushing over to me, 'are you sure you've never done that before?'

'No, I'd never even seen one before today,' I say.

'You could perhaps join the races!' she says.

I laugh.

'No, I am serious. Though maybe your aunt wouldn't like it because they allow you to wear a pair of loose trousers.'

'Trousers? Really?'

'Yes, really.'

I continue smiling, and though I would love to ride the velocipede again, the idea of racing it does not really interest me. I only want that feeling of blood pumping through me.

'I have so missed physical activity,' I tell her, as we walk back to the mound.

The others are standing when we arrive at the blanket. Oskar is looking at me with something like wonder. He claps, but doesn't say anything.

Joan rushes forth. 'You were both marvellous,' she says. 'I'll definitely try next time.'

Miss Taylor smiles gently. 'You must be famished after that,' she says.

And when she says it I realise, yes, there is a great emptiness in my stomach; I'm almost dizzy with it. I sit, and she hands me some bread and cheese from her basket.

'Thank you,' I say. And as my heart rate begins to slow, and I take small bites of the food, I look around and wonder, with these people, with this open space, whether I could be all right with living here, after all.

Faye and I had European bicycles, with the big swooping handlebars, for cruising. The bike didn't need to be part of my fitness routine as I had that worked out already, so I was happy to have it for leisure. Sunday rides along the bay. Stopping for smoothies, sometimes for lunch. There was a nice little café, with all the organic and gluten-free BS we coveted. One time we went at night so we could see the penguins down on the pier, but we forgot to check the weather and we got absolutely soaked. At first we laughed, and kissed in the rain like in some corny movie, but it was Melbourne and it was cold so that got tired pretty quickly and we rode as fast as possible home. In the apartment we looked like drowned rats, to use a common Australian expression, but being in range of towels and the heater we were able to laugh again.

A week after we broke up, I rode my bike into the city, but then got drunk and took the train home. I never picked it up.

We were so close to each other, or we would have been. I really do wonder how she would have taken it if I'd opened up to her. Are there really couples out there who know terrible, dark things about each other? And then does it make them stronger? Wouldn't they both have to have an equally terrible secret, in order to understand the other? Faye didn't have one of those. But that's unfair of me, isn't it? If I paint her as 'good' does that remove a dimension from her? No, it doesn't. Anyway, maybe she did have a secret. Or maybe she does.

I remember a friend who was a crime writer admitting to

me, after a few drinks, that he writes in the genre because he fantasises – graphically – about killing people. Faye always liked crime shows. She could get very angry, and even lash out physically – throw things. But that's just ordinary rage. Different from premeditated violent acts.

That last trip, with Leonora, was just as vivid as any other.

It's clear to me now – regretfully, shamefully – that I can't go back from my actions. That I must have tripped too many times, and a link has been forged that possibly can't be broken. Unless, perhaps, I die.

Well, that will come soon enough.

Henry didn't tell me why the tabs shouldn't be taken more than three times. It seems there are many reasons. For the researchers to know this, though, I can't have been the only one. There must be test subjects out there frequently visiting other eras when they fall asleep. And to what effect? On them, on their hosts, and on history? But I can't let the world know what I've experienced without getting Henry in trouble, and without revealing that I'm still living. I guess I should let this record exist in some form after I'm gone, then?

It is getting colder, damper. Leonora is already well into winter. It does feel strange to see her own seasons, months, racing ahead of me. As I've said, if I tripped back further – perhaps to Elizabethan times – in one journey I might be there for months but then wake in the present and it has only been a night. In 1200 I could be there for a year. With Leonora, I sleep a few hours and witness maybe a day and a half. And then time moves fairly quick in between trips as well. Between trips to 1200 you may miss two years. Time damps down.

Is it day or night, William? I can't hear the birds.

I am so cold.

Ice under my fingernails, in the veins of my nose. Aunt Ailie's whole body shudders next to me in the cab.

'We are obliged,' she says to herself. Meaning that as Mr Stewart last called upon her – the last few times, in fact – it is time she called on him. But this is one of the coldest evenings of winter, a frosty pre-snow blue cold. I worry about the cat. Does he have a fire to curl up next to? Or a warm body? I know animals can be resilient, and Scottish animals, in particular, are used to all kinds of weather. But if the cat has been domesticated, which he seems to be, he will prefer the indoors.

I had a brief letter from home, from the new Mrs Duncan (I still cannot call her my stepmother). She tells me all is well, and that she and my father hope I am settled in. She tells me she saw a stoat with its winter coat, and she knew I'd appreciate that. But of course it just makes me ache for home. It is snowing there already, a white blanket settled over the heather. They mention nothing of having me for Christmas, or coming to visit me here. As though this move of mine were permanent. They are making me feel I cannot go home until I have something to show for my time here. A husband, no doubt. It makes me want to actively defy them. But how can I? To study one needs money, not to mention to be allowed. And a woman also would not be a candidate for apprenticeships in trades. It is the body that interests me. But I am not like Rebecca and Joan, not assured and independent. I never could be.

I press my head against the window of the cab, and then retreat quickly. It is frosted cold.

Mr Stewart lives in a tall tenement that faces Holyrood Park and Arthur's Seat. In the dusk, the great mounds look imposing, with deep contrasts between the snow and the Seat's craggy shadows. The clouded, setting sun pokes its rays, gloriously, through the ruins of St Anthony's Chapel, glimpsed in the distance before we pull up in front of Mr Stewart's residence.

As we ascend several flights of stairs we hear music, children bawling; smell peat and beef and onions. The stairs are grooved in the middle from so many footsteps. Mr Stewart opens his door immediately, joyfully. 'Come in!'

There is a short entranceway and he gestures for us to go into a sitting room at the left. In the room, the tall windows are hung with thick red drapes, and on the floor is a large rug under several mismatched, worn armchairs covered in pillows. The fire is going and the room makes me feel immediately comfortable. I stretch my fingertips under my gloves, working the sensation back.

'Sit, sit!' he says.

We move together to a larger lounge and he goes over to a sideboard to pour plum-coloured wine into glasses with thick, curled lips. He does not seem to have a maid. It's a small place in a noisy, tall building but it has a unique view. I can't tell whether he is well-off or not. He has the appearance of having 'just enough'; it's possible he has more but does not spend it on unnecessary items. Like new armchairs. Because these ones are certainly adequate.

'What an absolute pleasure it is to see you again, my lovely,' he says to me directly.

My aunt sits up straight beside me, but I see in the corner of my eye she is smiling. Surely she does not intend . . . Mr Stewart has to be thirty years older than me.

'A delight to see you, too, Mr Stewart,' I say.

'So what have you been doing, what have you discovered?' he asks me.

I tell him about the outing to the Gymnasium, and about the velocipedes, though I know Ailie doesn't approve. We make polite small talk about Edinburgh, the news, the weather. I ask him how his novel is going.

'Ah! It's in the bag, my dear. I'm already at work on the next one: about a young man who discovers a land of strange giants, but finds a way to tunnel under the ocean to return home. Of course, along the way he meets many other strange creatures. And a girl in their clutches!'

'It sounds amusing,' I say.

'It is rubbish,' he says, 'but these kinds of adventures are new to many people, and they like the surprise of them. People who haven't read the myths, you know?'

'You mean of the ancient world?' asks Ailie.

'Precisely.' He smiles warmly.

After our first drink, Mr Stewart serves a cold supper to us from items on the sideboard. He tells us it is too frosty in other parts of the apartment so we must eat in our lounge chairs. I try not to laugh at Ailie's face when he says this. Because we have to hold the plates, we can only use one utensil – a fork. Mr Stewart has no trouble bringing chunks of meat to his mouth and biting them off. I try to follow suit but am aware of being caught between being enthusiastic in front of my host, and not appearing too greedy or messy in front of my aunt. I bring the fork to my lips and attempt to nibble, to take in small pieces. Sometimes strings of meat come off and slap at my chin on the way into my mouth. Once when this happens I catch Mr Stewart's eye and he gives me a mischievous look. I smile back, even with a mouthful.

He takes our plates and sits them on the sideboard, tops up our drinks.

We continue to talk. He appears suddenly alarmed and leaps forward to catch Ailie's drink before she spills it, as she drops off in her usual way, her head lolling on her neck.

'Oh, here she goes,' he says with a laugh. He gets the drink out of her hand in time and sets it on a low table. Then he sits a cushion under her head.

The fire cracks and pops.

We are as good as alone, and I feel all of my recent experiences rush up and sit behind my teeth. I don't know if he's the right person to tell.

'Mr Stewart, when you are creating a character, do they take over you somewhat?' I ask with some hesitation. 'Do you think about them a lot?'

He frowns, considering the question. I notice the way many individual hairs in his eyebrows flick up towards his hairline. 'A lot of writers do, perhaps, but no, not me. When I sit down to write they just re-emerge, like friends coming around for tea. I don't need to think about them in between. I know they'll be there.'

So perhaps he wouldn't know what I am going through.

'Why do you ask?' he says. 'Do you have an interest in writing?'

'Not particularly, but I read and I am interested in the process, I suppose.'

'Some writers do say their characters haunt them. Think of Mary Shelley and her Frankenstein's monster, a beast born of a dream.'

I wrap my arms around myself.

'Would you like more wine?' he asks.

I shouldn't. I won't. 'Yes, please.'

'What is it that haunts you, young Leonora?' he asks.

My heart pounds. As he tops up my glass from the carafe, my face is level with his crotch.

'Nothing,' I say.

'I don't believe you,' he says, turning his back and placing the carafe on the sideboard. He sits again and looks at me. I don't know if I like that he can see something in me, but I am comfortable in this room, and a new environment makes me feel distant from my visions, which seem to be hovering, waiting, back at Ailie's.

'The idea of home,' I say.

'You mean the question of home?' he asks.

'No. The fact that I know where home is, but I cannot be there. So it haunts me.'

He nods. 'That's . . . very sad,' he says.

The silence is awkward. I've said too much. 'Is there something that haunts you?' I ask.

'Oh,' he waves his hand, 'the usual. A cliché. A woman. The one who got away.'

Maybe none of us gets what we want. Does this become something you just accept, as you get older? Ailie wanted a child; Mr Stewart wanted love; I want to live in the Highlands – to have physical duties but to be free in my thoughts, to use my hands while my mind has time to draw connections between ideas.

'I'm sorry to hear that,' I say to Mr Stewart.

'It happens, child. At least, for a writer, heartbreak is fuel.'

'I suppose everything can be fuel,' I say.

'Yes, nothing is wasted,' he says, perking up again. We both take a sip.

'I should get my aunt home,' I say, regretfully. The two of us do have a rapport. Perhaps he could still be the one to tell, though my heart races at the thought. Perhaps I would become a character in his next book – a haunted one.

I gently shake Ailie until she wakes and convinces herself she's been present the whole time, and we add all our layers of clothing before we head downstairs to our waiting cab.

All that velvet. It meant I had a line from the Beach Boys' song 'Surf's Up' in my head: 'hung velvet overtaken me / dim chandelier awaken me'. Eric was obsessed with the Beach Boys, I remember now. I haven't been able to listen to that album for decades without feeling a deep melancholic tide come in like the spray hitting the rocks on this side of the island, where I am sitting, watching for otters. It's sunny enough, today, but windy and rough. I'm watching for otters, for hours, because I need to see some life. The aloneness came upon me last night, oceanic. It's something I've felt before, even when not alone. I wonder if some of us are just born with it – a genetic trait. That perceptivity to one's minuscule, ever-solitary existence has a particular feeling, a weight: hung velvet.

After two hours, and no otters, I vomit onto the ground beside this seat that was set up for spotting wildlife. A robin has been keeping me company, flitting curiously back and forth from some stalks and ferns. The nausea stirs again. But I told William to leave me for four hours. He is good at taking specific instructions. I'm sick of the sight of him, and all he cannot be. But I'm fond of him, too, with complete awareness that it is only due to what I can project upon him.

Are these rantings, yet? Surely being alone so long, Lear on the heath, I will be mad soon. *A poor, infirm, weak and despised old man.* Do I wish for madness? It seems easier than being conscious, and going through the same cycles. Perhaps I've never been capable of feeling anything deeply enough for it to drive me crazy.

Oh – that could be it.

When Faye would fly into a rage and there I was, a mast, watching words whirl around me.

Or maybe I only felt emotions when I was young. And they were strangled just like Humbert's were when his first nymphet, his 'Riviera love', died suddenly. Only to be reawakened by Lolita.

I never had another like Eric, and if I was searching I didn't always know it. But Eric didn't die. He sort of . . . took up drugs.

Real nasty stuff, I heard. He had a feed but never posted, was just randomly tagged sometimes in photos, looking pale and straggly. And old. I never looked at them too long, and blocked him eventually. I didn't want to see him like that. I really, really could not.

The sun winks but then the wind bites. What is that? I think I finally see something! Or is it just another ripple in the water?

Leonora would sit here too, wouldn't she? How can I think that I am alone, when I have her? We've forged a connection, through time. I hate to admit it . . . but I'm glad it's not broken. For her it isn't pleasant. I wonder if she feels the way some people feel who have a close connection with what they think of as being God. Wouldn't His presence sometimes be a burden?

Yes, I definitely see an otter! No, two! Oh, this was worth it. A new sign of life for my dead eyes. The world hasn't ended. Euphoric adrenaline. The grin hurts my cheeks. I run my hand through my hair, which is warm from the sun. In my fingers a huge chunk comes out. I let the strands spread into the wind like the ashes of a loved one.

I wake in a panic, sweating but cold. How is she? I am worried. I miss her. This was an ordinary nightmare: a dog became wolf and its lips spread further and further back to reveal pink gums and yellow, sharp fangs. It snarled and sniffed. It knew I was there.

Why don't you come and take me already?

I can't possibly get up. My muscles are liquid as sweat. But there is that knocking. I want to tell William not to answer it, but my voice catches. It must be day. Light peeps around the blind on the small window. The cold damp fills my nostrils, a hint of fishbones.

Eric is still often the first image to come to me when I wake. His face, his boy chest and elegant, translucent arms; the scent at his elbow crease. Him, and now, Leonora. And then Faye slides in afterwards. Longing and loss shift to shame, and there are all these other waves of everything and nothing – feelings I'm not sure there are words for. But they've been captured in songs and paintings. And in that scene in the film *Midnight Cowboy* when Jon Voight changes the channels on the TV, accompanied by that aching John Barry score. There's that dog with the falsies in its mouth. Connected to the wolf in my dream. It's horror.

I told you there were no others like Eric, that is true. There were hardly any men at all. Before Faye I had a profile on an online dating site for a while. I didn't receive many messages but I ignored most of them anyway, and trawled through the profiles of the youngest men on there – only if they had that particular look. Mainly dark-haired, thin, insolent but sweet – one flavour coated in its opposite. I was too terrified to message them. One day, out of the blue, I received a message from a twenty-year-old. His pictures were a little blurry, but he looked younger than his age. In one of them he had in earbuds and wore a hoodie. He had a piercing in his lower lip. He was immediately sexually forthright:

Hey man

You like young cock?

I thought it might be a trap.

Hi, I typed, *what are you looking for?*

Can you send me some more pics? he asked.

Why don't you send me some? I wrote, and felt a stirring in my pants at the thought of it.

I gave him the email address I mainly used for porn subscriptions. He sent me a couple of pics. In one he was fully clothed, standing by a messy bed, and he was smiling – he looked so young. In the other he had his shirt off in front of the mirror – paper white and thin.

Your turn.

Send me your cock.

This was moving fast.

I don't know . . .

He typed: *Where do you live?*

I told him the suburb.

I scrolled through my phone, trying to find a half-decent photo of myself. I was fit. I thought, maybe I should take one of my chest reflected in the mirror. My face had piqued his interest, God knows why, but he seemed to want more.

Would he want to meet me, though? Or did he trawl for pics to fill some specific folder of unique porn – older guys, or maybe all kinds of guys, posing just for him? Because, though I felt shy about it, I wanted flesh, I wanted contact. Truth be told, I wanted romance. I wanted him to look at me the way Caravaggio's Bacchus, or the boy with the basket of fruit, invites in the viewer.

The pic sharing went on. He said he wouldn't meet me unless

he'd seen my cock. I asked him to share first. He sent me a photo. It was average sized and lightly curved, leaning up against his stomach with his hand on it, from a bed of neatly trimmed pubic hair. I could see the tops of his slim thighs with a soft blond fur on them. Heat rushed through me. How had I even gotten this far? Why was he so interested? I pulled my erect cock out of my jeans in the bathroom and took a picture, before pulling it off easily over his image.

Maybe this would be enough. But he did want to meet. Spent but suddenly brave, I said I'd pick him up in my car.

Bethea is in the doorway to my room. A room that must stink of sweat, piss, vomit and mould. I try to sit up, worried. I can only raise my hand.

'Dinnae worry yersel,' she says. And sits on the edge of the bed. 'I just came to tell ye that somebody's been askin aboot ye, in Gairloch.'

'What?' I manage to push myself up on my hand. Bethea reaches immediately in and arranges the pillows into a mound, so I can lean against them. I think suddenly of my mother. Have I robbed Mum of the chance to look after me? To put a wet washer on my forehead one last time? No, but if I'd stayed they'd have made me get the operations, one after another, dragging my worthless life out like a bad dance remix of Fleetwood Mac's 'Everywhere'.

'A woman,' Bethea says. 'I just heard her ask if anybody had seen a man ca'd Jeff, and she described ye. In the store there.'

All the questions jammed in my mouth. What did the storekeeper say? What did she look like? Was it Faye? My mother? A tracker?

'The storekeeper didnae know anythin,' says Bethea.

'What did she look like?'

'Like a bonnie pixie.'

Faye.

I moan, turn my head away from her. 'She needs to go away.' My face is wet.

Bethea puts her hand on my leg. 'Maybe she has already.'

Faye knows me so well; she knew where to look. Probably I had mentioned going to the place of my ancestors, sometime in our life together. And she probably knows it is an easy place in which to disappear. What would this have cost her? So much money and time. Why can't people let other people die? The ache is too much. I mustn't let her find me.

Bethea pats my leg again. 'Well, just thought ye should know.'

'Thanks, Bethea,' I say.

'I'll come by again.'

I nod. There is complicity between us. I don't want to infect anyone else, but I can see she is alone, her husband dead, and she is beyond caring about my choices. She will never ask more than she thinks I could answer. I don't really deserve to have this. Someone.

You know, we used to just put up twigs and sprigs,' says my aunt, taking in the colourful streamers, picture cards and flowers in Miss Taylor's home. In the corner is a fragrant fir tree, bedecked with sweets, candles and fruit, much larger than the crooked tree Ailie recently bought and decorated. This living room is of substantial size, uncluttered, all in shades of brown. My green dress matches the tree and is suddenly festive.

I clutch my hands between my knees, sitting on a russet-coloured lounge. My knees have been shaking all morning. My whole body is in tremors. It is warm in the room. I can't shake the visions. I can't close my eyes. It is getting so much worse. The woman with short hair is coming up frequently. And then there was a wild animal, hunting me down. The feeling of persecution when I awoke was palpable. I felt the floor of my room covered with knives. I didn't want to get up.

Edith came to help me do my hair and I saw her through a haze of fear. She remarked that I might be sick.

'No, I'm fine,' I managed to say. And on the tip of my tongue were other words that made no sense at all. *Everybody's talkin'* . . . In a foreign accent.

Edith has drawn my hair into a tight red clip and now I am bothered by one strand that is pulled too tightly and stings. I work at it with one shaking finger and see Ailie look at me with a worried expression. I try to smile. I am craving the sweets on the table. It is that time in the month where sweet flavours seem like they will create a soft lining for both my belly and my thoughts.

At supper, Oskar is across from me at the table. I look, he looks away; he looks, I feel his eyes. He sips and looks over the edge of his glass. I cannot think of what to say. He reaches for something and his chest shifts under his shirt. His neck elongates, white and ridged with tongue-holds.

'Eros.' The word slips off my tongue. Luckily, right at that moment someone has pulled a cracker and lollies spray across the tablecloth. I have no control over myself.

Dr Fallow is here. I can't tell him. I think about what the asylums must be like. Somehow I do have an image of them, though I have never seen one. Padded walls, a spot of blood on a pillow. Women with wild hair and cracked lips.

Edward, I see wolves.

Edward, I see a man in my looking glass.

Edward, I see the water.

Edward, I am starting to speak the words he hears.

Edward, I know a new word: 'fuck'.

I did try to start writing it all down. But I felt so ashamed of the strange words. What if someone found it? Ailie or Edith? But I can't go on keeping it in.

Oskar reaches across the table with a cracker for me to pull. I notice his long, thin fingers. I pull hard on it and the sweets shower in his direction, which means I have the larger half. He scoops them up and puts them in my palm. His fingertips linger and he looks into my eyes, but then he swallows and draws away.

With the food sitting heavy in our stomachs we crowd around the piano. Ailie stands back a little. I know she envies Miss Taylor her piano. It is yet another symbol of Miss Taylor sitting slightly above her, in ways that matter to my aunt.

We had learnt many of the carols at school and in church, and I sing them now softly, not wanting to be heard above other voices. My favourite has always been 'Away in a Manger', because I love the image of the baby Jesus surrounded by sleeping animals. The heat and smell and peace of them.

I need to relieve myself and so I leave the room during 'Silent Night' and pull on my cloak to go out to the privy. The air outside is grey, cold and crisp, and seems to hold Mr Dickens' ghosts of Christmas past, present and future. I hear the crunch of a footstep behind me, before I open the door to the reeking privy. I spin. It is Oskar.

'Sometimes it's good to get away from the noise,' he says.

His coat is slipped over his frame like a glove. A swell of desire rushes from my groin to my head and I feel dizzy. I try to grip the privy door but my hand doesn't quite reach it and then he is here and he catches me in his thin, strong arms. I smell his skin, the candied fruit on his breath. Our mouths come together immediately, opening wide, drawing one another's breath. I press my chest to his, move my arms to circle him. I can't think of anything but the skin beneath his clothes, and the organs beyond that. His blood, beating. There is no place for us to go but the stinking privy. Eyes all around us, from the tenements. We have no option but to pull apart.

When we do, and the cold air hits my face like a slap, rationality returns. We cannot do this, or it will create some external evidence of my madness. A woman who has burst from her corset, from the cage of her bones. That's what it feels like, like I am uncontained and spreading out.

I press a hand to his chest, half pushing him back, half just to feel the warmth. The look in his eyes I suspect matches mine – wild.

And so I picked up this twenty-year-old from a McDonald's carpark in the western suburbs. It was dark. He stared ahead at the road, chewing on his lip. My tongue was paralysed.

'Where will we go?' he asked, and when he looked at me his eyes were childlike, a little frightened, and that both repulsed me and turned me on. I wanted to let him out of the car and I wanted to make him come.

'Got any beer?' he asked when we were inside my flat. He stood in the kitchen with hands hanging by his sides from out of his hoodie. He had on jeans and those kind of canvas sneakers that smell after a while. A boy's shoes. I handed him a Coopers Dark and then looked at him properly. He returned the gaze and smirked at me while necking the beer. Less shy, now. He set down the bottle and went straight for my belt. I wondered if we would kiss at all. Maybe he wasn't into it. I didn't want to force my mouth on his if he didn't want me to.

He pulled out my cock, which was already hard, and nodded. 'Nice,' he said.

I rubbed the front of his jeans. He pulled off his hoodie and shirt and I felt a rush of lust and something more complex. Memory, perhaps. It hit me like sudden nausea. I moved my hand up to stroke his collarbone.

'Suck my cock,' he said. So bold. He pulled it out of his jeans himself.

I led him by the forearm toward the lounge in the next room.

I sat him down and knelt in front, took him in my mouth gladly. He began to say things: 'Oh yeah, suck it, spit on it.' How could he know what he wanted, at his age? I was envious. But also, there was something lost in that moment. I became aware of the orangey lamplight, the sound of my own mouth. Why was it a turn-off that he wasn't innocent? Such a beautiful youth – skin video-game white, perfect nipples, a line of soft blond hair down his front. But he'd done this many times before.

Still, he got me off easily, after he came in my mouth.

'You're super quiet, man,' he said to me afterwards.

'Mmm.' I nodded.

And then he thanked me and left. And I sort of napped on the lounge and woke, as usual, thinking of Eric. And with guilt coursing through me, to my fingertips, even though the lover had been of age. Maybe it was guilt about wanting him – and the experience – to be more than it was? Anyway, I still thought about it a lot when I masturbated, afterwards. The smell of his sweat and cheap deodorant. But not long after that I met Faye, and felt joy and love and subsequently pushed a lot of things down, deep down, but never deep enough.

You get the point.

Yesterday I sat watching for otters again, spasming with coughs, and I thought: I could just go over the cliff. It's small, but the water is cold and will probably kill me. I could put rocks in my coat pocket, like Virginia Woolf. I wonder if Faye has moved on from here, or if she's staying in Gairloch. It's as though she can smell my stink: my foetid, dying breaths.

The anatomy book lies open on a stretched-out neck, flesh peeled back, and I see that we are made of clusters and tunnels. Rebecca has added colours to the illustration: reds, pinks, blues. I resist putting my hand to my cheek to check everything within me is contained. Her face is near mine as she explains tendons and vessels, stretches of pink clinging to bone, that move now as I nod. Her eyes are wide and I can now see the back of them, all the spidery red. The vulnerable sockets.

'These colours,' I say, 'you know them from . . .'

'From the cadavers,' she says matter-of-factly.

A clock gives a chunky *tick-tock*. Joan is stretched out reading on the lounge behind us, one leg crossed over the other. Rebecca smells of something earthily floral, like a stem or stalk. They live with Rebecca's uncle and this is the old town, closer to Surgeons' Hall. A close space, in the middle floors. The uncle is away mostly, they tell me, but no one is supposed to know that. Rebecca shows me around. There are only two bedrooms. Theirs is dishevelled and musty, with one bed. It has a dresser and a quite-empty book-shelf. Clothing draped across chairs. The dresser is overcrowded: powders and nervine pills, Reid's Essence of Coffee, scraps of paper and a half-tapped inkwell. They do not mention the mess. It makes me scratchy, brings something up: my mother's face turned away in a dark room. But this is lively mess, busy mess, mess I couldn't hope to accumulate.

Rebecca keeps turning the pages – some images coloured, some as they were. She teaches, explains, but without pause. It's a lot to take in, this exposure to my workings. And nothing to explain *that*. The brain looks only like a lump – it could be in the sky or underground, a cloud or vegetable. Rebecca has given it no colour. Maybe *he* doesn't even live there; maybe he's caught in my chest or my elbow.

'You need a break.' Rebecca smiles. 'Tea?'

'Yes, please.'

Joan moves to the bedroom and closes the door, without a word. Rebecca brings out the tea tray. She frowns at Joan's absence, but says nothing about it. I see I cannot come any closer to her as a friend – not without upsetting a more established equilibrium. So here is someone else with whom I cannot share my burden.

'May I ask what began your interest in the medical?' I ask.

She takes a sip and sits the cup down. 'All my siblings died before the age of seven.'

'Oh . . .'

'Four of them.'

I cannot imagine having and then losing a family around you. I only had one loss that could compare.

'And I never could stop asking why, and wondering if more could have been done. And being the one who somehow lived, it seemed I had to have a purpose.' She sips again, looks intently at me. 'To just get married, I couldn't see that for myself.'

'I have such admiration for your determination.'

'Don't. It doesn't really feel like a choice.'

It feels like more of a choice, or at least a resistance to other options, than what has happened in my life.

Rebecca looks toward the closed door briefly, where Joan is, and even though she turns back to me and shrugs, she can't hide her worry. I have to go. I can feel the visions pressing, anyway, on the spidery red behind my eyeballs. I need to be alone with them. But I hope some of Rebecca's determination has been absorbed. I know where I want to be, at least – I have only to work against the wishes of others, and this encroaching presence.

Madness needs privacy. If I could only work out the words to this song in my head. But I am always sitting with Ailie. I have to turn away from her to the window and make the sounds with my mouth. She caught me rounding my lips at dinner. She said perhaps I should talk to Dr Fallow. But then she frowned and said maybe not, that it would be better for me to talk to him when I am feeling well. Because it would ruin my prospects with him, I suppose (though I see they are not there anyway, as much as Ailie wants to think they are). But I am getting desperate for a cure. And maybe Edward would have that.

William will be in Edinburgh in the early new year. I antici-pate seeing him so much. I hope he brings with him the smell of the Highlands, of the air and heather and his retriever. I will get as close as I can, and just inhale. I will beg him to take me back there. Although now, might these visions follow me and taint the one place I feel at home? I must find out how to leave them behind – leave Edinburgh, leave the man in the looking glass. Nothing would keep me here if I were able to leave, not even the irresistible draw of Oskar. Perhaps I need to go elsewhere, to Australia – it is the place that springs to mind – and drop *him* off. That is impossible. How will I get there and also find my way back?

Ailie and I are now in the middle of reading John Stuart Mill's *On Liberty*. Well, I am, and she pretends to know where we are up to. It is difficult for me to read about freedom and tyranny without relating these words to my own situation. Mill's number one basic liberty is a freedom of thought and emotion. The individual being sovereign over his own body and mind. But what if your thoughts are being suppressed, not just from the outside, but from some inner tyrant also?

And I think that Ailie wants me to know this text in order to feel 'at liberty' to pursue a life she perceives as being better than the one I had, one of a higher standing, but isn't that, too, suppressing the thoughts and emotions I have? It is the opposite of liberty; it is to put myself, potentially, in the hands of another tyrant. I feel I am pressing at walls all around.

A note has come from Oskar and Edward Fallow, inviting me for tea. Me alone. Ailie is unsure about letting me go without her, without a chaperone. I don't think it is because she is worried about me being alone with men; I think it is because she is worried about their impression of me at this time. I have been taking the laudanum regularly. It doesn't calm the visions but it softens my daytime reflections of them, the way they haunt my eyes, ears, tongue. It helps me appear functional. But this is not a way to live. Sometimes I do wish the perfect suitor would come along, whether I like him or not, because then it will be over with; I will be able to accept my fate. And if I cannot go *home* then what else is possible? But then, Miss Taylor. Rebecca and Joan. But one needs education, money. And to be happy in the city.

And to not be speaking in tongues.

Ailie and I arrive at the middle floor of a large grey building, on a wider street than ours in the new town. She had insisted on at least seeing me to the door. When we ring the bell she looks stricken, cannot decide if she should greet the men. 'Would it be ruder to leave or stay?' she mumbles to herself. 'I don't want them to think they have to invite me in,' she says, and rushes quickly away, her skirts brushing the stairs.

A petite maid with brown deer-like eyes answers the door. 'Mr Fallow is expecting you.'

The apartment is much larger that Aunt Ailie's, and also Mr Stewart's and Miss Taylor's. The floor is bone-coloured, cold-looking. I follow the maid into the lounge, where there are deerskin rugs, an unusual white stone fireplace, and armchairs also coated in animal furs. Near to the heat, the rugs and the chairs give off a smell that makes me think of Jesus in the manger.

Oskar rises from an armchair as though he hadn't heard me come in. When he takes my hand his slim fingers are cold, and shaking a little. As though he's just come in from outside.

'I'm afraid Edward was called away again,' he says.

'Oh.' I cannot look into his eyes. I smooth down the front of my dress.

'Virginia will bring some cheeses, and tea. Please, sit,' he says, as he sits himself across from me, leaning back and placing one lavender pantalooned leg atop the other. He wears a vest the same off-white as the floor. The light colours of his clothing make the pink stand out on his cheeks, which dimple when he smiles. A lock of hair has fallen in front of his eyes.

I am so afraid of what I might do or say. Despite his high collar I can see the frantic pulse at his neck.

'Thank you for inviting me,' I say. The words seem to bounce around the sparse, strange room, before being absorbed into the furs.

I resist the urge to rub my face against the animal throw that is behind me on the seat.

Virginia wheels in a trolley and then takes off an ivory platter and places it on the low table between me and Oskar. The product of an animal served on the bones of another. I don't know much about hunting – a man's sport – but I do feel strange about ornamented death, instead of killing to sustain life, as with food.

'Did you stalk any of these animals yourself?' I ask Oskar, as Virginia pours steaming tea into white cups.

Oskar uncrosses his legs and leans forward. 'Only this one,' he says, pointing at a deerskin on the floor.

'Do you enjoy it?'

'It's just something my family does.'

His eyes roam over my face. His lavender pantaloons hug him while he is sitting. They look soft – doeskin, perhaps. His legs are like a deer's, too, long and bony. I sip my hot tea, washing down the excess of saliva in my mouth. He leans forward again, slices a piece of soft cheese and adds it to a piece of fruited bread. He seems to think for a moment, then rises, still chewing, and goes out of the room.

He returns quickly, the maid following him with a small bag. She bows lightly to me and then leaves the room, moving towards the front door. It opens and closes.

'I've sent her on an errand,' he says, and a devilish smile breaks across his face.

I don't know what to do with my lips or my breath; they are twisted like the beak of a crossbill. I take some cheese and bread and let my mind focus on the flavour. The bread is a little dry and catches in my throat.

Oskar stands, sits again, then stands purposefully and comes over to my chair. 'Do you like the cheese?' he asks. There is a tremor in his voice.

I stand. My back is cold off the pelt. The fire is to the front of me, behind Oskar.

'I'm a little cold,' I say.

His face moves in slowly, questioningly. I open my lips. His hand grips my upper arm, hard. My tongue moves inside his mouth, tasting the sugar from his tea. I make a sound of wonder, and hunger. He presses his whole front into me, and I encourage, with a hand on his dipped lower spine. His pantaloons are indeed doeskin, and soft, I notice, as I move my hand to his buttocks, pressing him into me harder. He makes an 'oh' of surprise, pulling away momentarily, looking at me like he can't believe this is happening.

He moves from my mouth and kisses my neck. I feel desire, thick between my legs. There is an ache. He pulls me over to the rug closest to the fire, spins me around and begins to unlace my dress. With one hand I reach back and lightly brush his crotch. Again he makes that desperate noise, of want. He spins me to face him. He draws one breast out of my dress, gasps and leans in to take it in his mouth. Pleasure shoots through my body with his warm tongue on my nipple, gently agitating it. He does the same with the other breast.

I want to see it; I want to know what it is like. As he loosens his own collar and begins to undo his vest, I edge my fingers between the buttons in the soft lavender between his thighs and pull it out. Not pink like an animal's, but with the blood showing through. So hot and hard, straining at itself. Somehow, I know how it will feel to put my mouth on it. I kneel down, my dress half-off, and slide it past my lips and onto my tongue. Oskar moans deeply, puts his hands in my hair. The cock grows harder still. He pulls my face back and collapses on top of me. He pushes up my skirts and finds the split in my drawers. With his still-shaking fingers he finds that centre of me, pushes a finger up inside the hot wet ache. He leans down over my clothing, puffed out all around us, and kisses me hard. I spread my knees out further, showing him he is welcome. There is only this. Breath and heat and skin; the smell of hot fur; the sweetness of his lips. And then he pushes himself inside me, with a look of ecstasy, again as though he cannot believe it. There is a tearing sting at first. I inhale sharply. He pauses, touches my hair questioningly.

'I'm all right,' I say.

So he moves in and out slowly. His breaths are deep. I can tell he is holding back. It begins to hurt less. There is a pleasing throb at the front of my secret place, beneath my belly. I buck up to rub that against his stomach. This makes him lose control, and he pumps suddenly very quickly just a few times and cries out, and I feel his cock pulse inside of me.

He slides off me, panting slightly, and lies beside me on the rug. I worry about whether the seed will leave a stain. I pull my skirts down under me to catch it. I am still pulsing. I could keep going, or go again, or do something else. I wonder if he knows about that place on a woman, the place that makes her feel that uncontrollable spreading pleasure that he seems to have just experienced. If it is his first time, too, then he may not know.

He is facing away from me, towards the fire. 'Edward was not called away. He was always away.'

'You wanted to see me alone,' I say.

Oskar rolls onto his back and adjusts his clothes while looking at me. His cheeks are deep red with heat and exertion. A lock of his dark hair is stuck fast to his forehead. I move to sweep it off, but he flinches away. 'I cannot marry you,' he says.

'Then let us just be friends,' I say.

He looks puzzled.

I need a friend, I want to say. But that would be too much.

What does he need? Only this quick release? Is it just that there is no language for this in-between space we are occupying now, on the rug? No word that aligns it with good, anyway.

'Cover yourself,' he says, looking at my breasts still on display, then standing and leaving me alone. I could happily remain by the fire, half-naked, on the fur, feeling the press of heat and the sensation of softness on my shoulders.

There is that tune in my head again, like no music I have ever heard. Oskar, I need to tell someone. I need to get this out of me. Sadness wells up in my chest. I stand and fix my clothing, as much as I can on my own.

Oskar returns to the room with a lit pipe. 'There's a dresser in my room, so you can tidy your hair.'

I move to where he is gesturing. He meets me halfway, grabs my arm firmly. 'If you tell anyone it will only reflect badly on you.'

I stare into his eyes. They have lost their depth. 'Why do you have to make a pleasant matter unpleasant?' I ask.

Again he looks puzzled. 'I don't know what you mean.'

'Cannae . . .' I don't know how to articulate it. 'Can you not make me feel I am being punished?'

'You have lowered yourself; you must feel some guilt?' His hands are beginning to shake again.

I will not tell him, then, that I enjoyed it. That I would do it again. It seems that will make me lower still, in his eyes. I fight back tears of anger. I grit my teeth, and wrench my arm from his grip.

'I feel nothing,' I say. And I walk to the door.

I fix my hair in the window of the cab, which Ailie had arranged to wait for me.

I am not really numb; I am both awakened and angry, and still physically aroused, with his seed and no doubt my blood sitting beneath the layers of my clothing, a concealed secret.

I can't quite get my hair back into place. I am as tumbledown as an old town tenement.

If I had a husband, at least I would have room to express myself physically, in that way. But what if I was forced to marry someone with whom I did not have such a strong attraction? Like Mr Stewart, for example?

Closed doors on every side.

Faye and I met at a party. We'd both come with someone else and those someone elses knew everyone and we didn't, so we talked. We'd both recently watched a series that was streaming, about a cop having a life crisis who ends up in a small town blah-blah same old, but the character was just so compelling – we agreed on this. And we bumped devices to add each other to our feeds and I watched her world through this and then asked her out for a drink one day when I was bored and lonely.

It happened quite quickly. We had one of those subterraneous connections, expressed through the eyes. Like, even when our opinions differed, we were able to empathise, to a degree, with how the other had come to that conclusion. Through few words, we could see the landscapes of each other's childhoods, and certain defining events of life. I just wanted to know more and more about her, be around her. But it scared the hell out of me. At first I told her I was just really busy, that I could only see her once a week. She was really nice about that. But then I'd long for her and overanalyse the hours between her text messages. I'd wait for her to text first. I'd hold back on xx's and smiley faces but then go crazy if she didn't send them herself. She was all I wanted, then, but I wasn't ready to want that.

She was so patient, when I think about it. This one time she was over at my house, and we'd just fucked – me bending her over, standing up (she loved that), my fist in her hair – and we were lying side by side, limbs casually draped, and I told her I wasn't sure I could give her what she wanted, that I didn't know where my head was at, that maybe she had developed feelings I couldn't reciprocate.

She pulled away from me, but then looked back at me, with a strange sort of resigned mix of sadness and love. 'I'm glad you can be honest with me,' she said. 'That's really all that matters. And it's kinder than pretending.' She slid her singlet on over her head, but then stayed lying next to me, turned away. She sighed. My gut churned with horror. What if that sigh was the beginning of a series of sighs that would lead to a resolute, final sigh, wherein she decided that was as much as she could handle? And yet I didn't reach for her.

What I'd said was true and it was the opposite of true. She gave and gave and gave and I took and, really, I couldn't reciprocate fully. I am too selfish a being; I held on to my secrets. Time and texts and gifts and thoughts – she gave. I didn't feel good enough for her. But then I dragged those early months on and on because I fell deeply for her and I fell, too, for her falling. How could you give up a beautiful, good woman who would do anything for you? Once, also early on, she said to me, 'Maybe what you love about me is my capacity to love.' I gave no answer. 'I guess,' she said, 'that's as good a reason as any.'

I so wish I could have given her what she wanted. Instead I pushed and pulled, pushed and pulled. And she stayed, and she did coax me out, encourage me – the better parts of me, if you will entertain the idea for a moment that there was anything good to bring out. I grew happier and more productive at work; I was fit in a less obsessive way; I even danced occasionally to bad pop music. That made her happy.

And the sex was phenomenally good. She was open-hearted and also open-minded. She could take me in a powerful way but then the next night let me fold her over, let me blow on her cheeks. And once I got the terrain of her cunt I could make her come easily, and then enter her straight afterwards while her body still pulsed and vibrated. Her eyelids would be half-closed, almost like she was stoned, and that would drive me wild, especially when she had no make-up on.

Bethea has suggested I move from here. Because of the incident in town. I tell her I can't stomach a journey. But then, I definitely do not want Faye to find me. Faye, who I perhaps did not treat as a friend.

Bethea has still not asked who the woman is. She never pries. I've never had a companion that tolerates silence (and mess) so well. I'm not sure why there is collusion between us. Perhaps she has a secret, too. And people with secrets can sniff each other out. Or perhaps it's just the Scottish way, not to pry.

I think I trust her, but I'm also slightly nervous that if I let her put me and William in the car, she'll drive us to the nearest hospital. Sometimes women like to save.

Last night I was Leonora as she lost her virginity. Pleasure, pain and confusion. I woke up and I had come all over myself, and I felt guilty because she had not. That bastard. It might take time, sometimes, but it's not hard to get a woman off. But then, he wouldn't know or care, would he?

God, to be penetrated, though. I could come again right now, thinking of the way it felt for Leonora. As I've said, I never wanted to be a woman but there's something so fulfilling, or maybe relieving, about a cock inside you. It touches your organs, turns you inside out. It takes your breath.

It's typical that, despite me being so ill, my dick still works. I bet it wouldn't if I were back home and being operated on and loading up on drugs. But I'm not supposed to be feeling pleasure. Maybe that existence would have been more torturous. Yes.

Increasingly I think I've taken the easy way out. Let myself off the hook. I am suffering – in pain, and facing my thoughts – but would I have suffered more if I'd made myself live on? And continued to be around people?

Selfish to the end.

Leonora is selfish, too. She is not meek. She wants what she wants.

I don't know about going, Bethea. I don't know. It feels like prolonging. But then the horror of Faye suddenly finding me here, still alive, and forcing me onto a plane back to Melbourne. Looking at me in that way a person does when they care about you. Forcing me to talk.

No.

It is New Year's Eve. It is late. I am full and my head aches with the onset of my poorlies. But I am light as well, with the fizz of alcohol. Oskar has not come to Miss Taylor's house. Áilie is fast asleep, upright on the lounge. I stay sitting next to her, afraid of my own mouth. But I sip again and again at the dry, sharp liquid. *Spit on it.* In my head there are bodies in strange settings under too-bright lights. In here, the lamps have been turned down. Is this heat, this rage beneath it all, from me or *him*?

Miss Taylor takes to the piano again, and Rebecca stomps over to me and holds out her hand. She has loosened her dress. Her cheeks and nose are red. I let her pull me up to standing.

'You are allowed to move,' she says. Her teeth are large in her mouth.

I think of God. Would praying help?

'I wish Miss Taylor had a dog,' I say.

Rebecca is still holding my hand. 'You're drunk.'

'Yes,' I say.

'In the future they'll have a drug called ecstasy,' she says.

'You're right,' I say.

We are at the piano, now. Miss Taylor and Mr Stewart are play-competing on the keys. Joan is languidly leaning on the piano's edge. It is a silly song I don't recognise. We are done with the maudlin ticking over of one year into another, of 'Auld Lang Syne'. The new year is a vista of impossibility. I cannot think about it. I drink more.

One of the visions, lately, has been of a giant bug sitting on a wall, protecting a picture that he does not want his mother and sister to take away. That picture is anchoring him to reality.

It is the animals that anchor me, but in the city they are hard to get to. The cat only visits occasionally. I asked Ailie if I could get a bird, even though the thought of one in a cage is not ideal, but she said she wouldn't be able to stand the noise.

Rebecca is loosening my dress. Shame slides in from somewhere. I swallow it away. I can breathe now that my dress has been loosened. I can try to learn the words of the song.

With a tear on my eyelid as big as a bean, is how it goes.

I am assaulted by the vision of a flying machine. Great white wings and a low rumbling. It is too terrifying. I collapse onto the floor. Rebecca laughs, but then comes and sweeps me up under the arms, takes me to a corner away from the fire.

'Where are all the young men?' she asks. 'Miss Taylor is usually so good at inviting them.'

I smile. Where are the dogs, where are the men?

'I don't know who to tell,' I say.

She pats me on the shoulder, but stands and looks back toward the piano: the bright, loud part of the room.

'I don't know what will help,' I say.

She hasn't heard me. I don't want to cry. I am not close enough to anyone to share my tears with them. But that thought makes me well up further. I stare at the wall.

'You'll be all right?' she asks.

I nod. She goes.

My mind is as busy and loud as the room. My stockings are too tight. Where is my drink? I can't breathe. I start to undo my dress further. It is loose enough now to pull over my head. I draw it up, smelling trapped smoke and skin and dust, and then throw it on the floor. That feels better. I loosen my corset.

Mr Stewart notices. 'Oh my, looks like we're getting a show,' he says.

Rebecca squeals with delight, runs back over to me, picking

up the bottle of champagne from the table on the way. She holds it to my lips and, still seated, I instinctively reach for her waist. She feeds the champagne to me like a lamb on the teat.

Mr Stewart throws his necktie into the fire. The piano has stopped.

'I don't know . . .' says Miss Taylor, though she is smiling.

But Ailie wakes, inexplicably, as now it is quieter. 'What is . . .?' She stands quickly and moves over to us, shoves Rebecca out of the way. Cool liquid spills down across the top of my breasts. I laugh. For a moment all is light. Ailie mutters, wrenches me up and tells me to put on my dress.

'Dear Mrs Kemp, please . . .' starts Rebecca.

'Don't you speak,' Ailie says. Miss Taylor remains at the piano. Mr Stewart seems to have disappeared into another room.

I am dressed. I am dizzy. Ailie drags me to the door. I look back, smiling at them all. This year they know what they are doing. I wish them well.

In the cab my aunt falls asleep again. It is not far, luckily, because the streets are full of drunks and fire.

When we get up to her rooms she tells me wearily that we will discuss the matter tomorrow.

'And you will not be seeing them – any of them – anymore. We need to find the right circles for you to move in.'

Just when I have begun to feel some warmth, when I have come closer to friendship, with the possibility, too, of confession and aid. Have found people to potentially learn from, to learn how to become what one wants to become.

In the dark room, the moon glints off the looking glass. I can see the whites of my eyes.

I guess you and I will be alone now. Is that what you want?

She sees us. She looks us deep in the eye.

I wonder about the characters in books I have read. Did they see me too? Some, yes. Like Aschenbach.

It's discomfiting when books do that, though. Sometimes terrifying. And yet afterwards, you cling them to your chest.

It has been a winding drive south to the ferry, during which I largely snoozed. When we exit the car in the bowels of the boat, an announcement comes through about it being a rough day, but that the crew will endeavour to make the crossing as comfortable as possible.

Once up the stairs, Bethea darts for a table and seats with a view to the back of the boat. I'm not such a fan of 'riding backwards' but she's done this many times before and I guess has her comfort zones. The décor is browns, mismatched plaids, on carpets and chairs. It reminds me of a Sydney pub, but with the peaty smell of Lagavulin, the boat's 'malt of the month', instead of Bundy and Coke.

The table secured, Bethea goes to buy chips – crisps, whatever – and a cup of Earl Grey. I look around at the windblown Western Scots, loose-chinned English, smooth-skinned Germans, some young, clean-faced mod-types – Asian and white – in jeans and backpacks and caps. Majority male. Majority white. Whisky tourists. Digging in bags for pre-quartered sandwiches and flasks or returning from the bar with armfuls of crisps and plastic cups.

I'll miss my tiny island. The path I wore from the room to the kitchen to the otter seat. The familiarity of the bathroom.

A non-man as my only companion. The candles. The faces at the edge of sleep. It is only the fear of being found alive that is taking me further away, into the Hebrides, where Bethea owns another house. Larger, damper, she tells me. Large indeed, I hope, if she is staying on. Has she nothing better to do? I guess, in bereavement, she mustn't.

Our silences go well together.

But when I scream at night in terror or shame or pain, what will she do? It just erupts, a foaming spray.

Bethea is back from the kiosk and munching inelegantly, staring out at the water. Her pale face is scrubbed and unreadable. She wears layers of wool, pilled and old.

Maybe her face is not inscrutable; maybe I have never been a good reader of women's faces.

I can't think about the fact she knows I'm dying. The fact she is letting me do it in front of her. Her compassion is too much to bear. Did her husband die horribly, or quickly? Either way, she's done this before or she's playing out what she wished she'd been able to do. That gives me some use. Maybe I am supposed to do one good (however skewed and strange) thing before dying.

She munches and I think I'll be fine but then we hit the open water and the sea rises up on one side and then the other. My head feels fuzzy and my stomach complains with a belch. There must be somewhere outdoors I can sit.

'I'm going for a walk.'

She nods.

I find the stairs and walk slowly and carefully up, blocking a fit couple in their sixties in full waterproof gear.

On deck the air is thick and salty and a relief. The only seats are facing backwards. Nonetheless, I sit and watch the mainland recede while my hair ferals about my head. It is not raining, at least.

'Whisky or wildlife?' asks another loner, with an American

accent, binoculars around his throat. I don't want to make conversation, mate, I just want to sit and control my breathing.

I say the first thing I think of. 'Seals.'

'You're Australian?'

'Good pick. Whereabouts in the States are you from?'

'Toronto.'

'Shit, sorry.'

He waves it away. Happens all the time. I feel bad. But maybe now he'll leave me alone.

'I'm going for the birds of prey,' he says, 'eagles mainly. And a bit of the whisky too.' He whites me with his smile.

'Well, enjoy,' I say, and stand up before another question can come. I stumble, embarrassingly, and bile rises. I cling to the ferry's edge and make my way around the side, where there is, thankfully, no one. But no seats, either. I place both hands on a rail behind me, and lean back into the wall. And watch the islands coming into view.

I can't see much in the grey spray. The isle probably looks as it did, if not in Leonora's time, at least a hundred years ago. The permanence is comforting. There are still green remote places like this, producing spirits that taste like salt and smoke, that transport you through time – via sensation. They've been doing this a long time, but I guess we get bored of all that is good and have to invent new forms of technology to turn experience up a notch. Go beyond Proust's momentary madeleine effect and make it into something clear that can also be captured, pinned down. Nothing is allowed to stay unexplainable, at the tip of the tongue – *What does that remind me of? A banana lolly, my first kiss at the carnival?*

Maybe if life were all sensation. Wait, no, that's what I have been denying myself my whole life. Because sensation is not always equal on either side. The other party might be consumed, like a dram of whisky.

I go downstairs as we come into the dock. Bethea holds out

her arm for me to take. I hate that I need to. But the stairs are steep down to the car hold. We take them very slowly. I vomit just outside the passenger door – it smells of cured meats – and a few people avert their eyes. I get in the car, leaving the puddle. Bethea says nothing but hands me a half-full bottle of water. I watch the door of the ferry open. The land bobs and swings in my vision. Soon it settles as the ferry is secured enough for us to drive out.

"It's no far,' says Bethea.

'I'm okay,' I say.

She drives like all the Scots seem to, fast and hogging the road but then gliding to the edge when someone has to pass. Fast but friendly. A little toot on the horn here and there in thanks. All the colours of green on this island, farm to bog to forest. Coloured wildness all over the peat. Large tracts cut out and black. Disparate guesthouses, farmhouses, white brick distilleries with their distinct pagodas. Small curved beaches with black driftwood, starred with pebbles. Highland cattle in their long burnt-orange coats and a man shaking out the grain for them, smiling at my gaping tourist mouth. Black sheep, and white sheep with black faces. A hen harrier guarding a junction on a pole.

Down a long dirt driveway we turn, with greenery overgrown and flattened by wind encroaching upon it. Small birds swarm like bugs. Bethea's house is large and brown, like a jutting cliff. She often has it rented out all summer, she tells me. Mainly whisky tourists. But the biting wind on the island means it isn't so popular in the colder months.

I lean against the car as Bethea unpacks everything. Once the bags are out – including William neatly folded in his box – she reaches in and pulls out a knobbly old shillelagh, and hands it to me. 'Was ma da's,' she says.

I take it and give it a go, leaning into it. I'm surprised by how well the walking stick fits me, or suits my temperament. The illness has aged me about forty years, it seems.

'All I need now is a pipe, maybe some tweed,' I say.

She laughs, her eyes crinkling. 'Tha' can be arranged! There's a woollen mill up the road that's been here longer than yer colony.' Her smile fades quickly. 'Right, then,' she says, picking up one bag and heading for the door, her sturdy arse wobbling with the weight of it.

I wake up and for a moment I think I am the bug I saw on the wall in my vision. I think I cannot turn over because my back has become a hard, round shell and my many tiny legs are sticking up in the air. But then I see my own hand reaching, and the panic slowly ebbs, like dissipating smoke. I stay lying in bed, where I am confined. Ailie would not let me leave the house, and still isn't letting me. She is displaying rage through her tight lips, disappointment through lowered eyes.

So I am confined, until she decides what to do with me. I am also ill. My body aches, and I have brought up meals. My clothing is loosening again. I will be back to my old physique, though not due to trudging across moors in fine air. By the time William arrives, I wonder?

Edith brings in porridge. Through the sheets the bowl warms my belly. 'Could you refresh my hot water bottle?' I ask her.

She smiles sweetly, but there is an edge of something beneath it. Perhaps because a maid would not have the luxury of getting sick like this, or going mad.

The porridge is made with butter and salt. It is rich and gets stuck in my throat. The few drops of laudanum left in the bottle call to me, but I know I must save them because there might be spies, now, if I try to venture out again for more.

I close my eyes and there is an image of a mother and her daughter standing in the doorway. I snap my eyes open. They are from that story with the bug. How do I know it is a story? It is within me like a memory, because of the emotions it draws forth. The mother cannot look at me.

Here is a real memory now: sipping milk and water from a bowl, my mother with her arms around my shoulders. I can't see her face, ever. I can only feel the weight of her arm, her presence, her eyes on me. If I try to remember her face it blurs further, and slips away to the side of my vision.

I jump when the door opens again. Ailie stands halfway in, one large hand resting above her bosom. She clears her throat. 'How are you feeling?' she asks.

Alone. It takes a moment for me to summon my voice. 'Perhaps getting better.'

She nods. She stays where she is, as though I will jump at her, like an unleashed dog. 'It's very important that the laird is making time for you, you know.'

I just cannot wait to smell the Highlands on him, to be brought closer to home. 'I know, Aunt.'

She wants to ask if I'll behave. Her frown shows her worry.

'He knows me, Aunt. It will be all right.'

'Yes, yes, of course.' She has talked to me about suitable behaviours, and public decorum, but never addressed the issue directly, just gathered worry in her eyes like bunched cloth.

She will be coming with me to see William at the inn where he'll be staying. We will no doubt ask about his wife; I will ask about his dog, I will ask about Chapeltown, I will ask about my father. It will all break my heart.

William suits the opulent room on the top floor of the hotel with a view of the castle and the mound. His blond hair is as clean and glossy as the gold brocade that hugs the curtains and hangs from the bed canopy, which can be glimpsed in the far room. We are in the sitting area – Ailie, myself and the laird – with a young maid flitting in and out topping up tea. A tray of sweets sits on a low table in front of us, and I accidentally choose a large, hard piece, which diminishes my ability to talk. I am overwhelmed, anyway, and Ailie is doing enough talking for the both of us. She was delighted, when we arrived, to see the laird be so familiar with me, though I knew he hid the full extent of his affection. I was glad to see it still in his eyes. As Ailie talks and I wrestle with this rock in my mouth, his eyes move often to me.

A small whiff, I catch, of grass and dog, but the fire is also going and he is freshly washed, so the smell of the Highlands has not permeated the room. Probably just as well, as it may have made me faint with want. It is really even too much to see him sitting here, so formally, nodding at my aunt, as she tells him about the improvements to sanitation and plumbing in the city, and drops the names of famous architects, and then scientists and artists and authors, whom she has met.

'My dear old Charlie, he was rather a good friend of the poet Thomas Aird when Aird was editor of the *Herald*. And Aird was a friend of De Quincey, you know. Charlie's poems sadly were ahead of their time, misunderstood . . .'

'That's fascinating, Mrs Kemp. Please, have another biscuit.'

'Oh, I couldn't possibly, but you are so kind. Leonora will have another one, though – won't you, dear?'

I nod and lean forward to take a chocolate-coated biscuit, even though I have no appetite. I feel William's eyes on my wrist, my hand.

I've got you under my skin, sings a voice in my head, rich as the chocolate. I shake my head to clear it, and Ailie gives me an alarmed look.

Take me back home, William.

Ailie draws a breath but I cut in. 'How is Aignish?'

William looks relieved to be able to address me. 'It is fine, dear Miss Duncan, your father and Mrs Duncan continue to care for it well.' He smiles warmly. I actually do not want to hear that. I want to hear that they need me. 'Winter took a while to come this year, so we are thinking it will last long, too. Remember the year when everyone had to bring the new lambs indoors because of the late snow?'

How could I forget? Their small bodies navigating the furniture; Duff whimpering and confused. They'd been inside for only a few days but I'd wished it were forever. Bring the outside in and the inside out. An animal in my bed; sleeping under the stars.

I say as much. Ailie cocks her head again. *Oh, Aunt!* Anger rises within me. She cannot possibly understand.

'Perhaps we should be going,' she says abruptly.

'Oh no, no, you just arrived,' says William.

'We must not overstay our welcome,' she says.

'Take more tea,' he says to her, and the maid is instantly at her elbow, filling her cup. The fragrance is lightly floral.

'Oh, thank you,' she says. A small silence follows. 'Leonora is getting on just fine,' Ailie says, then sips delicately. 'Very well indeed.'

William seems to detect something in her tone. He looks at me sideways as she sips again.

'Aren't you, dear?'

'Oh yes,' I say, and clear my throat. 'It's very different, you know, from home. The air . . . I've been a little ill.'

I imagine Ailie will be reproaching me with her eyes but when I glance over I see another familiar look on her face, and I lean across to rescue the cup of tea before she spills it on herself. Her eyes droop; she falls gently back onto the cushions.

William looks startled.

I can't help but giggle. 'It happens often.'

'Oh!' he says. 'Well . . .'

'It's really so nice to see you,' I say.

'And you, Leonora.' He remains with his eyes on Ailie.

'She won't wake for a while.'

'We may speak a bit more freely, then?'

'Yes,' I say, my heart swelling. 'Oh, how I miss home.'

'It can't be so bad.'

'It is just not my place, here.'

'Have you made friends?'

'I've tried.'

'Friends like me?'

I don't answer. My lips tremble. Here I am presented with another opportunity. Here, finally, might be the person with whom I can share this burden.

'I . . .' The tears come in a rush.

William stands quickly and comes over to me, touches my hair gently. 'Leonora, Leonora, it can't be that bad.'

'It's not just Edinburgh. It's . . .'

The maid enters and William springs back. She seems to assess the situation, and leaves again. I hear a door slide across.

'Tell me.'

His voice is so soothing. But my words are mad. How can I tell anyone? But if I don't, it feels as if my well will fill up and overflow, and I don't know what form that will take.

'It is madness,' I say.

'What is?'

'I . . .' I look up into his eyes. 'I am haunted.'

'What do you mean?' He frowns.

'I see visions; I hear voices.' After the words come out, I am hit by a wave of fear instead of relief. 'I have strange melodies in my head that I've never heard before.'

William drops his hand from my hair. 'When did this begin?' He sits back down, away from me.

'At first it wasn't much – I just felt this . . . presence. But now, at times, it overtakes me. They are like the memories and thoughts of someone else, inside my own head.'

'This is indeed madness,' he says, looking at me with pity.

'No, well . . . I don't know. I thought, could it be something of the spirit world? But then, I have never believed in that, either.'

He says nothing.

'I have nae told anyone. I didn't think I could. But it's been such a burden.' The thickness of the word *burden* in my accent.

'Why tell me?'

'You know me.' I look into his eyes. He looks away. It is too much for him to contend with. I have made a mistake.

'It will be all right, Leonora. These things are understood much better now. There is a whole science devoted to the mind.' He points to his own head.

'Oh, it's so hard to explain. I'm sure that's what any lunatic would say, but it feels truly to be something external invading me. I mean, some of these visions are of a world that does not exist, one I couldnae possibly have invented!' I am exasperated now. And only making it worse. William remains looking away, at the gold brocade. These are ravings. I am not unintelligent; he is not unkind. 'Look, William, I am glad I have told ye, to get it off my chest, but you do not need to take it on. Please, you can forget it. I will be all right, as you say.'

He remains frowning. 'You were always different,' he says.

As though I have let this in.

He glances suddenly at Ailie, who is rousing. I quickly wipe my cheek. William picks up his teacup.

'No thanks,' my aunt says sleepily, smacking her lips a little, 'but Leonora will have another biscuit.'

I sleep on the top floor under the sloping roof, because it's what I got used to on my small island. Away from the ground that is waiting to swallow me whole. These stairs are an ordeal, but with each painful step I remind myself that that's why I'm still here, to feel this. A plate with a lonely sausage and an overcooked fried egg sits on the kitchen table.

It is warm in here with the Rayburn on. Bethea is in the sitting room, tsking at the way the pages of her paperback curl in the damp. Her large underpants hang on a sagging line in front of the stove, with its hotplate covers thrown back like blown skirts. The *drip-drip-drip* onto the stone floor. I know I should wash my own clothes. It has been some time. I am turning wild. My hair is a wet sandbank pushed back in a heap from my forehead. It's too matted to even finger-comb. Bethea says nothing about the smell. I've never been a naturally smelly person, but I nonetheless used to sluice any hint of dirt from my skin, showering for two minutes twice a day, in the morning and after exercise.

Faye would tease me about how anxious I'd become if it'd been too long since I'd showered. I'd try to subtly sniff my underarms when she wasn't looking. I washed all my clothes after one wear. Except a jacket or two. Faye would wear one long vintage cashmere wool coat every winter, all winter, like a dressing-gown. By the end of the season that dried-out sweat smell – reminiscent of a teenage boy – would become apparent. Though I was obsessed with keeping myself clean I never minded this with her. She was thrifty and so she avoided the drycleaners and just gave the coat a wool wash once the weather warmed up, leaving it to dry flat and stinking like an animal in the bathroom for days, before putting it away for next winter.

Before sitting to eat, I duck around the clothes to sit a heavy kettle on the Rayburn's stovetop. The fire is freshly stoked and the plate is nice and hot. When it steams I make strong tea, no sugar or milk. The egg and sausage turn out to be, unsurprisingly, rubbery and tasteless.

So Leonora has told someone about me. But I am no longer telling anyone about her. I'm no longer speaking aloud to William with Bethea around. Instead, I'm writing in a curled-edge notebook. But who will ever read it? Her story is not really even mine to tell.

Once the pot is boiled I take my tea into the lounge room, hobbling and falling into the other armchair across from Bethea.

'She liked those, my wife,' I say, nodding at the thriller she is reading.

She lowers it slowly. 'Is that who was askin aboot ye?'

'She's not my wife anymore.'

'Divorced?'

'I didn't quite get to the paperwork.'

Bethea frowns deeply. 'I dinnae think I want to know.'

'You don't need to.'

She looks for a moment as though she will ask more. But then she brings the book back up close to her face. She must need glasses.

'How did he die?' I ask. Her husband, I mean.

She sighs. 'An accident.'

I don't push her. I look up at the bookshelf behind her. It's mostly pulpy crime, romances, historical fiction. I take up my well-thumbed copy of Kafka's stories, sitting on the table beside me. It's only been a few days but this is my chair already. I sit here most of the day, read, despair, dream, remember, think about taking up the shillelagh and walking. Want the air. But mostly don't. Want to die, but don't die. Don't want to die, either. Thank Bethea in my mind, but then am repulsed by her kindness, and her mouth noises. Her bad cooking. I should just not eat. Her wool gives off a reek of trapped smoke and something greener.

'What did ye do?' she asks, snapping me from my thoughts, but not lowering the book or looking at me. 'Tae want tae be this far away?'

'I just want peace,' I say. 'I have a right to it.'

'Do ye?' She still is not looking at me.

'Doesn't everyone?'

'Doesnae yer wife?'

If I had the energy to get angry. I mean, why now? Is she feeling some sisterhood-like complicity with a woman she's never met?

'You don't know anything about it,' I say, moving to stand, pain shooting through my abdomen.

'I dinnae, I'm sorry,' she says, lowering the book again, her pale moon of a face remaining tight.

I cough and pain shoots again through my abdomen, and lower, and then wetness spreads beneath me in the chair. I call out with shock and pain.

'What is it?' She rises.

'I've shit myself,' I say.

'Poor bairn,' she says, chuckling. She throws her book down and goes to get a towel. I sit alone in the shameful sticky stink, spot a rabbit shooting by out the window.

I've been both afraid and ashamed, in the days since we saw William. But I have also been mostly free of the visions, as though the telling did open and release them, like steam. I have been able to finish my meals, and can sit up in the evenings and read to Ailie without tiring too quickly. My aunt has been out a lot, since that day, though hasn't told me much about what she is doing. She leaves me sitting and staring out the window at the grey city, Edith tidying around me. I hope I will see William again, and that he will not tell my father. Or perhaps that would be good – that my father would then send for me, see that Edinburgh is not treating me well. That it is driving me mad.

Today the sun glints off the windows on the building opposite, across the alleyway. I could almost like the place.

I have a line in my head from *Cosmos*: 'It is an inherent attribute of the human mind to experience fear, and not hope or joy, at the aspect of that which is unexpected and extraordinary.' Humboldt is talking about comets, 'stars with fiery streaming hair'. I would embrace this unknown if I could, but I do not even have a word for it. Nor do I know if it is natural. If it turns out to be as fleeting as a shooting star then I will be grateful.

I hear Ailie on the stairs – that neat footstep could only be hers – and then the door is unlocked and opens. I smile at her but she looks stricken, guilty.

'What's wrong, Aunt?' I ask.

She leaves the door open and I hear other feet on the stairs – men's feet, boots.

'Now, Leonora, the laird and I had a word, and I just didn't know what to do. I spoke with Dr Fallow, and he thinks . . .'

I close my ears. My body is on alert, full of flicking tails. I see the open door and I run towards it. There are two men on the stairs in white. I push past them and they grab for me when Ailie shouts. I don't have on any shoes, or a coat, but I run out into the cold, bright street, knocking into a man so his hat tumbles onto the footpath. I look to the left and right, and run in the direction of the old town. The feet are now coming after me.

On Princes Street four well-dressed people are crowded around a velocipede, viewing it like an exotic creature. I push past them and mount it, pulling my skirts up. They exclaim; one even laughs. And then I am off. On the footpath there are too many people. I move onto the road, but it is bumpy and reverberates painfully in my groin and lower back. I push on. I weave between two cabs, and a horse shies and whinnies. Faces are a blur, noise rises and falls but mainly I hear my own panting breath. The focus and movement of my limbs clears my head. I don't know where I am going or what I will do when I get there.

I have been fast and those who were chasing me – both the men in white and the tall man who must own the velocipede – have fallen away. I dismount and run the bike, my stockinged feet aching with the cold, up the Royal Mile, dodging the legs of beggars and trying not to look into children's faces. I cannot be confronted by that at this moment. Here is the druggist, and near it the entrance to that underground chamber. I lean the veloci-pede against the shop window and immediately urchins surround it. I enter, the bell tinkling. The man who last served me, and whom I saw cloaked in that underground room, is already serving a customer. I wring my hands and pace, but he does not look at me. Will he let me hide out in that chamber?

He is taking a long time with the hunched-over woman. I cough behind her, and they both turn. The agitation must be showing on my face because he says 'excuse me' to the woman and comes over, with a puzzled expression, perhaps unsure where he has seen me before.

'May I hide in your . . . underground?' I ask.

He looks around at the woman, frowning. I feel I've kept my voice low.

'Please.'

'It is there for a specific purpose.'

'I need to commune,' I lie. 'I need to access the visions.' As I say this, I shiver. I don't want to access them. But down in that darkness, what if they do take over again? And how long can I stay there, anyway? Even if he lets me down there I have no money, no other clothes, no hat, not even any shoes. He and his wife, and their community, are strangers. They have no obligation to look after me.

Oh, I trusted William to be a friend. Perhaps I should have trusted someone else, like Miss Taylor or Mr Stewart. Or would they have told Ailie, too? No matter what, I might have ended up here, ragged and alone in the old town, bare feet on the floor just like when I was a child.

'You must wait, Lass,' the man says, turning back towards his customer.

'I cannot; they are in pursuit.'

'They?'

Now I realise how that might have sounded.

'People are not understanding of my gift,' I say, my eyes pleading.

He puts up his hand to say: just wait.

One of the children outside has managed to mount the veloc-ipede, and three others are pushing him away from the window, laughing. But as it clears a cab pulls up at some speed, sleek black horse bucking at the halt. They have spotted the velocipede. My stomach clenches like the claw of a hawk.

'Sir!' I exclaim. He is handing the woman a brown paper bag. Is there an entrance within this room to the underground?

I push past the woman and run behind the counter through the door that is flipped up. I remember the druggist emerging from somewhere beneath the counter last time I came in. The two men in white burst through the front door. The druggist and his customer exclaim. There – the trapdoor. I lift it and take the stone stairs, slip, slide down painfully on my behind. There is a lamp lit in this first small room that looks like a living area. I hope it will connect to the greater structure. I hear snoring from the bedroom – his wife must be taking an afternoon dot. I don't go that way, then, but into a dark hallway. It smells of moss. At the end of it is a wooden door and I push, hearing the men clomping down the stairs behind me. I am winded and sore from my fall, and tears are beginning to choke my chest. I must go on, I must go on. The door gives and I see nothing but black. I run forward, my hand trailing a cold wall. A sob escapes and echoes around me. They are close now, I can hear their breaths.

'Miss Duncan!' one man calls angrily.

Soon the wall falls off at my right, and I think I am in the main chamber. I walk forward. Perhaps I can hug myself against a wall and stay completely quiet. Perhaps there will be more openings.

They are right at my back; I feel one man's hand swipe out and disturb the air; I feel it as a whisper on my neck. They are being quieter now, too, realising they will have to find me in the dark. I am at an advantage now, without my shoes. But my feet are completely numb. I ache all over. I try to breathe as quietly as possible, and try to remember the way to that small cell.

And then light – the druggist with a lamp, the two men backlit silhouettes. I gasp and turn and trip on a chair. I am on the icy floor. And then their hands are on me, dragging me up, gripping hard at my arms and waist, as though I will wriggle free like a cat that hates to be held. I thrash my head back and forth.

No. No. This can't be happening. Please let me go, let me go home. I will be well, then.

'Come with us now,' one of the men says, gently.
'I want to go home,' I say.
'Everything will be all right.'
I know that they are lying.

PART FOUR

Waking is coming to the edge of a moor in the fog, seeing ghostly dots of candlelight and heading towards them; seeing brighter lights further in the distance, unnatural. Taller buildings than in Edinburgh. Moving machines that make the noise of thunderclaps. So waking is like heading into another dream. There are small arched windows atop long rectangular windows in the ward. Light. So, morning. The other bodies mumble and shift. The ward has been warmed by thousands of dank hot breaths in the night. *What is this quintessence of dust?* So this is madness – jagged thought; words and images familiar and conjured. Father made it clear in his letter that he knew of everything that had happened. Yet he knows nothing. He thought that it could be I wasn't ready for the city – but between the lines of his letter is the question of men, of William and Oskar; that I wasn't ready to meet them, that my mind is having trouble processing what the body comprehended. He blames me, but he also expresses guilt, for the first time, about sending me to the city. *I should have known*, is his most mysterious line.

Father, I feel that no matter what choices were made, by me or you, this otherness might have descended. This double behind my eyes, with its illustrations and wants. It frightens me, raises the hairs on my neck. Maybe I can still run away from it, find a crevice within my own mind. Or maybe I can confront it, draw it out. Are those the methods they help you with here? The physicians and the nurses and attendants? So far I have only experienced deep, drugged sleeps, which cannot be my cure.

Maybe it works for the ones who seem to have snakes for bones, who *mutter-mutter-mutter* while jolt-shuffling and lashing limbs out. I close my eyes again. I hear a song. It clangs in my head like a wooden wheel sliding off a large stone. I see a bard with hair the colour of a robin's flush, and winter skin. I cannot tell if this bard is man or woman. Maybe it doesn't matter, in the place where the other lives.

My body is unmoving under a rough blanket, my nightdress patterned with small stars. They let us keep our own clothes, which Dr Fallow – who is a consulting physician, here – says is better than at some asylums. I sit my hands atop my groin, for warmth. I close my eyes again. There is William in the fog, calling for Roo. But no, the closer I get to him I see there is something missing in his eyes. It is a waterhorse, come to lure me. Or I am the waterhorse. My feet are caught ankle-deep in the bog. The heather grows up around me. A railway is being set upon me. We are all sinking in the bog. One day they will find our bones. A man-woman with red hair will find our bones, and sing about us.

Some people would have walked in here and seen the ancient claw-footed bath, peat stains like patches on a cow, and had a fit of ecstasy. That little wooden slatted mat, the ceramic jug with which to wash your hair and your dirty neck, lathering up with heather-scented soap, pouring it out too hot and then soaking too long until your skin puckers with memories of chlorinated green hair, musk sticks, sunscreen, Mum's voice, *Yes dear I can see you I'm looking.*

But I don't like to sit and soak in my own filth. To watch the scales and dust turn the water oily. Though you couldn't really tell if it changed colour, here, because of that brown water that tastes citric and sweet, like lime cordial. (Maybe there are so many nutrients in the water they are prolonging my life.) But I have no choice about the bath, when I get around to washing. There is no shower. There are some tubes hanging on the back of the door that I presume could make it into a sort of sit-down shower, but that still means sitting on your slippery crack, feeling the grit of your filth beneath you. These tubes hung in the same place in the other bathroom, too. I wonder if they're an innovation of Bethea's, or whether they're something all Scottish bathers have. And that tub in the kitchen sink, instead of just filling the sink itself. Baffling. But where I grew up the sinks were small, double, and stainless steel. And we used scourer-sponges, not a rag and a brush. How do these differences evolve? If a Scot moved to Australia would they take up the shower and the scourer-sponge? Or seek out bath tubes and sink-tubs?

I have too much time to consider insignificant matters.

There's no point, when there will be no decisions in my future like: sponge or rag? And yet, it keeps my mind from flapping about on other useless considerations, such as *why did I put her through all that*; such as *have I altered history*.

So I haven't bathed much, though I should. Getting in and out, too. Creak with a side of groan. Leonora likes a bath. More than me, anyway. She – I – am small and dove-pale, soft as breath. Sometimes when she is alone she runs her hands over her body, not even down there, but across her own arms and chest, her thighs, and she experiences a surge of comforting endorphins, as though that feminine casing, those tiny fine hairs and the sensitive cups behind elbow and knee – as though it is enough just to have that. And I am enclosed, gloved-up inside her, a sensate voyeur. So many things I wish I'd known before.

In Edinburgh baths are necessary to soak off the soot but in the Highlands she was happy with, or made do with, a splash from a bucket or jug of fire-heated water. And not every day even then, as it went.

I am in the bathroom now because I found a brochure on ticks in a folder and I can't stop checking myself – pulling down my socks, taking off my pants, being faced with my pale blue sagging underwear, and patting my underarms. Do they go into your crack, in your earhole? Why do I even care? Lyme disease might just help speed up this process. It's something about how small and insidious they are, though. The way they burrow, like a negative thought.

Some days he stays away. I am not lying on a bed in a dank room, high up, with pain in my muscles and an ache in my groin. There is no mechanical man standing over me. I am not beating my shins with my fists. I am not hungry. Is there a woman? With long grey hair? Is she crazy too? I don't want her to be there. I don't want to be helpless. I should have died.

If he did die, the air would stop rippling ahead of me. He cannot stand that the wife has sought him. The shame is in him like a sickness. I hunker down over myself. This other woman, she touches my shoulder, but I feel grotesque. Is that him or me? Is she a nurse? The images are of boys, naked, slim, and with no hair on their chests. Their penises stand up. Their eyes are black seals' eyes, wet.

It would be late winter now, in the braes. Oh, to be back by spring, or in summer when the dragonflies and damselflies are numerous, in lace-winged bright emeralds. The peat will have dried. The chickens will be pink from ash. Mr Anderson misses me, perhaps. William misses his mother, still. I miss the sun and the grass. I miss space. I miss the colour blue. I miss time alone. I miss Duff.

An attendant held a mirror up for me yesterday and I saw myself in my eyes. Those moments when he is weak flood me with hope.

Dr Fallow is visiting. Usually I see Dr Lock, who sees all the patients in the acute ward, and administers treatment. Edward does not normally see patients in private; his role is more academic – implementing asylum-wide practices, recording the effects.

'How are you getting on?' he asks me, in this wood-panelled office. His chair seems larger and higher than mine; he spreads across it, arms out like the wings of a bat.

'I want to go home,' I say.

'How are the visions?'

I still feel embarrassed that he knows, and something like anger rises as well, because no matter how I try to explain the visions words never accurately represent them.

'Honestly, they have calmed.'

'Well, that is good news.'

'Who is that?' I ask, pointing up at a portrait of a man with two amused chins and a black dog under thumb, a book in his other hand – the word *Lunaticks* on it.

'Oh,' says Edward, 'that is a man to admire – Dr Battie. If it wasn't for him you might still be being bled and purged, or chained to a bedpost.'

'A woman was chained to a bedpost just yesterday.'

Edward's hands come in from his elbows; his fingers steeple. 'Only while sedation took effect. It used to be a hysteric was chained up for days, thrashing about. Most inhumane.'

'Aye.'

Edward leans forward and sips from a cup of steaming tea on his desk. I drink in the smell. We aren't allowed it, as it is considered a stimulant.

'How is my aunt?' I ask.

'Quite upset. She feels she failed you. But otherwise she is well.'

And still grieving for poor old Charlie. I should have asked her more about him. I was so caught up in controlling my thoughts, what I felt. And my anger over her not having been there for my mother.

'And how is . . . how are the others?' I ask. He frowns. How are the well youth? How are the learned and robust women and men? How are those who do not suffer visions, who pour champagne down their throats?

Edward actually ignores the question. 'It's good we managed to put you in the acute ward, you know,' he says, raising his chin, 'as hereditary lunacy is still considered incurable. You should, technically, be in the chronic ward.' He looks towards the building across from us, with its face-like façade. 'It is not so nice over there.' As though he has done me a favour.

But I don't understand. My father is not mad; my mother . . .

'What do you mean,' I say, 'hereditary?'

'It means to have inherited the traits of the parent . . .'

'I know what the word means,' I interrupt. 'But my father and mother were never mad.'

He cocks his head at me. 'Oh . . . you don't know.' He looks truly sorry, but then brightens. 'Maybe knowing is better. It may help you. I believe in patients aiding their own recovery.'

'My father?'

'I think you know it was not your father.'

My head spins. I clutch the armrests of the wooden chair. I only remember my mother in bed – but it was a physical ailment, was it not? As I crawled upon that floor, and cried myself to sleep. What floods back to me now is an image of her lying rigidly still, and a fly landing on her face. She blinked but did not move. I swatted the fly away, tried to curl up with my head on her chest, on her scratchy dress. Her unresponsiveness. I had pushed this from my memory. I feel ill.

'Why has this been kept from me?'

'Perhaps there is some shame about it, in your family,' says Edward.

A sob wants to erupt, but I fear it. I fear that sedatives will be shoved down my throat the moment I show emotion. I need to be alone. But there is nowhere to be alone. Edward has a look of pity on his face.

I must write to my father, and to my aunt, to ask them more about my mother. For how long was she mad? Is that why she and Father stayed in Edinburgh? Because in the Highlands there were no doctors with appropriate knowledge? But then the clear air, the animals, and so much to do with one's hands . . .

It's possible that my father did not bring my mother back out of shame.

No one wants to think such a terrible thing of their parent. But then . . . sending me off to the same fate, by making me go to Edinburgh. Or perhaps he saw it coming – and again he didn't want it to happen around him. He has his own madness: a fear of insane women. I see how selfish, or how blind, my father is. How much he needs life to be easy. But I also hope I am wrong.

I attempt to breathe deeply. Edward stands and I do too.

'Let's get you back to the ward,' he says.

He steers me by my upper arm from the office down an empty hallway, then unlocks the door to the corridor of my ward, which leads to a living area, dining area, and the dormitories. In the hall, a woman called Maude dances in a beam of sunlight. There is an excited commotion in the living area.

'This is a kind of therapy we're trialling,' Edward says. 'I think it'll be just right for you.' With that, he squeezes my arm and turns. I feel grateful for this moment of gentleness. People are not all one thing or the other. And sometimes they are only unkind because they think they have to be.

I try to peer past the backs of other women – dressed in drab grey and dirty stripes, with oily hair falling out of rough buns, or almost-bald heads for those who have had their hair shaved off. And then I hear a *woof*. At the same time, I see a cat jump up into one of the far, tall windows, a woman's gnarled hand reaching out to stroke it. The cat hisses and the woman backs away. Someone moves in front of me and there I see two dogs – old, and a complete mix of breeds, one tan-coloured, the other dark. They are being pawed by the women, and are panting happily as an attendant looks on, smiling.

'What's happening?' I ask.

'New friends, new friends!' says Mavis, a woman in her mid-thirties who looks much older, whose belly flops about softly under her loose dress due to multiple pregnancies.

The grief of learning about my mother still sits heavily upon me. But I crouch and one of the dogs, the tan one that is some kind of terrier, runs towards me. She jumps instantly to my face and licks it, her ears flattening against her skull, her big dark eyes soft.

Bethea has been looking at me strangely today, as though she's cottoned on to something. Cottoning on – is that an Australianism? If it is, I think it's one of my favourites.

'Bethea, you look as though you've cottoned on to something?'

She gives me a sideways look. We are sitting in our usual chairs, mine with a whiff of Pine O Cleen but no shit. Then again, can I really trust my senses at this point? Today's ache is reserved for the back – all across it, from my intestines, up my spine, to my shoulderblades. As though I've carried a large woman – Bethea, perhaps – over a threshold.

When Faye and I got married I performed that gesture, but she was tiny and light. We laughed, as I'm sure couples do. You can't imagine anyone taking it seriously. I watch the memory from a distance, like Jimmy Stewart's character in *Rear Window* watching the newlyweds from his chair across the space of the courtyard. Just like those fictional newlyweds, Faye and I drew the blinds down and didn't leave the room all weekend. I've never had such an appetite. For food, I mean, but yeah, probably for sex with a woman, too.

Faye used to sometimes express feelings of inadequacy because she wasn't fluid in her sexuality, like many of her friends. To her, being sexually fluid seemed like a political act. 'I just don't think about the sex part, with women,' she'd say with disappointment.

I always remained silent. I couldn't even tell her *that* about me, that I was fluid, or bisexual – whatever label you want to give it. Maybe because she wished she was. But more likely because my feelings for men were so specific. Men, boys. I suppose I could have at least opened up to her about having same-sex attraction. But then I would have had to lie directly if she asked me whether I'd had any experiences in the area.

But she would have asked me that anyway at some stage, right? All couples have that conversation: *How many people have you slept with? Have you been with anyone of the same sex? Are you into anything kinky?* All that stuff. I don't remember. I guess it would have been early on and I guess I lied to her a lot.

I can't think about the fact she could still be searching. Wasting her money, wasting her life. Don't care about me, Faye. You don't know who I am.

Bethea sits down her thriller, a completely different yellowed paperback than yesterday – she tears through them – and says, 'I found your notes.'

Cold replaces the hot pain in my back, travels right up my spine through to the tip of my head. I feel bile rise. 'My notes . . .?' *Play dumb.* Which ones, though? I have been keeping Leonora separate from my other thoughts, the horrible 'me' stuff. It feels as though that might help with my 'infecting' her, to keep them physically separate. I'm kidding myself, no doubt.

'About the woman,' Bethea says. 'Is it a novel?'

I clear my throat. 'Well, I'm not sure. Just ideas at this stage.'

'It's very vivid, though. Didnae know you were a writer.'

'I never have been before.'

'Ha.' She looks out the window. 'Have ye had a close look at the books on tha' lower shelf over there?' she asks, with a sparkling grin I haven't seen before, her tea-stained teeth all on show.

I twist in my seat but can't make them out. I stand, pain darting from hip to shoulder, and hobble over. There is a whole shelf of books – hardbacks, and different-sized paperbacks, with garish covers – written by one Bethea Scott.

'Oh!' I turn around, smiling, showing I'm impressed.

I have to find somewhere better to hide the notes on Leonora.

She is mine. It is obvious that Bethea writes pulp. Or wrote pulp. I cannot let her twist Leonora's story into some hand-wringing gothic romance that will move it away from the facts. Why couldn't I be holed up with a literary novelist, with whom I could entrust the story? The handwritten notes don't have all of the story, anyway. The earlier stuff is in William. I must find a way to get him working, as I can't plug him in, and consolidate everything. And do what with it? Incriminate myself? No – it's imperative, or else I might die and Bethea will fill in the blanks and tell it wrong.

I never thought about the fact I could write it as a novel! No one will believe it is non-fiction anyway. I could consolidate everything and send it to a publisher – or at least a better writer. I will rack my brain. With me removed from all the notes, I'm sure it will read like a good Victorian tale.

And that's honouring Leonora, surely. And also acknowledging what I've done. Perhaps I'll code in some warning about the technology for some clever person to find.

But really I'm too sore to think about it. I slump back into the chair.

'Any bestsellers among them?' I ask Bethea.

'Aye,' she says proudly. '*Escapades* was translated into eight languages.'

'Impressive,' I say. 'Is it a romance?'

'Not entirely. I was quite well known for crossing genre boundaries. They often ended up pretty dark.'

'Was?'

'I've no written much since . . .'

Since her husband died.

'It's nice tae catch up on readin',' she says, waving the book in her hand. She shifts forward in her seat. 'Ye want some eggs?'

I don't have an appetite today, but I say yes, as it's something to do until I fall asleep again and be Leonora. I don't dread the nights so much now that there's another warm body in the house.

I should be feeling worse about the institution . . . I put Leonora there.

As Bethea is leaving the room, pulling down her wool jumper over her large arse, she calls out, 'Oh, I forgot tae tell ye, ma nephew is comin tomorrow tae help us out a bit. I need this garden cleared up.'

'Oh?' *How old is he?* I want to ask. 'Staying here?'

'Well, no sure, I think he's got a friend on the island; that's why he's comin over.' She's paused in the doorway. 'So he might be stayin further north a bit, but sometimes he'll stay here, yes. He's a nice lad.'

Lad. Young. But then that's just what people say about people younger than them. A nephew. He could be thirty. Bethea is old, to my eyes. But maybe her sibling is much younger. I feel hope rising, despite myself. Hope at being able to sit, from afar mind you, and watch him tilling the grass. Tilling? This isn't the nineteenth century, I forget. With a lawnmower, then, sinewed arms on display. It might be enough to finally do me away.

In the letter to my father I asked about the nature of my mother's illness. I wanted to know: did the mind affect the body, or the body affect the mind? Or does he believe these maladies were unrelated? How long did it last for, or how long did my father know about it? And what was done? I don't want to ask if she suffered while dying. I have vague snatches of memory about her sickbed, and that is enough. It is simply too sad.

I didn't ask why he never told me. I don't feel I can face the answer just yet.

My conversation with Edward has had a strange effect. It has made me decide to at least entertain the idea that these visions are entirely my creation – even though I have never seen such things. The imagination is no doubt powerful. And if my mother suffered from lunacy then possibly I am doing so, too. Through my interests in the medical, I do know that in order to cure something its cause must first be found, and acknowledged. A tumour can only be removed if it is discovered that the symptoms in the person are due to the tumour. If I admit that I am mad, I can then find out what it takes to become well.

The tan-coloured terrier, Crombie, has really taken to Mavis, and she talks to it like one of her children as it sits by her on the bed. Perhaps it can sense her losses.

I wait and wait for the animals to come to me, not calling them because that would be selfish. I make eyes at them and receive a wag of the tail and sometimes a happy bark, but they remain mostly nestled in the arms of other patients. I understand.

Those patients are in need. Have been through more. The dogs know this. The cat is partly there to chase away mice, but she does like to settle in and purr upon anyone sitting in a particular armchair in the living area.

When we eat, around a long wooden table, the animals are shut out. We've all taken to eating much quicker – slurping the watery porridge or sliding meat down our throats – in order to have them back quicker. The pets are like royalty. They glow and are worshipped. Respected, too.

Last night as I lay in bed, hearing whispers through the bricks, I felt anticipation. I moved in and out of sleep and witnessed *his* fantasies about who the nephew would be. No, how can I put this now that is healthier? I fantasised about who the boy would be. How old. Or I imagined the man's fantasies from somewhere deep in myself.

I am struggling with putting it like this. I long to be able to speak to my mother, to ask her what she went through. Did she hold another person within her mind, too?

Perhaps collectively it is mad women who are imagining the future.

Today is the day. But I seem not to be able to get out of bed. The pain has moved from my back down to my pelvis and my legs. When I don't come down for breakfast Bethea brings me up a plate of sausages. She has her screen tucked into the small breast pocket of her jumper. I see it and suddenly crave all the images of the civilised world – flood me with them! Cary Grant's smile, a silver skyscraper, a cricket pitch, a Vegas stripper, a Mustang, a Lichtenstein (and I hate Lichtenstein), an Ikea-white living room with ocean views – and the sounds, oh, the sounds of Gershwin's 'Rhapsody in Blue', and then Brian Wilson, who loved that song, and then something sped up and electronic and entirely artificial. Something from 2024. Give them to me now.

But it's quiet and cold and close. And I'd feel like a child to ask. And I'm supposed to be denying myself. For whatever reason they're made, I stick to those sorts of vows – of discipline, of deprivation – I always have. But something else occurs to me, too.

'Bethea, how do you charge that?' I ask, my mouth full of charred meat. There is no electricity on here. It is naturally the way I tried to exist on the other small island. The Rayburn heats water, and there is gas, and there are fires.

'Solar, of course.'

'Oh yes.'

Does William have a solar panel? I look over to the box sitting in the corner of my room. Bethea is about to walk out.

'I wonder . . .' I say.

She stops. Follows my eyes.

'Do ye need it, though?'

'I . . . dictated some notes,' I say. Not telling her they relate to Leonora's story. Bethea might become too curious. 'Just memoir-type stuff.'

'Oh?'

Why does she look so interested? Oh God, now I'm going to die and she'll know that, too. The secret nobody has known. Now I *must* find a way to get William on, so I can write up the notes related to Leonora – extract them from the other stuff, my figuring out of my disgusting self.

And I do miss the way he – it – used to lie down on the bed next to me. As pathetic as that is.

The pain turns to quick, minor cramps, and I sit the plate on the bedside table and lie all the way back down, flexing and pointing my feet to try to get the blood moving down there and ease them out. Bethea is fart-arsing around getting the place ready for her nephew.

'How old is your nephew, Bethea?' I call out as casually as possible.

'T'be honest, I forget,' she says with a laugh. I roll my eyes to myself in bed. 'Last time I saw him he was mibbe about eleven.' My cock immediately stirs. I pause in my flexing and pointing. 'S'pose he might be about fourteen?' she calls.

Don't walk in now, I think. Don't walk in and see my reddened face, my beastly tongue hanging out.

I wake to the sound of sobbing. The light comes in sharp, with dust motes dancing in its widening trajectory towards the floor. Mavis' back shakes on the bed two down and across. The woman next to her mouths silent words at the roof, her hands in prayer position.

'Come on, Crombie,' Mavis says, then cries a little more. Crombie stays by the door, spread out near the beam of light.

I sit up and experience a head spin. I didn't eat enough yesterday, after reading my father's letter. I stand very slowly and walk down the central aisle, touching Mavis on the shoulder but continuing on to the dog.

I crouch. Crombie raises his head slowly, the red and yellow hairs around his lips wet with spittle. 'What's the matter, boy?' He rests his head back on his front paws with a whimper.

'Something's wrong,' says Mavis.

'Shuddup,' another woman yells, pulling a pillow over her ears.

Did Mavis know, like this, when something was wrong with her children?

I gently push the dog back so he is lying down with his tummy exposed. His teeth go for my hand and I wrench it back, though it was just a nip. His belly is extended. He has eaten something he shouldn't have.

Mavis continues to cry, and I shush her gently. 'It'll be all right, Mavis.'

The attendant stands silently watching by the door. I don't

know this one; she seems to be new. She is young, as young as I am.

'Do you know how I can find out what he's eaten?' I ask her.

She shrugs. If I raise my voice, I may be deemed hysterical; I may risk being moved away from the animals, away from Mavis. I pet Crombie on the head and go over to Mavis. I sit on her bed and put an arm around her. The rest of the ward is awake now, too, looking at the dog, looking at us.

'We'll have to wait for breakfast,' I say to Mavis. 'Then we can ask for Crombie to be taken care of.'

'No!' she cries. 'Don't let them take him away.'

'Mavis, calm ye'self; we will work it out.'

Her crying becomes louder, uncontrollable. Crombie's ears rise, though he remains where he is. Tess, standing by another patient's bed, gives a *woof*. Mavis jumps. She trembles. The attendant opens the door and leaves the room.

'Mavis, Mavis,' I say, 'please try to stop crying. It won't be of any help.'

'Just look at him,' she says. 'It's my fault.'

'How?' I ask.

'It's always my fault. I have . . .' she raises her shaking hands in front of our faces '. . . don't let me touch you!'

'This is not your fault.'

'I only fell asleep for a moment,' she says. 'I was so exhausted.'

'I know.'

The attendant comes back with another attendant and a nurse in tow. They don't move towards the dog but straight over to us.

'Yes, it's my fault,' says Mavis, unresisting, reaching her arms out to be grasped by the two women. 'But please help him,' she says to them, before turning back to me. 'Please help him,' she repeats to the room. When they leave, the other patients' eyes remain on me.

'Is the dog all right?' asks an older woman whom I've never heard speak before.

'I . . .' I'm so worried he may not be. And now it is on my shoulders. 'I can only guess what the problem is.'

'Will you fix it?' another asks.

I walk back over to Crombie and stroke his fur. 'I'll do my best.'

As we move into the breakfast hall I ask for permission to speak to the cook. The young attendant forbids it, her reasoning being that it will look like I have been given special treatment.

'Well, can you ask the cook for some rice or potatoes?' I try. 'Not for me, for the dog.'

The attendant gives me a strange look, and shakes her head, then goes to stand by the door.

I sit back down at the table and all eyes look expectantly at me. I fight the burn in my throat.

'Right,' I say to the group. 'I think that the dog may have swallowed a cooked bone from our chicken last night.' A few faces look determinedly down at their plates. 'Please – you weren't to know, if it was you. But cooked bones can splinter. Try to remember it from now on.' There are a few nods. 'It sounds strange, but if we feed Crombie more solid foods – potato is good – then we can cushion the bone fragments, in a way, make them easier to pass.'

'What about our porridge?' asks a tall sallow woman. Some of the others hug their bowls to their chests. I smile at her and nod, but at the same time our eyes flick towards the attendant. How would we get a bowl of porridge out of the dining area?

The woman next to the sallow one – buck-toothed Abigail – says, 'Ooh!' and indicates the pocket beneath her skirt, grinning. Soon afterwards, we arrange through whispers the swapping of bowls – so we still all have one in front of us, while the remnants of porridge in most of them are deposited into Abigail's pocket, which she reties under her dress at the end of the meal. We are all smiling lightly – there is a sense of camaraderie – though we smell darkly of fear and sweat. These women are my peers, my neighbours, possible friends. We have met misfortune.

As with my own poor mother. Who never recovered after I was born. That is what my father told me in his letter. And they did stay in Edinburgh for the doctors, he writes. This time around, he thought I'd be well there, young and resilient and unencumbered. He expressed much regret.

I have made many mistakes in my life. I do not know how to make up for them.

As we exit the dining hall, the young attendant grabs the skulking Abigail firmly by the arm. 'You cannot save food for later. You must eat your fill at mealtimes.'

Abigail is shocked. We walk on, pretending not to notice. Again, that burning throat. You try and you try and nothing works.

Back in the ward Crombie lies in the same position, breathing heavily. There is an older, friendlier attendant at the door now, one who doesn't speak much and who more often overlooks our outbursts. We sit on the cold floor in a circle around the dog.

Abigail with her now empty wet pocket sits next to me, shaking her head. 'I'm so sorry.'

I rub her arm.

And then, from the corner of the room a skeleton-thin mute called Vanessa enters the circle. At my eye level are her exposed ankles, narrow as wrists, with stockings bunched. She bends and sits right by Crombie, with audible cracks in her limbs. She reaches into her bodice, at the top where her breasts should be, and pulls out a slice of bread. She holds it by Crombie's nose, and he tentatively gives it a sniff and a lick before taking it in his jaws. From the other side of her bodice she pulls another slice.

I know the dogs are due to go outside soon. The bread should help the shards of bone pass through.

'Thank you, Vanessa. Thank you.'

I'm finally out of bed. But lulled by the painkillers that have helped me, I snooze in this uncomfortable white wooden chair in the wild garden of the property, notebooks tucked in an inner-jacket pocket, trying not to look like I am waiting. He has probably already gone by me, seen me drooling. No matter; he doesn't have to like me. No one ever need like me again. I'd like to think that Leonora would have, though, that healer of animals.

I can't tell what time or even what temperature it is. My body gives false readings; my skin presents itself to the world as cadaverous already, impenetrable. What am I doing out here? Faye could drive along that high road and see me as a speck in the distance – I feel certain she'd recognise me, even from there. Or Bethea could be poking around, trying to turn on William. 'Turn on', ha-ha, I wonder if the robot services women as well. It's probably been a while for her.

No, I'm sure she's not. No doubt she'll take the nephew out for drives or walks or whatever, which will give me some time to work out how to get William on and talking, so I can extract Leonora's story and then burn, burn, burn myself into the ground.

I feel like the only person I would tell my thoughts to now would be Faye. Ha.

That's a silly thought.

The front door squeaks open behind me. I'm too nervous to look.

'S'cuse me, Mr . . . Jeff, um, me aunt wants to know if you're up for some tea.'

I turn my head slowly. Bird legs in black jeans, swept-across fringe, small pink mouth. Oh dear God. He's coming towards me.

'Jeff?'

I am on the verge of explosive tears, or maybe about to vomit. I clear my throat. And again.

'Yes please,' I manage.

'Righto.' He bird-hops inside, leaving the door open.

I don't deserve this. Or I am mad already and have imagined it. A wee Scottish Eric, an image of the one who gave me life, this troubled life, but the depth of beauty that is life. My cheeks are wet now. I must dry them. I said I don't care if he doesn't like me and that's true, but I also don't want him to be so disgusted that he keeps away, well away from me. No – he should. Oh, but when you've seen. I am so weak. So terrible. How much of life we spend trying to hide our utter desperation for a glimpse, a small touch, a taste, of that which we find exquisite.

It's Bethea coming out with the tea tray, spoons jingling in cups. He's close behind. She sits the tray on the little white table that only just accommodates it, and pours, humming. He stands with arms akimbo, then lifts one hand to push his thick hair back, but it falls immediately again over his forehead.

'What's wrong with ye, then?' he asks me.

'Bleddyn,' Bethea says firmly.

Yes, what *would* she have told him? And how would she have explained my presence? She gives me a conspiratorial grimace.

I clear my throat again. The shock of his beauty remains. 'Just, ah . . . spot of TB.'

Bethea raises her eyebrows.

'It's made a real comeback, you know,' I add.

'Consumption, eh? Not the best place for you then, is it?' he says, and then crinkles his eyes up exaggeratedly in a grin. 'Should be down in Spain, *mate*.' His attempt at saying 'mate' with my accent is amusing. I give him a half-smile, realising I probably look like a squashed toad.

Hopefully he doesn't know too much about the symptoms, or can't pick the symptoms of my own disease, my rot. Hopefully he won't realise I am dying.

Bethea will have a lot on her hands when that happens. I wonder if she can still play dumb, though, express shock and say that I had told her I was being treated? That I was in recovery? Wouldn't be very believable. Or maybe all this time she actually *hasn't* known I am dying. No, I'm sure we share this secret knowledge. I mean, look at how I'm falling apart.

Both Bleddyn and Bethea sit down on the other white chairs, and we peer down to grass and trees and rocky outcrops and ocean, to the two buzzards crying and circling. Bleddyn slurps when he sips his tea. Bleddyn – little wolf. I am so glad for the blanket across my lap. I will have to carry it around with me everywhere I go.

And then, unexpectedly, they return. Worse than they've ever been before.

The woman with the short hair says words I do not understand, like 'Vegemite' and 'jumper', though when I am inside the vision I am him and I understand the words, and I know that I both want to be here with her and I don't. I am regretting the third beer (pronounced 'bee-yah') because I've bloated uncontrollably like a woman on her period. Faye bends over to pull another beer out of the Esky (she's one ahead) and I stare openly at her arse.

Esky. Esky. It dances around in my head all morning when I wake and stare at the white walls. I've missed breakfast.

He stood up then and cupped his hands beneath her cheeks.

I woke and was surprised not to see that swollen organ between my legs.

The vision was accompanied with such sadness, too. And something else. Something like when I was supposed to meet my schoolhouse friend Abby but I was hawk-spotting with Mr Anderson and I plain forgot. And then I saw her by the low stone wall. That feeling in my gut when I saw her face. It was a feeling like that.

Someone's face, a familiar face, is above me now.

'Esky,' I say.

'You're not making any sense.'

I go back under with him, into the water. A boy is swimming nearby, and he reaches out his pale white hand and touches the boy's shoulder. The boy turns his wet head, looks alarmed, looks toward the shore.

I wrestle myself into the now. I don't want to know.

'Jeff!' I call. I know his name and he knows I know. I begin to shake. 'Jeff. Jeff.'

It is Edward, talking now to a nurse. She says I've been talking to myself, moaning. He glances at me. 'Leonora, you're awake.'

My words are caught. Jeff got my tongue.

'He knows what he has done to me,' I say.

'Who?' But then Edward frowns. Perhaps he fears I will say his brother's name. 'Leonora, I'm afraid we have to move you.'

'Is the dog well?'

'They are both all right. You are not. And you are causing a disturbance.' He looks genuinely distressed, his chin dimpling as he gazes down at me over his collar. 'We need to isolate you – and then we can get to the bottom of this.'

'It's not because of my mother,' I say. My body still shivers, vibrates. I try to remember to accept that this is a mental condition, that I need to be cured – but it is too palpable. Jeff: existing, somewhere in some other time.

It is Jeff who is holding on to me. Not the other way around. Perhaps because he could not tell Faye all about himself, or the older woman he sits with now.

Yes, I see you, Jeff. I see it all. I see that you need to finally show your insides. But *I* don't need that. I need to be out of here. I need the grass. I need to live. Don't take me with you into that bloodless otherworld. Please, cut me off.

I've been rooting around in the box William came in, looking for another source of power. I take frequent breaks, sitting, frustrated, on the dusty carpet. I shuffle over to the robot and run my hand through his hair and down his neck. Wait – there is a bump, small, at his hairline. I push down on it and voila, a flap of neck springs open at the back, containing the solar panel. I knew he'd have to have one. It is the cheapest and most abundant source of power, though some corporations engaged in the ongoing resource wars would still have you believe that we need to push aside the populations (and remaining wildlife) of nations in order to get at their coal.

The company I'd worked for had been embroiled in this. On one arm they still invested in old energy sources and stymied renewables, while on the other they developed and pushed 'adaptive' technologies, like weather shields for buildings, temperature-control clothing, genetically modified food and drinks, and so on. The biotech and neurotech arms were only partly about finding ways to improve quality of life – they were also about finding novelty forms of entertainment and creating the kind of tech that would be highly sought after (bringing in huge amounts of revenue). Like my friend the magical little tab. It was my job to market the tech-tainments that made it past testing. And it was simple. The tab would have been simple, too: Now *here's* a way to adapt to climate change and war – just sit back, relax, get out of your head. *Mind your heid.* It's not the fault of scientists and designers like Henry, it's just their job; it's just the way it is. If they don't create these techs then some other clever person will.

Okay, so now I need to get William into the sun, and not draw too much attention to what I'm doing.

'Cor, what's he?' The lad is at the door to my room.

'Oh, hello, Bleddyn. It's just an andserv.'

'We never had one like that at school.'

'It's a banned model.' I give him a conspiratorial wink, then feel stupid for it. 'Actually, I wonder if you could help me.'

'Yeh.'

'Just gotta get him into the sun, for some juice.'

Bleddyn nods, his arms akimbo again and his hip bones sticking against the lip of his jeans. His shirt, tucked – some collared, floral polyester number from a bygone era. The kid has a bold style. He moves over to me and bends to put his lean hands under William's shoulders. Bleddyn's hair flips off his forehead, catching my face. I inhale, subtly. He tests the weight, seems to decide it isn't too bad, and then pulls him up to his chest. 'He's pretty light!'

'So you can take them with you when you travel, I guess.'

'Feels strange. 'Cos it looks so human.' He peers down at the sleep-mask of William. Two pretty things side by side. This is why we live, I think. And then: how can I even deserve such a sight? And with Leonora all fucked up, seeing my sights, too.

I'll die soon, Leonora. I'll leave you alone.

Though I have actually been feeling good today. What if the doctors are wrong? Or liars? What if they wanted me to just spend all that money on drugs and operations? What if it was just some infection, and it's going away? Fat chance . . . And I *should* die. I need to.

Bleddyn looks up at me. 'C'mon, then.' He smiles. The smile is a dart.

I creakily stand and follow him. He switches to carrying William behind him, one arm hooked back over the torso. Bleddyn's joints are flexible. William's lower body thuds gently on each carpeted step. Bleddyn goes slowly.

'Where is your aunt?' I ask.

'Dunno,' he says.

He pulls William through the kitchen and out the back door; across the path made of large rocks (some a bit wobbly) through the weedy garden, scaring off a rabbit; and to a grass patch he's just mowed, from which there is a dip and, in the distance, the sea. The briny wind pushes Bleddyn's hair into his eyes and he shakes his head to clear it. Then he sits William down, crosses William's legs, and pushes his head down so the neck is exposed. William looks as though he is sulking, picking at stalks of grass.

Bleddyn flops onto the ground next to William, stretching full out so I can see every rib through his shirt. His eyes are closed so I can have a good long look and hold the image in my mind. I've done this for as long as I can remember. I was born with some inbuilt knowledge of ephemerality. I drink in images like whisky. It actually helps. I have many pictures of Eric, frozen in time. Faye, too.

It's hard to have this kind of personality, though. A voice inside that prods you and says: This is a moment. Remember it. Because as soon as you realise it's a moment, you depart yourself. You are on the outside or in the future looking back on the moment and the image, instead of being fully present in it. My future is so short that I am merely storing this particular image for tonight or tomorrow, not years from now.

Bleddyn opens his eyes. 'What?' He sits up on his elbows.

'What's that?' I say innocently, peering out over the garden at the salt spray, and at one of the buzzards rising on the current.

'How long till he works?'

'Not sure.'

'Get some sun, then. You look like you need it.'

I obey, sitting down next to him. Not too close. I lie on my side. The grass prickles, but it's not like it is in Australia – not pungent, not full of stinging bull ants and crushed eucalyptus leaves. Even the bees here are softer – large and fluffy, like toys. Though I haven't seen a bee in Australia since I was a child. I do think about the ticks, but I don't care anymore. Let them burrow.

Soft, yellow eyelid light, rising sweet grass, soft, quiet. So quiet here now.

I have that sick-stomach urge to weep again, a weight pushing down on my lungs, and a hot throat. I don't expect you to feel for me. I don't even know who 'you' is anymore; I've vowed to destroy this (and yet I'm still addressing you, as though I want you to be here with me); I don't know what the fuck I am doing on the grass; I want to roll back over (is he looking at me?) and touch his cheek, or his stomach, concaved below the ribs with his arms under his head like that, chewing a piece of grass and projecting an image of what he wants to be, as young men do – not a single fucking worry. My lust (love? So close to the idea of transience – have I always fallen quickly?) is always tinged with envy, ever the beta-male, fighting for a position, to be fit, to not seem desperate, to not seem earnest, to be functional, to be successful, to not be weak, to not be suicidal, to not be *me*.

Oh God, imagine . . . Imagine if he just rolled over on the grass and flung an arm over me. Does anyone's life ever work out like that?

We hear the car rolling up the drive.

Bleddyn springs to his feet. 'I'm starving,' he says.

The woman is back, to feed us. It shouldn't be that way, but it is. I remain on the grass with William, then realise this might draw attention to him. I sit up carefully, keeping my eyes to the grass to fight a head spin, then I push William, in his cross-legged position, to a spot that won't be as visible from the back door, hidden by a few plants. The game will be up if Bethea decides to do some gardening or walk down that way for some other reason, but I need him to charge so there isn't much I can do.

'Jeff!' Bleddyn appears at the back door, excited. 'She bought *chocolate.*'

I walk towards the house.

I'm not sure if it is memory or vision. Sitting on the floor by the bed and the bed is moving, squeaking. My mother is lying on her side with my father behind her. His hand is across her breast, coming from behind her. The lower part of her body is covered by a blanket. She reaches out her hand and gently touches my head.

This is a small room, with padded, wailing walls.

If I could be any creature it would be a falcon, just to see Scotland from above, and to soar.

I hope Mavis is well; I hope the dogs are too. I do think my father loved my mother – he wasn't to know this would happen to me. But if only he had let me stay.

The porridge today is extra watery, and lacking salt. In Jeff's time he pours oats from a small pouch and there are bits of dried berries and he adds milk and puts it in a magic machine and the porridge is ready. How could I invent such a thing?

I told Edward of some of the things I've seen and that was possibly a mistake, but then how will I get better if he cannot help me figure it out? A doctor must not look incredulous, but he struggles terribly with that. Most people do. They cannot imagine seeing the world the way another does; they cannot experience life outside their own head.

It is cruelly cold at night without the other bodies around me, and with just a scratchy blanket, as though I am being punished. I may have screamed last night; I may have screamed for a while.

If I am a lunatic, can't a lunatic still have purpose? Or are they only ever a burden? Could not my imaginative life be incorporated into a way of living? Oh, but it would be a burden to others at the times when it takes over, when he takes over; when I see, confusedly, through his eyes.

I keep thinking about the anatomy book that Rebecca showed me. I press my hand to my abdomen and think of the womb beneath, and the intestines, and the bladder – how some emotions seem also to be felt in these organs, such as fear, and anticipation. I think about when a dog barks and its lower abdomen squeezes. I think about the busted body of a rabbit all ready for stewing up. My fingers twitch. I want to put my hands inside of animals.

Jeff is weak, in mind and body. He thinks he will die soon. He convinces himself that he wants to. But he clings to life, with a somersaulting seal-heart, with fresh beauty for his eyes, and Highland air in his lungs. For some reason I cannot hate him. Perhaps he truly is my invention; that would explain my response.

I tried to get up this morning. I got as far as the stairs and I looked down and they appeared like the drop of a cliff. It's not so much an ache today as something pressing on my chest, and a sandiness in the eyes after staying up writing before a rough sleep. Have you ever thought about those words, 'rough sleep'? You don't have a soft sleep or a smooth sleep, but you can have a rough one. I am trying to recall why I kept waking, anxious.

Bethea has come in with porridge – far sweeter and superior to the muck Leonora is getting. I hope she can somehow share the taste from my receptors. Bethea is very quiet. I decide not to ask about Bleddyn.

I drift off again looking at a crack that meets wall to ceiling, so familiar to me now it has become an old friend. It is phallic in shape, long and curving up and over, but then I would notice that. When I wake I think, with panic, that William is sitting on the floor in the room. I can't recall bringing him back in yesterday. So I hope it was Bleddyn who brought him, and that he has remained off the whole time.

But – the voices in my sleep. Was it not my own voice I heard?

No. Surely not. Bethea has respect for privacy.

But I must turn him on now and start to write down those early notes so I can then delete the memoirs with which they are intertwined. Once everything about Leonora is separate, I'll find a way to send it off – maybe Bleddyn can help – and then I will delete the files and burn this too. This – I persist. Facing myself?

Or some human urge, not yet stymied, for articulating one's experience of the world, one's surroundings? Some final attempt at understanding? Though I know that's impossible.

At the moment I stand from the bed there comes a crack of lightning over the blue-black sea, seen through my small window. When the thunder follows, the glass in the window vibrates. I suddenly worry that Bleddyn is out there – for I can sense he isn't in the house. I stand and stare out, but my breath keeps steaming up the glass, and I soon give up.

William. I move over to the door first and close it softly. Then I activate him.

He looks at me calmly.

I ask him to speak my notes back to me, slowly, with pauses, and with the volume down low. Luckily the storm will help to cover the sound. As William does so, I begin to write down Leonora's story, by candlelight, being swept up and amazed by it again. My stomach rumbles and my hand cramps but I continue on for as long as I am able. When I am in too much pain, I shut William down (I am still not letting on to Bethea that he is functional), and add the notes to my most recent ones about Leonora, in the top drawer of the bedside table.

It is calmer now, and though I am hungry I lie back down. I'm hungry for a glance of Bleddyn, too, and I wonder if he's been out somewhere during the storm, drenched like Heathcliff running from the Heights.

My hand has had a chance to rest. I don't hear anyone stirring, in the quiet aftermath of the storm. There's a leap of panic when I remember the voice. Did it not sound like it was me, talking downstairs? It's coming through clearer, now, away from that immediate place of exhausted sick-waking, that red-eyed swirl-space. Could Bethea have done it, truly? Accessed the recordings? Because Leonora's story intrigues her, no doubt. But she sure would have gotten more than she bargained for.

In fact, she may have sent Bleddyn away, if she knows all about

Eric and me. Shame tendrils – up my chest, up to my cheeks. I can do nothing but lie back on the pillow and worry and wait. And if Bethea goes out today (oh, please) maybe I will get down the rest of Leonora's story and then I can at least work out how and where to send what I have. If there is any conclusion, in the coming nights, I could send that off separately. I must make sure someone else owns it, not the pulp writer, not the woman in the sweaty knits. No.

Bethea has been gone for a day and a half. Has she left me to rot? Bleddyn is nowhere to be found. I have made slow trips downstairs and have now eaten all the oatcakes and scraped out the jam.

I have finally finished writing down Leonora's story to date. To her madness, her isolation. I found an envelope, and enough stamps to wall the paper and send it across an ocean, but I don't know how to get it to the post office, or who to send it to. What the fuck is my purpose? I am planning on burning the rest of this soon.

But Faye. Perhaps she should know, after all. So she doesn't miss me too much once she hears I am dead.

Bethea is back. She comes straight up the stairs and with each footstep I feel more like a naughty kid who has wagged school. There are myriad things she might explode with.

'I missed you,' is weirdly what I say.

She tilts her head, and then frowns deeply, and then sits a plate of food in front of me. 'Had some things tae take care of,' she says. 'Ma husband's other life.'

'Oh. You . . . could have warned me.'

'I told ye.'

'What?'

'Ye were delirious that day.'

I don't know whether to believe her.

'Where's Bleddyn?' I ask.

She frowns again, and leaves the room and closes the door.

After days of eating barely a thing I am ravenous, and I wolf down the sausages and bread, and wash it all down with lukewarm, sugary tea.

I feel strange. I must have eaten too fast.

I have vomited on myself. I call and she doesn't come. She is not my nurse, I suppose.

Oh, I feel terrible, the worst I have felt. Is this finally . . . ?

Is Eric still alive? Will Leonora get back to the Highlands? Is Faye still out there, roaming? The envelope . . .

There *was* a delirium. She'd said, 'It's not right what you did to her.'

Not him, *her.*

This is . . . pain.

It is quiet upstairs, finally. She can no longer hear him spluttering, moaning, and choking. It will be a mess, she thinks. The body. No one ever knew he was here, except Bleddyn. She will tell him that Jeff has gone home to Australia.

That poor woman, searching for him. Would she go on and on? That was what life was, for some women – they tied themselves up with worry. It gave them purpose, while the man simply dreamed. And if there was any truth to those notes, the other woman, too, would now be free of him. It was so selfish of him to hold on for so long. Men do not know how to sacrifice themselves, she thinks. Only for other men, or for governments. Never for us. Though they might convince themselves they do. Just like Robert did.

She plods up the carpeted stairs, her hands out in front of her to catch a fall, as she always does. She can smell the sick at the top of the stairs, in the corridor. When she gets to the room she takes a deep breath, facing away, before looking in.

His torso is side-on but his legs are twisted to the front, quite unnaturally. The vomit is filled with blood. She steps around a pool of sick to get to the robot, sitting on the ground. She claps and the robot blinks its eyes open, looks at her.

'Help me,' she says.

It stands up and surveys the scene, expressionless.

I wake and all I can hear are birds. My chest rises and falls with quiet breaths. I cannot feel him; I have not dreamed of him.

I wake and I have dreamed of deer, of home.

I wake. The memories remain as though they are my memories, or vivid stories that I have been told and have imagined fully. They are still accompanied by emotion. But there are no new ones cropping up. Has he died? Have I killed him? The idea comes with a strange, mixed sensation of delight and loss. This room, in its isolating, plain horror, comes into full relief.

I wake again. I will request a session with Edward. I am convinced I can make him see I am well again. Well enough for now. I fear I won't remain so if I'm made to stay here, staring at these walls.

She has landed back in Australia on a fiery day, but she carries the cold of Scotland in her bones.

Months later, a letter arrives. There is no return address on the envelope.

Dear Faye,
By the time you read this I will be gone.
I loved you, truly. But I also desired young men, or boys, barely on the verge of adulthood, arguably innocent. This is why I could not hold on to you. I am wrong. Don't waste any more time having decent thoughts of me.
Everything I touch crumbles.
You hated my self-pitying moods.
But this is beyond that.
Please see enclosed.
J

His writing had been affected by the illness, she sees.
He is truly gone. But finally, here he is.

A woman emerges from a moss-green copse of trees. The rustle of her skirts in grass; birds rise in flushed dusk. The golden dog bounds to her. Home, here. The laird's friendship and guilt made a clearing for her, a new life and emergence of practice. Her own dwelling on the property. Working with the animals – learning anatomy, their tunnels and clusters, with Mr Anderson's help. Only so much you can learn from books. Only so much about people, too.

Entering the house, dark rise of stairs, and the laird and lady's chambers. There had been a slow acknowledgement of her fit, something exploratory and kind. Their soft hands on her, the laird and his wife. Leonora's hands the roughest, on her curves and in his curls. Afterwards, back to her hut and study and Duff curled in a sun-spot. Next to her, some rare caramel William gets from abroad.

And forgiving the father, because he did not know ways forward. And because Edinburgh did open a mind's door towards this path of working with the animals. The path that feels right for her. He listens better now, too. She writes short notes to that city – the aunt, who after all did her best, and Miss Taylor, Mr Stewart, and Rebecca and Joan.

The laird's little dog still barks sometimes, at her ghostly corners. It's best, still, to stay away from the looking glass. Or one feels bound.

No, go to her own small garden and dig beneath the top layer of soil. Turn, turn. Brush back hair with dirt.

ACKNOWLEDGEMENTS

First of all, I would like to acknowledge the fact that I have used real places in this novel but completely invented residences, people and events, particularly in Chapeltown and Tomintoul. With Edinburgh, I have alluded to some historical events, such as the first women studying medicine at Edinburgh University, but my characters are not based on any of the real women – those incredible pioneers known as the 'Edinburgh Seven'. The main texts I drew on for detail and inspiration in regards to the Leonora chapters were *The Tales of the Braes of Glenlivet* by Isobel Grant (compiled by Alasdair Roberts); *Women of the Highlands* by Katharine Stewart and *A Year in Victorian Edinburgh* by Lynne Wilson. I am deeply indebted to the authors of these works. A huge thanks must also go to the Tomintoul Museum, who let me take photos of pretty much every exhibit and also kindly answered my emails. Also very useful were the Surgeon's Hall Museum, and *The Scots Herbal: The Plant Lore of Scotland* by Tess Darwin, and for general flavour, *Sunset Song* by Lewis Grassic Gibbon and *Crowdie and Cream and Other Stories: Memoirs of Hebridean Childhood* by Finlay J. Macdonald. Thank you very much to Tina and Norm, formerly of Cardhu, who hosted me, took me on that first drive on the road to Braemar where I experienced a form of falling in love (with a place), and for lending me some of the above books. I'm grateful to Ian Hume for his notes and comments on the use of Scots language. For the Jeff chapters I'd like to acknowledge the inspiration of a man I saw give a gaga-eyed lecture on Caravaggio's nudes, and also, for the general concept of the novel, Kathleen Taylor's *The Brain Supremacy: Notes from the*

Frontiers of Neuroscience. Thank you also to Angie and Dick and the retrievers in Bunchrew; to the laird, lady and child inhabitants of a tiny island micronation; and to the Fletchers, and Kate, on Jura, for so kindly letting me commune with Orwell. *Slàinte*, Scotland.

And my deepest gratitude to:

Peter Bishop, for the advice you gave me in my early twenties (to abandon a work but keep writing), for your capacity to deeply engage with a work, for your constant enthusiasm in regards to *this* work but also your integrity towards writers and writing in general. To Martin Shaw, my wonderful agent, who loved and understood *Spectre* from the get-go, and who has also been a great long-time supporter of Australian writing. To Jane Curry, Eleanor Reader, Zoe Hale and the PBB/Ventura team for getting behind this novel in every way, and being so excited, communicative and organised. To Kate Goldsworthy, the most attentive, thorough and caring editor – you are wonderful. To Lee Kofman for your generosity and insight on my draft. To Donna Ward, thank you for being there through this, and for being such a champion of my work. To Sonja Meyer, my amazing sister, an early reader and forever invested in my success and fulfilment. To Mum and Dad, for forcing my work upon your local book club. If they thought the last one was weird . . . To Gerard Elson, for everything we've shared, and for being such an encouraging companion during the gathering of this, and for always engaging with and believing in my work – DSL. To Josephine Rowe, for being a dear friend, a wonderful reader, and for sharing the Jura night sky with me. To my whisky buddies, the muses Top Gun and Ice Man, and best bud Cap, and to Lagavulin 16. To J, thank you for the poetry. To my Echo authors, who have taught me so much, and made my life far richer than I could have imagined. To my colleagues for embracing my double literary life. To Mallory, my faithful hound. And to the person with whom I can be my full self, Christopher Zavou.

NOTES ON THE USE OF DIALECT

Some minor changes appear in the rendering of Scots dialect in this edition compared with the original Australian publication of 2018.

Leonora speaks in a Highland dialect with her father, their acquaintances, and others in Chapeltown. She has known the Laird, William Wink, since they were children together and she speaks to him in the same way.

When Leonora moves to Edinburgh, her way of speaking changes because of her aunt's influence over all areas of social etiquette and engagement – they are Edinburgh New Town dwellers and mixing with Edinburgh's well-heeled classes. As well as this, the language of ideas pertaining to Leonora's interactions with the women from Edinburgh University's medical school and other members of the literati, as well as the visions of the future, leaching across from Jeff's mind into hers, are expressed in a more homogenised form of language.

A number of online resources, including the *Dictionary of the Scots Language*, and the editor's dialectal knowledge, were consulted in checking the dialect. Stylistic features include present participles ending in "in" – rather than "ing", and without the use of an apostrophe, in line with most standard sources on Scots (for example, *Education Scotland*, accessed January 2019).